THE CROW MAN

Robert Denton Brownell

For Mom

THE MEETING

E ben stepped into the cool water of the quietly bubbling creek and relished the feeling of his feet sinking down into the mud squishing between his toes. He never tired of it; an exotic, almost guilty pleasure that was his alone to enjoy. Taking a deep breath and stretching his arms widely, the boy smiled and took in the smells of the shaded bit of woodland he often retreated to. Throwing his heavy, sweat-soaked straw hat onto the shallow bank he splashed the clear water on his head and sat back enjoying the feeling of it running through his shock of blonde hair and down over his face. In the distance through the long grass at the edge of the field, through the trees and the endless green corn fields he could barely see his house and surrounding farm buildings awash in the shimmering sunlight of a hot Iowa July afternoon. The heat of the day distorted the structures and made them seem as though they were just a dream or an artist's rendition of the world on this sweltering afternoon. Here, he was completely alone with his own thoughts and dreams of what he hoped his future might be.

Eben continued swishing his hands back and forth in the water. He immediately felt better as a small breeze blew through the trees. Pausing a moment, he watched as a crawdad scuttled to safety in a darker, less disturbed pool well further on down. Overhead, the hot wind blew harder and rippled through the long branches and blew down along the water where the boy, still squatting in the shallows, delighted in the feeling of it against his sweat-soaked shirt. Yes, this was his world.

Hearing a noise in the distance, Eben bounded halfway up the bank to hide behind a tree where he could see the outside world. He watched the house and outbuildings awhile. Nothing moved other than his father's cows pressing against one another in the shade of the ancient grove of oak trees lining the south side of the farmstead. Deciding he was safe, he slid down the muddy embankment and thrust his feet back into the water. Feeling pure contentment, he lay back on a mat of dead leaves and stared up at the wispy clouds slowly crossing the afternoon sky above.

Freedom he thought. Freedom from his chores and his brothers and sisters. Freedom from the heavy leather razor strop his father used on his boys to remind them to be humble, hard-working and obedient servants of God but Eben thought otherwise. The creek and timber offered an escape, something he looked forward to when the endless days of school, work and church often became too much for his confused young mind and free-spirit. It also offered a forbidden and tempting door to the outside world. His father's property was at the very edge of the sprawling, rural Community of God his family belonged to. The other side was another world where everything was different, strange and oftentimes fascinating to young Eben Wittmer. The small stand of timber he found refuge in followed a bend in the creek which extended out into the English side, the closest way into the nearest town, Kamron, Iowa with its strange outsiders and their clothing, cars, music, shops and everything else so foreign to the boy.

Eben, along with everyone else under the age of eighteen were strictly forbidden to leave the Community unless they were with an adult. To do so was considered something of a crime. They were continually warned it was not their world, but a place full of evil and corruption where the word of God was not taken seriously. Eben's oldest brother, Josiah often spoke of crossing the creek telling everyone he'd never come back. He fought with their father, Gideon, about the things he wanted to do in the outside world. To Gideon, an Elder in the Community and therefore an important man, it was all nonsense. Josiah was expected to come back to be baptized and marry. As the oldest son, he would eventually be installed as an Elder as tradition dictated but the boy wanted nothing to do with the strict life already laid out for him.

Eben was jarred out of his daydream by the sharp crack of a tree branch breaking. Pulling himself up slowly, he crept through the underbrush to hide behind another tree. His eyes caught a flicker of something moving a good distance down the creek. A chill ran through his body fearing that it might be his father. More than likely however, it was probably a deer spooked from its daytime hiding place or a squirrel but he was still cautious just the same. Maybe, he thought to himself, it was the Crow Man.

Whatever it was, Eben waited afraid it could be his younger brother or sisters who had stumbled upon his secret hideaway. He hated the thought. Josiah had shown him this secluded place when they were small boys and they'd made a pact to never to share it with anyone else. Over the years Eben came here as often as he could but Josiah rarely did anymore.

Eben strained his ears hearing the faint rustle of footsteps in the undergrowth coming closer until suddenly, he saw a splash of color moving through the trees. Relief washed over him once he realized it was a girl and not his father. She wore a bright purple dress covered with odd looking colorful flowers which hung down to just above her knees and clung to her womanly curves due to the gently blowing wind. Her red shoulder-length hair was pulled back in a ponytail with an orange piece of cloth. She would walk several steps, pause to raise a strange black box she carried on a strap around her neck and look through it. After doing this several more times, she walked farther to sit on a fallen log only a few feet from where Eben was hidden. He'd seen English girls before when the family would go to town, but he and his brothers and sisters were forbidden to stare at them. Without his parents here to scold him, he gawked at the girl trying to take in as many details of her as he could. From the looks of her Eben guessed she was about his age, fifteen or sixteen.

A trickle of sweat ran down his face causing his nose to itch. Releasing his grip on the branch to wipe it away he slipped in the mud. In desperation, he grasped a low branch which snapped loudly as it broke. Rolling down the embankment head over heels, he fell into the water with a loud splash. In a panic, he jumped to his feet ready to run but his curiosity got the better of him. Peeking cautiously over the edge of the ravine he was horrified to see the girl standing there staring down at him.

"Hello," Eben said sheepishly.

"What are you doing?" the girl asked backing up several steps. Her large blue eyes stared at Eben with surprise and fear.

"I, um, fell in the water."

"No kidding. What are you doing down there?"

"Nothing, I was just..."

The girl backed up a few more steps with fear etched on her face. "Were you watching me?"

"No, well, I mean, yes. You walked up on me. There's never anyone out here."

"Oh. My uncle owns this land. He said his property ran along the creek. I'm not trespassing am I?" she asked nervously. "I was just taking pictures of the birds and animals."

"No, you're not trespassing," Eben replied. "My father owns the land on this side. That's our house back there."

He pointed to the well-kept farm house and outbuilding three-quarters of a mile away.

"Mr. Robinson is your uncle?"

"Yes, Uncle David."

"What are you, a member of the Community?" she asked.

"Yes. You're English. I can tell from your clothes."

The girl frowned not understanding Eben's reference to outsiders. "No, I'm an American."

Eben smiled. "My name is Eben Wittmer."

"I'm Wendy Harrison," she answered, also smiling just a bit. "I'm staying with my Aunt Shelly and Uncle David for a few weeks. I live in St. Louis."

"I'm very pleased to meet you Wendy."

"You are?" Wendy asked. "I mean, I'm glad to meet you, too."

From across the fields Eben could hear his father calling his name, his voice distorted and carrying on the wind. It made him jump. Looking back at Wendy he replaced his hat and flashed a smile at her.

"I have to go now. My father is looking for me," he said squatting down to pull his shoes and socks on over his wet, muddy feet.

"Oh, well, okay."

Eben climbed to the top of the ledge and waved. "Goodbye."

"Yeah, bye."

Eben allowed himself one last look at her before ducking into the corn field to run for home.

Eben ran through the shoulder-high corn away from the timber breathless and drenched in sweat. Upon reaching a grassy water-way hidden from the house, he made his way up to the farmyard behind the barn. From here, he ducked into the tall weeds lining the fence. With another glance back to the trees along the creek he thought about the odd girl he'd just met. He hoped his father hadn't seen the two of them talking.

"Eben! Where are you boy?" he heard his father yell. "Eben!"

Rounding the corner of the barn, Eben approached his father who stood scowling with impatience.

"I'm here, Father."

"Where have you been? We've been looking all over for you."

"I was just walking out along the fields. Looking at birds."

"Mmm," his father replied, stroking his long beard. "Why are you all wet?"

"Oh, I fell in the pond. I slipped in the mud." The pond was on the other side of their sprawling farm from the creek.

Again, Gideon grunted and stared at him from under the broad straw hat he always wore. "Well, you, Josiah and Isaac are coming with me to mend fence. Some of Hershberger's cow's got out and into our west field."

"Yes, Father."

"Come, before it gets too late."

Eben followed his father and climbed into the back of the wagon where his younger brother Isaac waited. Josiah sat glumly on the bench seat next to Gideon who took the reins. With a gentle slap, the horses plodded out onto the gravel road. Eben sat in the back among the fence posts, wire and tools his brothers and father had loaded earlier and stretched out in the bright sunshine. His wet clothes clung to his body steaming in the heat. Removing his socks and shoes, he threw them to the side hoping they'd be dry by the time they got to the west field.

It was a beautiful day; hot and sunny with a slight breeze blowing from the south. Eben dozed on and off listening to the rhythm of the horses clopping along the road and the cicadas and grasshoppers whining in the weed filled ditches. Red-winged blackbirds and swallows dived and wove through the sky around the wagon adding their chirps and cries to the symphony. Eben couldn't stop

thinking about Wendy. A smile crept across his face trying to remember every detail of her. She was certainly pretty, he thought,
and the tight dress she wore...

"I wonder who that is," Isaac said pointing down the road. A
cloud of dust blew out into the fields, stirred up by two men on
horseback. Shading his face from the bright sunlight, Eben could
barely make them out.

"Sentinels," Gideon muttered softly. "Must be changing the
shift at the crossroads."

The boys watched in silence as the two groups converged on
one another.

"Brother Gideon," both men said touching their hats in
greeting.

"Brother John, Brother Eric," Gideon replied with a slight nod.

"It's a hot one today," John said gazing skywards. "Looks like
rain."

"Yes, God be praised, we need it."

The two men continued on their way.

"Father?" Isaac asked once they were well down the road.

"Yes, son."

"Why do they always guard the roads?"

Gideon continued staring straight ahead, his face devoid of any
expression. "They do so to keep the English out. We can't have
them snooping around in their cars and bringing vice into our
Community."

"I want to be a Sentinel when I grow up," the child said boldly.
Eben and Josiah gazed out into the fields doing their best to ignore his comment.

"No son, you'll have the farm to take care of some day. It's your
birthright. Those men come from families with no land. Though
they're perhaps some of the most faithful and loyal men we have,
they are nothing but common laborers. God has provided you with
your place, they with theirs."

Josiah coughed and turned to spit in the weeds at the side of the road. Eben noticed his face burned a hot, deep red.

The Sentinels were the police force of the Community. Day and night, groups of two guarded every road into and out of the Community to, as they claimed, keep the English out. Their real purpose as Eben and everyone else knew, was to keep people in. In addition to watching the roads, the Sentinels also made monthly rounds stopping at homes in the middle of the night to collect what they called 'church tithes'. This usually consisted of meat, eggs, dairy products, grain and sometimes even livestock. If anyone ever dared object, they were often beaten in front of their family as a warning to others to pay their dues. Their leader was a large, brutish man by the name of Leroy Fisher who liked to think he excelled in his role as Head Sentinel. His chief lieutenants were his brother Lev, Paul Himschoot and Arlen Kopp. All four men were universally disliked and feared by everyone as were the band of men they employed.

Reaching the west field, the four set to work repairing the holes in the fence. Josiah, Isaac and Eben dug holes next to the ancient posts which had broken off due to age and the cows' habit of leaning against them to scratch. The afternoon air quickly became warmer and downright sultry. The boys dripped sweat as they dug into the rich black dirt down to the brown clay beneath which didn't dig as easily. After unloading the new posts and wire, Gideon went to work helping the boys dig new holes humming as he worked.

Eben threw a shovelful of dirt to the side with thoughts of Wendy still flooding his mind. He smiled to himself. *She certainly looked strange* he mused remembering her colorful clothes and the way she wore her hair pulled back and uncovered. Women in the Community wore plain dresses which hung to their feet and covered their arms completely. All had their hair done up in a tight bun which was covered with a lace prayer covering or bonnet. A stirring sensation began between his legs as he remembered the shape of her body especially the curves around her breasts and hips. Eben muttered her name as he worked; *Wendy. Wendy Harrison.*

"What are you mumbling about, Eben?" Josiah asked quietly.

"Nothing."

"It has to be something."

"It's none of your business, Josiah, so leave me alone."

"Well now, could it be that girl who's been down at the creek lately?"

"I don't know what you're talking about," Eben said trying to head Josiah off.

"You know what I'm talking about. Did you see her when you were down there today? Because I saw you going down there."

"No! Just drop it will you?"

"Who is she?"

"I don't know what you're talking about," Eben whispered angrily.

Josiah's forehead was creased with concentration while he continued to dig. "I might have to come with you the next time and see her for myself."

Eben felt his face flush with anger. Since Josiah was the oldest he was always trying to outdo his younger siblings, something Eben resented. "I saw her first so you just stay away."

Josiah laughed and opened his mouth to say something but was interrupted by Gideon.

"What are you boys talking about down there?"

Eben stopped and looked up at his father who stood leaning on the post-hole crumber, eyes intently focused on his sons.

"Nothing father. We were just talking…about school."

"School, eh?"

"Yes, sir," Josiah answered throwing a shovel-full of dirt out of the hole he was digging. "Eben was asking how hard his math was going to be this year. I was telling him about it."

"Hmm…well don't be whispering and telling tales and such, especially around your mother. You know how she dislikes whispering and mumbling. If it can't be said aloud it shouldn't be said."

"Yes Father," both boys replied.

"You're not trying to lead him astray are you, Josiah? Because you've done enough to yourself already."

"No."

"You make sure you don't."

Josiah frowned and nodded. "Yes Father."

Once the new post holes were dug, the four set the new posts in them, shoveled dirt back in and tamped the soil down tight. New wire was stretched between the posts with Isaac cranking on the come-along. Josiah, Eben and Gideon then set about nailing it to the posts with fencing nails to complete the repairs. When the job was finished, the old broken posts and the unusable wire were carefully loaded in the back of the wagon to be taken home and piled behind the barn in the old granary.

"Come boys. Looks like a storm is coming in."

The boys turned to look at the northwestern sky which had begun to turn a dark bluish haze. In the distance thunder boomed. Isaac, Eben and Gideon ran to gather up the tools while Josiah untied the horses. Once the tools were loaded Gideon snapped the reins and guided the horses out onto the road. For the entire trip home they watched the sky with tense faces as it continued to darken and rumble. Bits of lighting began stabbing along the horizon several miles away causing Gideon to snap harder at the horses to bring them to a trot.

After running the horses at a fair pace for most of the way home a cold breeze on the front edge of the storm blew through the fields churning up dust from the road as rain began to fall in big, cold drops.

"Just in time boys. Praise the Lord," Gideon exclaimed guiding the horses into the shelter of the barn. Outside the wind intensified bringing with it slashing sheets rain.

"Josiah, Isaac, unhitch the horses, brush them down and feed them. Eben, give me a hand unloading the wagon."

Isaac, always happy to do anything with the horses jumped down from the wagon and began the long job of unharnessing them while he hummed a hymn. Eben and his father climbed down and went to the back of the wagon and unloaded the tools. Retrieving a steel brush from the workbench they took turns brushing the dirt and clay from each tool before putting them back in their place along the wall. With the other two boys out of earshot Gideon looked over at Eben in the light of the lantern he'd just lit.

"So, you were down along the creek today. Down in the corner where the woods are."

Eben froze and lowered his head to hide his face beneath the brim of his hat. His father hadn't asked a question. It was an accusation.

"Um…"

"Tell me boy."

"Yes Father."

Eben picked at a piece of dirt stuck on the end of the shovel not wanting to look at his father.

"Look at me."

Eben looked up to see his father staring at him with cold dark eyes.

"Each one of you children has been told never to go down there haven't you?"

"Yes sir."

"Then why do you persist? I will not have you defy me."

"Why? What's so bad about going down there?" Eben asked raising his voice.

Gideon slapped Eben hard enough to knock his hat to the dusty floor.

"We don't talk back in this family!"

Eben glared at him.

"Don't push me son."

With a grunt, Eben picked up the shovel. For a moment he considered hitting his father with it. *Yes, it would feel good to give a little back,* he thought to himself.

Instead, the two continued cleaning tools in an uncomfortable silence. Eben could tell his father wasn't finished with him yet. He could see him becoming angrier.

"Your lies and your deceit! Why Eben? Tell me!" Gideon finally said throwing his arms in the air.

"I don't know Father," Eben replied. His father, his teacher, even his friends badgered him constantly about his temper. He told things the way he saw them but he always seemed to be wrong in everyone else's eyes.

"Try harder! I don't have to remind you that lying is a sin as well!"

"Yes Father. I'll pray about it tonight."

Eben wiped his nose and turned back to cleaning the shovels while the rain continued to splatter in the barnyard. A loud clap of thunder rumbled overhead shaking the barn. Gideon stood for a moment staring out at the storm with his hands on his hips.

"The creek and timber are a bad place Eben, and I forbid you to go back down there. You can't leave the Community. To do so makes you vulnerable to the wickedness the English seem content living with. You, me, all of us here are under the protection of God but only here. Do you understand me?"

"Yes Father, I won't go back," Eben answered without looking up.

"Good, finish up here and help the boys if they're not done with the horses. Then come in and wash up for supper. Your mother and the girls should be about ready for us."

"Yes Father."

Eben watched his father run through the rain to the back door of the house and disappear inside before throwing the shovel into the wall.

"You old man!" he shouted. "What do you know about anything? Stupid old man!"

Eben stomped back and forth fuming with anger, his face burning from where Gideon had slapped him. He'd never said anything about something bad at the creek before. What did he mean? Why was it such a bad place? He intended to find out.

JOSIAH

Josiah hunched over his plate inhaling his supper like a man who hadn't eaten in a week. His right hand held a fork which moved in a blur between the plate and his mouth. In his left hand he held a piece of bread, his fourth since the family had sat down for dinner which he used to sop up every last drop of the chicken gravy he'd poured all over his food.

"This is very good Mother. Your gravy is the best thing I've ever had. I could drink it."

"I'm glad you like it," their mother, Mary said. "Would you like some more?"

"Yes please," Josiah mumbled through a mouthful of chicken before handing her his plate.

Mary, who hadn't had a hot meal in years stood and went to the wood burning stove.

Eben pushed a half-eaten piece of chicken around his plate while he daydreamed about the strange girl with the red hair he'd met earlier in the day. The more he thought about her the more exotic she seemed be. Despite what his father had said, he was

14

already planning his next trip to the creek in the hopes she'd be there again.

Josiah dove in before she'd returned the plate to the table.

"Thank you Mother."

"You're very welcome."

While he Josiah ate, he stretched his long legs under the table and accidently kicked Eben in the leg. Lost in his daydream, Eben jumped from the kick.

"Watch your feet, Josiah!" he said angrily kicking Josiah's leg. Josiah looked up with a smirk on his well-tanned face and kicked Eben much harder.

"Oops, sorry about that, Eben," he said through a mouthful of cooked carrots.

"Stop it now!" Gideon roared reaching over to swat at Josiah with his fork.

Eben felt his face flush. He waited a moment then kicked much harder the second time but Josiah pulled his feet back just in time. With his head down, Josiah continued to stare at Eben through the thick, dark hair spilling over his eyes. In one swift movement, he returned the kick where it landed squarely on the front of the seat. For one terrifying moment Eben felt his chair fall backwards and balance for just a second before tipping back completely with a loud crash.

Eben lay on the floor for a moment trying to regain his senses while Josiah, Isaac and the girls howled with laughter. Enraged, he jumped to his feet.

"I'm going to kick in your ugly face!" he shouted taking two giant steps towards his brother. Gideon reached over and grabbed him by the arm.

"Stop it!" he said in a low, menacing voice. "Pick up your chair and sit down."

Eben pulled against his father's strong grip. He intended to punch Josiah as hard as he could.

"I said sit!" Gideon shouted. "We don't fight at the dinner table."

"Yes, Father," Eben replied casting a dark look at Josiah. "But he started it."

"Do you want to go out to the barn and talk about it? Both of you?" Gideon asked. Both boys shook their heads and looked down at their plates. "Good. You sit down and eat. You keep those oversized feet to yourself. Understood? This is your last warning."

"Yes Father," both boys muttered.

Eben brushed himself off and picked up his chair. Across the table from him, Josiah continued to smirk at him from under his mop of hair. The family continued with dinner while the girls chattered on about the new kittens they'd found in the barn earlier. After finishing another plateful, Josiah lazily pushed it away and leaned back in his chair.

"Mother, may I be excused? I'd like to set up the checkers board."

"Go ahead," Mary replied. "But no fighting over the games tonight."

Josiah stood and grinned at her while he rubbed his belly. "Why mother, I'd never think of such a thing. It's just a friendly game after all."

"It is? When is anything between you two a 'friendly game'?" Mary asked. The entire family laughed. In addition to being stubborn, Josiah and Eben were fiercely competitive, especially with one another. It didn't matter if they were playing chess, running, milking cows, seeing who could brush his teeth the fastest or even going to the outhouse; everything was a competition and they often became heated.

Josiah lingered in the doorway wearing a look Eben knew all too well. "Do you remember last fall when I picked more corn than Eben did?"

"Yes, Josiah, you've told us every day since last October," Gideon growled. Eben clenched his teeth wishing he could smash Josiah's head in with a chair.

"I guess we all know who does the work around here," Josiah continued looking directly at his brother.

"Josiah! I'm going to…!" Eben shouted. He began to stand until Gideon's fork thudded onto the top of his head.

"Silence! Josiah, out!"

Josiah disappeared into the front room laughing quietly to himself.

"Eben, are you finished?" Mary asked trying to change the subject.

"Yes, mother."

"You didn't eat everything on your plate."

He stared at the piece of half-eaten chicken and potatoes still on his plate. "I'm sorry, Mother. I guess I'm not too hungry tonight. I think I got too hot today."

Mary eyed him suspiciously. "If you're done would you bring some water in for the dishes? It's your turn tonight."

Still angry about being punished, kicked earlier and hit on the head with a fork, Eben pushed himself away from the dinner table wiping his mouth on his sleeve. He stood quickly stomping his feet on the bare wooden floor and made sure to push his chair back noisily into the table.

"Is that necessary?" Gideon asked in frustration. "Do as your mother asks without your rudeness."

"But I don't feel good."

"That's too bad. Isaac had the flu last month and still managed to do his chores. Go do it."

Knowing he couldn't win especially after the day he'd had, Eben reluctantly gave in. "Yes, Father."

He skulked to the back door and retrieved the bucket and thrust the screen door open causing it to bang on the side of the house. He filled it from the pump and lugged it into the kitchen where he dumped it into a large brass pot warming on the stove. After three trips back and forth it was finally full.

"I always have to do everything around here," he mumbled once he thought he was out of his parent's earshot. He kicked the bucket across the yard to the well. "It's not fair."

This caught the attention of his mother who followed him outside.

"Why must you talk so much?" Mary asked in a hushed voice. "Do your chores and do them quietly. I will not have your sullenness and disrespect. Do understand me?'"

Eben knew from the look in her sharp blue eyes not to argue. He didn't mind making his father angry but his mother was a different story. He didn't like upsetting her.

"Yes, Mother, I'm sorry.

"Good, bring in ten more, the girls are going to bathe once we're done with the dishes."

Eben did as he was told and brought in ten more buckets full of water in silence thinking the entire time about how everyone seemed to pick on him. Seeing his mother washing dishes with the girls made him feel even worse than he already did but he knew he had to apologize to her before he went to bed. Otherwise, he knew, it would eat away at him making sleep impossible.

"I'm sorry, Mother. I shouldn't have been rude to you."

"Thank you," she replied giving him a quick kiss on the cheek. "Sometimes you just need to take a deep breath and relax before you talk back and stomp around."

"Yes, I know."

"Okay, good. Now, go play your game."

Eben skulked to the living room where Josiah sat on the floor in front of the checkers board with a sly grin on his face.

"Ah, my next victim. Come, Eben, sit here and play me," he said rubbing his hands together. "I've schooled Isaac enough for tonight. You're next."

Eben sat on the floor opposite Josiah and quickly set his pieces out on the board.

"Are you going to whine and cry like a dumb girl tonight when I thrash you?" Josiah asked softly.

"No, I'll be celebrating and watching you cry your eyes out you big dumb cow."

Josiah hooted with laughter and moved a piece forward. "Go, it's your turn."

The first two games went quickly but as they set up their pieces for the third game they'd settled in to their normal intensely heated matches. Neither would make a move without giving it some fairly serious consideration.

Ten minutes into the fourth game, Eben studied the board carefully trying to calculate his move. Josiah had unwittingly fallen for the trap he was about to spring. A smile crept across his face once he realized it was going to work much better than he'd realized. Picking up his piece, he jumped Josiah's red checker deliberately taking his time.

"Oh, no!" Josiah exclaimed.

Eben finished the move and without taking his fingers off the piece, jumped Josiah's remaining five checkers in rapid succession.

"Looks like I won the game."

Josiah stared at the board with disbelief. "How did you do that?"

"Skill, I guess."

"Yeah, skill my foot. Set it up again."

Two-hours and nine games later the boys, tired and falling asleep on the board, wearily climbed the steps to their bedroom.

"How many games did I win tonight?" Eben asked mockingly.

"I don't want to talk about it."

"What's that, Josiah? Didn't I win ten out of the twelve we played?"

"Shut up."

"Are you a sore loser little Josiah? You going to cry now?"

With a growl, Josiah grabbed ahold of Eben's foot and began pulling. "I'm going to throw you down the steps!"

Eben wrapped his hands around the stair rail and hung on for dear life. He knew Josiah would indeed throw him down the steps, since he'd done so before. The boys struggled for a moment until the balusters began to snap, creak and sway from the stress being put on them.

"Let go, you're going to break the balusters again!"

Josiah wouldn't back down and continued pulling on Eben's foot. "I'm not going to break anything. You're the one hanging on to them!"

"Stop it!"

"No! You stop it!"

"Idiot!"

"Chicken liver!"

"What's going on up there?" Gideon shouted from the living room. "Because if you two break the stair rail again, I'll beat you both with the pieces just like I did the last time!"

The boys paused each intently staring at the other waiting for one to give. With a huff, Josiah finally released Eben's leg. "Just you wait," he said under his breath. "No one calls me a sore loser! Or an idiot for that matter!"

Without hesitating, Eben kicked Josiah squarely in the chest sending him clattering down the stairs where he crashed onto the landing below with a thud. Smiling broadly, he looked down at his brother who was clearly angry and a bit dazed.

"Idiot," he said before running to his bedroom. Downstairs, he could hear his father's voice rumbling with displeasure. He knew Gideon would more than likely make Josiah sit downstairs at the table until he cooled off to prevent the fight from spreading upstairs.

Eben undressed, climbed into the bed he shared with Josiah and lay awake thinking about Wendy. Everything about her was mysterious and intoxicating. For an hour he stared out the open window at the rustling leaves of the maple tree wondering what she was doing just a mile and a half away from where he lay in bed. Soon, he drifted on into a light sleep dreaming about her climbing in the window and slipping into bed with him. Just as he reached out to touch her Josiah stomped into the bedroom and threw his clothes on the floor. Eben's dream instantly evaporated.

"I just got to sleep," he mumbled.

"So what," Josiah replied. His face wore an all-to-familiar mask of trouble. Eben turned on his left side away from his him as he flopped into bed with a grunt.

"So, tell me about this girl you met down in the woods," Josiah said not wasting any time. "I want to hear all about her."

Eben covered his head with a pillow and pretended not to hear but Josiah began poking him in the back.

"Don't ignore me, Eben. I'll keep doing this until you tell me.

"I have nothing to say. I was down there and yes, there was a girl there. That's it."

Josiah poked harder. "I think there's more."

"Stop it or I'll punch you!"

"You can't hurt me you little girl."

Eben rolled over and took a swing at Josiah but missed.

"Okay, okay," Josiah said holding his hands up in mock defense. "Relax, I'm done."

With a huff, Eben flopped back onto his side and pulled the covers tightly over his head. Despite being exhausted, he tossed and turned but sleep wouldn't return to him. All he could think about was Wendy's freckled face, her hair, her pale white legs disappearing up into the dress she wore, Wendy climbing in the window....Despite not wanting to tell Josiah or anyone else about her, he wanted to brag a bit too. He enjoyed making Josiah squirm whenever he could.

"Hey, Josiah, are you awake?"

"Yes."

"The girl down at the creek, she's the Robinson's niece."

"What's she look like? What's she wear? English clothing?" Josiah asked sitting up abruptly.

"She's short and ugly, with bright red hair," Eben replied. He hoped by telling Josiah that Wendy was ugly he'd lose any interest he might have in her. "And, she wears strange clothes. I don't even think they're English.

"What do you mean? Strange how?"

"I don't know, just strange."

Across the room, Isaac stirred in his bed. He'd gone to bed several hours earlier hoping for at least an hour or two of interrupted sleep. "Why don't you two be quiet? I'm trying to sleep."

Josiah turned and cast Isaac a wicked look. "You lie down and shut up, Isaac, or I'll come over there and make you."

"I'll tell Father."

"No you won't because I'll paddle your behind. Lie down and go back to sleep."

With a sigh of resignation, Isaac rolled over and covered his head with his pillow. Josiah leaned back over close to Eben.

"Let's hear it."

"Well, she has red hair. Her clothes are very strange, not like the English girls in town wear."

"Different how?"

"I don't know. They look like they were fancy once, but now they're torn up. She wears a scarf around her neck that is an odd pink color. Her dress barely came down to her knees. You know, I've never seen a dress so short." Eben said.

"That low?" Josiah asked. His eyes became wider. "Could you see anything?"

"Yes, her knees."

"Her knees?"

"Yes, they were…nice knees."

"Oh…"

Eben continued: "She also has strange looking shoes. They don't have tops or sides, but these straps held together with a buckle of some sort."

"What's her name?" Josiah asked leaning back against the headboard. "Did she tell you her name?"

"No, I didn't really talk to her."

"Eben!" Josiah warned waving a finger.

"I told you, I don't know!"

Josiah pulled his knees up to his chin grinning even wider now. "Next time you see her, ask. I'm curious. Tell me, does she have a car?"

"Yes, Josiah, I'll make sure to ask her name. You must think I'm stupid."

"No, not always."

"I wondered if she drives too now that you mention a car," Eben continued. "She looked like she was about our age and all of the English kids get to drive cars when they're old enough."

"That's all very interesting, Eben. Very interesting. I think I'll just come along and introduce myself sometime."

Eben felt the familiar anger return. "No! I met her first! You can…you can just stay away!"

Josiah reached over and playfully poked Eben in the back again. "I'll do what I want. I'm sixteen now, remember?"

"You know we're not supposed to go down there. What if father catches you?"

"Ha! I don't care what he thinks. The first chance I get, I'm leaving this stupid place."

"You've been saying that for years, Josiah but you've been sixteen for months and you're still here. Are you afraid?"

Josiah frowned and looked over to make sure Isaac wasn't listening. His shoulders slumped as his cockiness evaporated. "I don't know how I'd live out there but if this girl has a car, well, it might be my way out. It'd be a start anyway."

"That didn't stop Tim," Eben said referring to a friend of the boys' who had left earlier in the spring. "And no one's heard from him. Maybe he found a job and somewhere to stay."

"Yeah, I thought of the same thing. He had to have known someone. You can't just go out there and expect the English to give you a job and a place to live. They won't."

"How do you know?"

"I don't, but it can't be easy. All I know how to do is milk cows and work in the fields."

Eben shrugged his shoulders and turned to look at Josiah in the moonlight cascading in through their bedroom window. "Maybe the English farmers hire Community people who have left."

"It's not the same. You've seen the machines they use for all of the work. I wouldn't know how to use them," Josiah said softly.

The boys sat for several minutes thinking about the foreign outside world.

"So, where do you think Tim went? And what about Elizabeth Beiler?" Eben finally asked. Elizabeth was his age and had run away from the Community the summer before even though she was only fourteen at the time. She and her family were the closest neighbors to the Wittmer's just a mile and a half down the road. Eben had always had a crush on her and often thought that once he reached the age when boys begin thinking seriously about girls she would be the girl he'd want to marry someday.

Josiah shook his head and sighed. "It's hard to tell. You and I only know a few people who have come back after being out there but they won't talk about it. No one does."

Eben smiled and glanced over at Isaac who was snoring gently in his bed. "Maybe it's something else."

"What?"

"Maybe the Crow Man got them."

"What? Eben, you know that's forbidden!"

Eben snorted with laughter and rolled over on his side, ready to sleep.

WENDY

E ben hid behind the curtains in his parent's bedroom watching the entire family disappear down the gravel road in the wagon. Once they crested the hill by the Bieler's farm they'd be a good mile and a half from home and on their way to his grandmother's house further on. By his calculations this would give him a good three or four hours before he'd need to be back at the house in bed looking and acting sufficiently sick.

Without hesitating, he stomped down the stairs and out of the house into the steamy cornfield. The rough leaves of the plants scraped his bare arms and face but he didn't mind. As he reached the edge of the field he stopped and peered through the dense plants to the patch of woods lining the creek. A strange mingling of fear and dread suddenly overcame Eben and he wondered for a moment if he shouldn't just turn around and go back to the house. Wiping his brow on his sleeve he waited for a moment trying to decide what to do: Should he do what he desired or should he simply follow his father's orders and stay away from the creek and the freedom it offered him?

Eben quickly made up his mind and pushed on further through the field. Emerging from the corn, he casually strode out. Just as he'd hoped, Wendy sat on a log on the other side of the creek in the shade. Eben wiped his perspiring face with a damp shirtsleeve and took a deep breath of the humid, lifeless air.

"Hi Wendy!" he said with a wave.

"Eben! Hi! I was hoping I might run into you again," she said standing.

"Oh, I had to wait for my parents to leave. They took my brother's and sister's over to my grandmother's house for dinner."

"What? Why didn't you go?"

Eben kicked at the dirt not wanting to tell Wendy the truth. "Well, um, I told them I was sick."

"Are you?" Wendy asked backing up a few steps.

"No. I just made it up. I didn't want to go."

"Why not? Don't you like her?"

"Oh, I love my grandmother but I was hoping I might see you today instead."

Wendy blushed and gave Eben a funny look. "Aren't you sweet. I want to hear about them."

"Who?"

"Your brothers and sisters silly. You have brothers don't you?"

"Yes, two. Josiah who's a year older than me and Isaac's eleven. And, I also have three sisters; Miriam is twelve, Rebecca is ten and Lydia is seven."

Wendy's face lit up. "Come over here and tell me about them! I don't have any brothers or sisters. What's it like?"

"What?" Eben asked.

"Having brothers and sisters!"

"Oh, I don't know. I could do without them."

"But why? I always wanted to be in a big family but my parents couldn't have any more children after me. I've always envied people like you."

"Well, it's not so great."

"You're just saying that! I always wanted a little sister to play with and do girl things with. It would be so much fun!"

The two stared awkwardly at each other from across the creek.

"Why don't you come over here and sit here in the shade. It's too hot to be standing in the sun. I want to hear all about your family. And you," Wendy said gesturing to him.

Eben paused. He'd never crossed over to where she waited. Unconsciously, his hand reached up to rub the sore spot on his cheek where his father had slapped him the night before.

"Um...I'm not allowed to leave this side. It's my father's property, the Community. I'm not supposed to be over there...or even down here."

Wendy looked at him with surprise. "Why not?"

"I'm just not supposed to is all. My father says that side is bad."

"That's nonsense. There's nothing bad over here. Just me," Wendy said with a grin.

Eben stared back at her and returned the smile. *Wow,* he thought. *She's beautiful.* "Well, okay, but I can't stay long."

Eben made his way through the timber and stopped just as he was about to cross the creek. Standing in the cool fast-moving water he felt his heart pounding in his chest while an odd feeling suddenly came over his body making him feel nauseous and dizzy.

"What's the matter?" Wendy asked.

"I...don't know. I don't feel well all of the sudden."

"It's just the heat. Its awful today. Come on." Wendy said holding her hand out to help him up the bank.

Eben gulped and looked at her hand before grabbing a tree branch to pull himself up. Tradition in the Community dictated that boys and girls should never touch one another until they were married.

"Um, I could have helped you."

"No, it's alright."

"Oh, well anyway, I'm glad to see you again."

"Me too," Eben replied blushing.

The two sat on the log staring at one another for a moment, neither knowing what to say first.

"I shouldn't be here. If anyone knows I'm down here I'll never be able to sit down again," Eben said with a coy smile.

Wendy laughed again and leaned back to get a good look at him. "Your people are so stuffy about everything. Don't you get tired of the rules and the old traditions?"

Eben wiped his brow on his sleeve again and gulped. He still didn't feel well and the heat of the hot morning was quickly becoming intolerable.

"Well, there are a lot of rules, even some no one knows about until you break them."

"That's nuts. Why so many?"

"I don't know. There are rules for everything. But, I suppose we're used to it."

"Are you?"

"No. I'm always finding a way to get in trouble with my father and my teachers."

The two laughed.

Suddenly Eben heard a loud click and looking up, was horrified to see that Wendy had done something with the strange black box he'd seen her with before.

"What are you doing?"

"I'm taking your picture silly. So I can look at you in my scrap book and so I won't forget you. I take pictures of all of my friends."

"Is that a camera?"

"Yes, but…"

"The Community doesn't allow people to photograph us."

"But, why?"

"It's a show of pride. It violates Exodus 20:4: "*Thou shalt not make unto thee any graven image, or any likeness of anything that is in heaven above, or that is in the earth beneath, or that is in the water under the earth."*

"Oh, Eben! Do you really believe all of that?"

Eben thought for a moment. His head was really spinning now. "Um, well, I don't know. It's just how it is. Please don't take another one!"

"Okay, I won't. But can I look at it before I delete it?"

"I, yes. I don't know."

Wendy pressed some buttons on the back of the camera and smiled. "You have such sad eyes for such a nice looking boy. Do you want to see what you look like?"

"No, thank you."

"You're sure?" she said holding the camera out. As she did, her arm brushed up against Eben's. His entire body immediately stiffened but he didn't pull away. Her skin was strangely soft.

Eben allowed their touch to linger for a moment wondering if she'd done it on purpose. Clearing his throat, he pulled his hand away to casually run his fingers through his hair.

"I'm sure."

"There," she said pushing a button. "All gone. Do you mind if I write some things down?"

"Why?"

"I'm just curious. I like to keep a diary and I'm interested in learning about you and how you live."

Eben shrugged his shoulders thinking it an odd question. No one in the Community seemed to object to pencils and paper. "Yes, if you want to, I suppose that's fine."

"Oh, goodie!" Wendy squealed digging into the colorful bag at her side to pull out a pen and notebook.

The two sat in silence again watching two squirrels run and play in the timber. Eben knew his friend John had no problems talking to the girls at school but for some reason, it made him nervous even though he had three sisters.

"Why do you come down here?" he asked. "I mean, you could go into town and do all of the things the, well, English kids do."

"Hmm…I don't know, it's quiet and I can watch the birds and animals, write and take photos. Besides, my aunt and uncle are really boring and I don't have a car."

Eben nodded. She'd answered one of Josiah's questions without him having to ask. His mind raced trying desperately to think of something else intelligent to say.

"You don't mind talking to me?"

"I don't know…why shouldn't' I?"

Eben blushed again more deeply. "I don't know. I've never talked to an English girl before."

Wendy grinned flashing her straight white teeth. "There you go with the 'English' thing again. Two times!"

"I'm sorry."

"Oh, Eben, it's okay. I kind of like it."

"What do people out there call us?"

"Oh, a lot of things. My aunt and uncle just call you 'Community people'."

"That's not so bad. What else?"

Wendy's face clouded over. "Nothing, Community or they call you all farmers. That's all."

Eben could tell she was being evasive. Since he'd never talked to anyone outside the Community he was curious. "Are you sure that's all?"

"Um, yes. Why don't you tell me about your family now?"

"No, I want to know. I won't get angry. I promise."

"Well, okay. Some of them think you're all a bunch of religious fanatics. They call you the Kool Aid drinkers."

Eben looked at her with surprise wondering what Kool Aid was. "What does that mean?"

"Do you really want to know? It's not very nice."

"Yes, please tell me."

"Oh, um, well, it means you're brainwashed. That means none of you can think for yourselves because you let the Bible and your preachers do all of your thinking for you. I don't believe that though!"

"That's a bunch of horse dung!" Eben answered. "The Bible is a guide for us to use as we live our lives!"

Wendy laughed with obvious relief glad she hadn't offended Eben. "Oh, I know. Most people out there aren't as religious as the Community people are. They just don't understand how you all live."

"But that doesn't make sense. What is there without God?"

"I don't know, Eben. I suppose I've never thought about it before. I guess they just don't have time for it. You know, like a person can't believe in God and have fun at the same time."

Eben shook his head in wonder. "Sure you can. He gave us everything. All He asks is that we be faithful and live by His word. It doesn't take a lot of time and it doesn't stop us from living good lives. We just don't drink, smoke or do bad things to each other."

Wendy continued scribbling furiously. "But don't you think some people use faith to hold total power over other people with threats and violence? That's what brainwashing means too."

"No, that doesn't happen here," Eben replied softly. Squinting his eyes, he looked up at the sun trying to guess the time. From the looks of the lengthening shadows on the east side of the trees he knew it was time for him to go back.

"I'm sorry, Wendy but I have to get back up to the house. My parents are going to be home soon."

Wendy pouted and put her pen down. "Darn it, I was really starting to enjoy our visit."

"I was too."

Eben stood and brushed himself off. "Do you think we could talk again sometime?"

Wendy hopped to her feet grinning from ear to ear. "Yes, I'd like that. When would you like to meet again?"

"It all depends on whether or not I can get away from my father. It's hard to do during the day."

"How about in the evenings? I could possibly come here at night."

Eben thought about how he might make it work. He knew he'd have to be especially careful. "Yes, I might be able to but I can't guarantee I'd be here. It depends on a lot of things, like my father."

"Well, how about this then," Wendy replied. "I'll have the same problem trying to get out of Uncle David's house late at night too but I can try. How about we meet here at midnight in two days and if one doesn't show up, then we try again each day after until we do catch up."

"Okay, in two days at midnight!"

"I had fun today, Eben."

"I did too," Eben replied turning to leave. "I hope to see you on Monday."

"Goodbye! I hope you feel better!"

Eben waved and began laughing hysterically before plunging into the corn field.

REVEREND STOHLFUTZ

Wendy brushed Eben's hair back from his forehead and kissed him long and passionately.

"Eben, I want you," she murmured. "Please…"

Eben returned the kiss with enthusiasm letting his hands wander down further than he'd ever dared. To his surprise, she moaned softly while he took pleasure in in the feel of the soft skin of her back. He reached further feeling the roundness her hips then moved them further down to her thigh. Eben's heart pounded wondering how far he and Wendy might actually go. He'd never done this before but it didn't seem to matter. Wendy moaned softly and pressed her body against his. He moved his hands further…

"Oh, Eben. Yes, like that…"

Suddenly, Eben felt himself falling into a dark abyss. Sound and light came rushing back causing him to catch his breath with a loud snort. Feeling a pull on his arm, he opened his eyes to see Isaac next to him with a smile on his face and a firm grip on his right arm. He suddenly remembered where he was and blushed.

"Oh, no."

Reverend Stohlfutz stopped speaking and stared at Eben with a look of utter contempt, a look almost every member of the Community had received from the old man on many occasions. With a deep frown crossing his wrinkled face, he closed his eyes tightly and shook his head. A long bony index finger drummed away in the air trying to capture the thought which had escaped him. Nearly everyone in the Community meeting hall turned their attention to Eben for a moment, then back to the Reverend who cleared his throat noisily and continued droning on in the oppressive heat of the morning.

"Way to go you idiot," Josiah whispered through the hand covering his mouth. Further down to his left, Gideon scowled and shook a finger at him.

"Sit up and behave," he mouthed.

Eben blushed a deeper red and tried to straighten himself on the uncomfortable wooden bench the family shared. He was convinced that the long oak benches, built by the first Community settlers in the 1850's, were intended to make people and their backsides suffer no matter how they positioned themselves. But no one ever sat on them for minutes; Reverend Stohlfutz's tedious sermons often lasted up to two hours, sometimes more, causing everyone in attendance considerable grief. Eben remembered seeing more than one person over the years either pitching forward or falling backwards off the detestable back-less benches when fatigue and boredom set in. He was glad Isaac had caught him just in time. Sometimes, things more embarrassing than simply falling happened; his friend, John, had wet his pants during church services several years before when the boys were younger. And worse, no one was allowed to get up and leave during the sermons either. John had been forced to sit in the mess, re-faced and shamed for a good hour while the Reverend continued on and on.

With a deep sigh, Eben squirmed desperately trying to find a comfortable position. To his horror, he realized a large bulge between his legs poking out at an angle and it was obvious. Deciding it would be best to just ignore it, he sat up to gaze at Stohlfutz trying to act as though nothing was wrong. Josiah snickered even louder. Eben glanced at his father out of the corner of his eye but was rewarded with what the boys called his, "wide-eyed crazy look."

Within minutes, the heat-stricken congregation returned to the sermon vacant-eyed and weary while Stohlfutz discussed the evils of the outside world and the dangers associated with it. Eben lowered his head and yawned. He and everyone else attending Sunday services in the sparsely furnished meeting house wished Stohlfutz would step down and let the Elders appoint another one of their own to do the preaching. They all knew however, he would never do so and he reveled in the power and prestige he believed the position gave him. Eben and Josiah hated him and were fairly certain Gideon did too.

Abe Stohlfutz was a tall, skinny man, bald on top with long white hair growing out on the sides of his narrow head. A long, un-kept beard hung to his chest while an unusually large nose and hollow, sunken cheeks gave him the look of a ghost. These unfortunate looks were heightened by a set of narrow, dark eyes which seemed to stab into the soul of everyone he encountered. His fingers too, were long and bony, tipped with long, sharp finger nails. Most people in the Community, especially the younger boys such as Eben and Josiah, often joked quietly about how much he resembled a buzzard or another kind of unpleasant bird. Some even went as far as to say he was the Crow Man himself which brought more hoots of laughter.

At seventy-two years old, Reverend Stohlfutz had been preaching in Meeting House Number Two for nearly fifty years. There were four Meeting Halls in the Community, each built geographically so every family had easy access to the required Sunday services and everything else Stohlfutz, who was also the Head Elder in the Community, deemed necessary to ensure the spiritual well-being of his flock. Most men only served for a few years, then stepped aside to give other men the opportunity to preach and lead their home congregations. But not Stohlfutz. He wouldn't give up what he considered his God-given station which he used to further his own interests while admonishing and generally making life unpleasant for those under his guidance. Every family throughout the Community was expected to make a donation of either cash or goods each Sunday for the upkeep of the meeting hall, the purchase of Bibles and so on, but everyone knew Stohlfutz pocketed the money and kept the goods for himself.

Stohlfutz's wife, Anna, was as skinny and frightening looking as her husband. She never smiled nor did she ever engage any of the women of the Community in small talk. She, just like her husband, used her position as his wife to satisfy her own means. Eben knew his mother detested the woman and refused to have anything to do with her even when the rest of the women would serve dinners for various church and Community functions.

He vaguely remembered a time when he was very young when Mrs. Stohlfutz had screamed at Mary for something during one such get-together. Mary, never one to take abuse from anyone, had stood up to her. A smile crossed his face recalling his short mother standing toe to toe shouting back and forth with the old witch who had completely lost her composure during the incident. At one point, a completely enraged Mrs. Stohlfutz took a swing at Mary who sidestepped the blow. The old woman lost her balance and lurched forward into a long table piled high with food for the upcoming dinner. Plates and crockery shattered, food went flying into the air with Mrs. Stohlfutz ending up in the middle of it. Mary then stood over her shaking a finger in her face while hissing something unmentionable. To most women in the Community, Mary was a hero but it came at a cost; she was officially admonished for one year which meant she couldn't attend church or any other Community functions. Mary didn't mind however, and much preferred staying home with her children than having to engage with Mrs. Stohlfutz or anyone else in what he'd heard her quietly refer to once to as, "that dreadful church."

The Stohlfutz's lived comfortably in a typical two-story Community home with two of their eight children and a teenage girl who they had taken in after her parents had died in a house fire. The younger children, Thomas, was Isaac's age and Elma, was Lydia's age. As they were too much like their parents, they were universally disliked by everyone, especially Isaac who'd had a long running feud with Thomas since the boys were five. Eben and Josiah knew of the trouble Thomas caused for Isaac and often found themselves in trouble for teaching the mean boy a thing or two when he pushed Isaac around. The adopted girl, Katurah, was much different from her host parents. A pretty girl with long blonde hair and a naturally kind disposition, Eben knew her life wasn't a happy one. She rarely spoke to anyone at school and often showed up with bruises on her face and hands. Josiah guessed she had more that couldn't be seen because some days she walked with a limp and couldn't sit at her desk properly without wincing in pain. Both boys had tried speaking to her several times as she was their age and pretty, therefore a good potential marriage partner, but she preferred spending her recess time alone with a tattered teddy bear she carried everywhere. An occasional "hello" or a simple "yes" or "no" was all she ever said to anyone.

Eben's eyes wandered around the meeting hall playing a game in his head in which he'd name every person in order of their birth in each family beginning with the parents. There were the Beiler's; Malachi, Sarah, Jen, Noah, Daniel, Luke and Abigale. The Miller's; Gabriel, Evelyn, Ada, Barbara, Collin, Freeman and Grace. Along the back wall stood several Sentinels, one of whom met his gaze as he worked his way through the Hostettler family. The man glared at him and raised a finger to vehemently point at Stohlfutz. Blushing, Eben quickly turned away.

Wherever Stohlfutz went, he always had at least two Sentinels with him. Stohlfutz claimed they worked his land as farmhands but everyone in the Community knew better. In addition to always being with Stohlfutz, these men were also always present during church services standing in the back or on the sides where they could watch everyone. No one dared object when they acted as ushers and passed the collection basket around making sure every head of the household contributed. To refuse meant a midnight visit.

Eben yawned again and felt his belly rumble. He wished he would have had more time to eat but he and his brothers were late getting up to do the milking. During the night he'd climbed out of his room and quickly run to the creek to see if he could actually get out of the house without being caught. Unfortunately, Gideon stayed up later than usual and it had been close to three A.M. before Eben finally got out and back.

Mary reached across Josiah and squeezed Eben's hand gently. He smiled when she winked at him. He knew attending church was a torture for her as well. As she did so, the Sentinel whose attention he'd garnered hovered at the end of the row scowling at them. Mary and Eben quickly turned their attention back to the sermon.

"The thief cometh not, but for to steal, and to kill, and to destroy: I am come that they might have life, and that they might have it more abundantly." Stohlfutz said waving his bony finger in the air. "And what did John mean when he spoke these words? Eh? He was warning true believers, much like those of us here in our sacred Community, to beware of outsiders, those who wish to take what you have. Your very souls! The walls of our Community are invisible, yes, for we cannot see them. But there are walls! Those walls separate us from the evil in the world out there, there in the English world where they worship their idols of money, possessions and live covetous lives in pursuit of pleasure."

Eben yawned again. Stohlfutz loved to criticize the English world but whispered rumors swirled about him and his wife going into town occasionally. With a sigh, he looked around at the other tired faces in the meeting hall. For a moment, he and Katurah's eyes met. Eben smiled at her and nodded and was surprised when she smiled back. She quickly looked away however.

"I am your shepherd," Stohlfutz continued. "And I am here to save all of you from yourselves and your pagan desires. Yes, follow my words and each of you will find salvation through the Lord."

Eben sighed deeply and watched as a bead of sweat dripped from his forehead and fell to the floor.

"And now, we have a young person with us today who was tempted by the very evil I've been warning you about," Stohlfutz said pointing towards the back of the meeting hall. Every person turned to look upon Samuel Schrock, a young man of seventeen who Eben and Josiah were friends with. His left eye was black and blue and nearly swollen shut. His right eye however, was wide open and looked upon the congregation with fear. Two Sentinels stood behind him waiting patiently.

"Come forward young man," Stohlfutz said gesturing to the boy.

Samuel hesitated turning to look at his parents who were seated nearby. His father stared straight ahead absolutely stone-faced but his mother looked at him and cried into a handkerchief. One of the Sentinels poked him in the back forcing him forward. Slowly, agonizingly, in obvious pain, he limped towards Stohlfutz on bare, swollen feet.

"Stand here before me," Stohlfutz ordered. "And face the people you turned your back on."

Eben and Josiah looked at one another carefully then turned their attention back to Stohlfutz. Samuel turned around with his one good eye fixed on the floor. One of the Sentinels accompanying him reached over and forced his head up with a thin wooden cane they carried during services.

Stohlfutz leaned in close, his mouth inches from the boy's ear. "There is wickedness in your soul which must be cleansed if you are to partake in the glory the Lord hath given us! Please, confess to those of us here, your family who has prayed for you and trusted you to live by the Word!"

Samuel looked at Stohlfutz apprehensively before reaching into his pocket to produce a wrinkled piece of paper. He began speaking in a barely audible, halting squeak. "I confess I snuck into town on many occasions without my parent's knowledge. I…"

"What's that? I don't believe they can hear you!"

Samuel looked at his mother and nearly collapsed as his legs began to give out from underneath him. Both Sentinels took his arms and jerked him upright. Taking a deep breath, he cleared his throat and continued. "I…I wore English clothing and I visited houses of ill-repute. I drank alcohol and I smoked cigarettes. I kept English money hidden in my home to use on my carnal visits. I have used the Lord's name in vain. I am covetous and I am a liar. I doubted God's love and I defied the will of my parent's and our blessed Community. Please, take pity upon me for I am a sinner."

Stohlfutz gently put a hand on Samuel's shoulder. "Thank you. Is there anything else you'd like to add?"

"Yes, I…I apologize. Please forgive me."

Other than the singing of birds floating in through the open windows not a sound could be heard in the hall and no one dared move.

"Now, we will all stand and condemn this lost soul."

The congregation stood as if Stohlfutz had pushed some sort of button and waited solemnly.

"Sinner!" a man shouted.

"Sinner!" shouted another.

Soon, everyone else joined in until their voices were a distorted chorus of shouts and jeers echoing off the bare walls of the meeting house. Eben half-heartedly joined in as was expected but with a few feeble shouts then stopped altogether. Beside him, Josiah frowned and jammed his hands into his pockets. After several minutes, Stohlfutz held his hands up.

"Very well, you may join the others."

Samuel was led to a bench known as the, 'sinner's seat' at the front of the meeting hall where four others sat staring ahead, absolutely motionless. Each was expected to hold a Bible at arm's length for the duration of the church service. If they wavered or collapsed from exhaustion, a Sentinel would strike them across the back and force them back into position. Every person who was condemned to sit here was usually struck multiple times before Stohlfutz finished speaking.

Josiah sighed quietly and poked Eben in the ribs causing him to jump. Eben waited a moment, crossed his arms, carefully reached over and pinched Josiah's arm as hard as he could. Josiah grunted and turned in his seat until Gideon cleared his throat. Both boys stared straight ahead at Stohlfutz as though they were paying attention to him but their eyes were fixed on Samuel.

"We have a number of young men in our little congregation here who are on the verge of manhood," Stohlfutz said gesturing towards the teenage boys in attendance. His eyes settled on Josiah and Eben briefly before moving on. "Young men who should be aware of what it means to be a man in our holy Community and the great responsibilities it entails."

"He's talking to you, momma's boy," Josiah whispered. Eben responding by pinching his arm much harder.

"Yes, there are great responsibilities for you. Responsibilities to your parents, your siblings and most especially, to your Community. But, do you find yourself tempted? Hmm? Tempted by the world out there? Yes, I think all of you are," he said turning towards Samuel and the others. "The English and their technology, they use it as a way to steal your souls. It's all iniquity, the pornography, the music, the money they live for. But how do you young men do what's right? You pray to the Lord and trust in him, and the Community, to guide you and show you how to live your lives in humble reverence. Look within to find salvation."

Stohlfutz closed his eyes and spread his arms widely. A smile crept across his revealing a mouthful of brown, stained teeth. "Let us pray silently while we give up our offering."

Eben suppressed a laugh thinking about his mother and how adamant she was about having her children brush their teeth. He was sure she had the Reverend in mind.

Josiah tapped him on the shoulder, then leaned over slightly and squeezed his eyes shut.

"What are you doing?" Eben whispered.

It was immediately obvious what Josiah had done. He looked at Eben with a screwed up face while he fanned his nose. "Eben," he whispered. "You're disgusting."

Eben opened his mouth to respond until Gideon reached over and tapped both boys on the head with the knuckle of his middle finger. Seeing it coming, Eben ducked away but Josiah shuddered under the force of the blow.

"Enough!" Gideon hissed through clenched teeth. Both boys sat red-faced as the offering basket was passed along doing their best not to laugh out loud.

"Josiah," Isaac finally whispered as he held a hand up to his nose. "Wow."

Arlen Kopp and three of his Sentinels approached from the rear of the hall and took two baskets from Stohlfutz's outstretched hands. Kopp and one man walked down the center aisle while the other two shuffled along the outside intently watching everyone. Upon reaching Gideon, a sneering Kopp handed him the basket. Ignoring the man, he threw a plain white envelope in and handed it over to Josiah. Josiah stopped and stared wide-eyed at the basket full of money for a moment before handing it on to the end of the row.

Eben watched Josiah's eyes become wider as the basket continued around the meeting hall. He continued to keep an eye on it as
Stohlfutz received it from the Sentinels and placed it on the table
at his side.

"Wow, that's really something, isn't it," Josiah whispered.

Eben shook his head in disgust knowing exactly what he was
talking about.

CHURCH MONEY

Once church services were over, people began to drift out of the miserably hot meeting hall into the sweltering midday sun. The heat and humidity had returned and was hovering at ninety percent making everyone in the Community miserable and wondering aloud when the summer heat would finally end. Eben and his friends, John and Zachariah stood under the shade of an ancient oak tree visiting about their summers and what they would do once they reached the age of sixteen. The boys had attended school together since they were five and were as close as friends could be. Now, as the oldest boys in the small two-room school building they attended, they looked forward to their last year together. Eben desperately wanted to tell his friends about Wendy but thought better of it. Rumors spread quickly in the Community and were often wildly distorted by the time they had gone through everyone.

"Do you think he did all of what he said?" Zachariah asked.

"Samuel?" Eben asked. "No, I believe he probably went into town a few times and got caught by his father. The rest of that stuff…well, everyone who gets in trouble confesses to the same things."

"He's getting what he deserves," John exclaimed. "He's a sinner and he has to make amends."

"But he only went into town. So they say anyway," Eben countered.

"Yes, but without his father's permission. He snuck around and did God knows what when he was there."

"Oh come on, John," Zachariah retorted. "He wanted to have a little fun. What's wrong with that? Everyone goes to town to run around once in a while."

"I never have, not alone anyway. My father forbids it and I follow the rules."

Eben and Zachariah snorted at their friend.

"John, you're always taking things a bit too seriously. Doesn't it hurt being so uptight all the time?" Eben asked throwing a pebble in John's direction.

"No, it doesn't. I grant you, we're all sinners and we have to work at being forgiven. Samuel doesn't obey his father and in turn, he's not obeying the word of God. He's consciously sinning with no regard for forgiveness. Let him suffer until he sees the path I say."

The boys stood in silence for several moments trying to think of something else to say.

"So, have you heard about my father's cows?" John asked his friends.

"No, what's happened?" Eben answered leaning back on the tree glad the conversation was on to something else.

"My father rents the field just down from your father's corner on the creek. We've had cows in there all summer."

"Next to the Robinsons?" Eben asked.

"Yes, they're in the Yoder's field. Some cousins to my family."

"We're all cousins in one way or another. Especially to the Yoder's," Eben laughed.

John snapped his fingers and pointed at Eben. "My mother was a Yoder and so was yours."

"And my father. And me!" Zachariah announced proudly.

"So, we're one big happy family. *Everyone* that is," Eben replied happily.

"You should know," Zachariah said poking Eben. John quickly shushed him and shook his head.

"What do you mean? I know my parents are second cousins. Big deal."

"Um, I'm sorry I said anything."

"No, Zachariah, your sister married Den and they're related. A Yoder marrying a Yoder, now doesn't that sound kind of strange," Eben retorted. He cleared his throat and raised his voice to imitate Stohlfutz's high pitched whine. "Do you Sarah *Yoder* take Den *Yoder* to be your lawfully wedding husband?"

John erupted in laughter but Zachariah looked away with pursed lips.

"Just drop it, Eben. I'm just having a little fun with you. You know how everyone seems to be related here. It's a joke."

The boys sat in the shade for a few moments in silence watching their families slowly file out of the church. Eben knew whatever he had meant wasn't a joke but he was willing to let it drop.

"About our cows…," John said still red-faced from his laughter.

"So you have cows in the Yoder's. Big deal," Zachariah muttered.

"Ha, ha. We've found some of the calves dead."

"Dead from the heat? We've lost some too," Eben replied wiping his brow on his white shirt sleeve.

"Coyotes maybe?"

"No."

"That couldn't be," Zachariah answered. "Coyotes don't kill cows. They just tear on them after they've died."

"Well, if it's not the heat, what then?" Eben asked throwing another larger pebble at John.

"I shouldn't say this but I will," Zachariah said carefully looking back towards the crowd lingering at the church doors. He leaned in close to his friends as a smile crept across his face. "But I think it's the work of the Crow Man."

"What? You know you're not supposed to talk about that!" John hissed.

Wondering when his parents and siblings would finally come out of the meeting hall, Eben sighed and removed his straw hat to wipe his forehead. He hoped they hadn't been cornered by the Reverend for his mother's sake. Despite making an outward show of disliking Stohlfutz, Gideon however, always seemed to find time to have whispered conversations with the man whenever they saw one another.

"Not a word of this to anyone," Eben said quietly. "My father has gotten strange about us going to the creek."

"Don't you and Josiah go down there sometimes?" John asked.

"Yes. He caught me the other day and knocked the stuffing out of me."

"Why?"

"I don't know. He's always told us to stay away from it. Up until this year he just shouted at us, now he's smacking us."

"It's because the Crow Man lives in there," Zachariah declared.

"Could be," Eben said with a wink towards his friend. "I've heard strange things at night you know."

"You're both crazy!" John barked. "It's a sin to talk about it and you know it!" He waved his stick at Eben and Zachariah. "You're both a couple of dumb fools. The Crow Man isn't a wild beast. It's just another name for the devil."

"How would you know? We've all heard the stories," Eben said pushing the stick away.

"Because, I'm smart, that's why. Don't you read the Bible? The devil has many of different names. He just happens to be what someone in Community made up a long time ago to scare hollow-headed fools like you."

"What about Ben Isler? Remember? They say he'd packed a bag and was supposedly running for town when something caught him. He told someone it was the Crow Man and it kept him hidden in a dark place for weeks and tortured him. That's why he stayed. It made him," Zachariah said.

John shook his head. "You're an idiot. Everyone knows Ben is crazy."

"Oh, yeah? My oldest sister said he was as normal as could be when they were growing up. It was only after he tried to leave that his head was messed up. He was gone for a long time too, then, he just showed up at church with his family one day."

"I remember that," Eben said. "He was really skinny too, and he didn't talk to anyone for the longest time."

"There he is, right there," Zachariah said with a nod of his head. Ben walked slowly out of the church meeting hall behind his wife, Annalise, who happened to be Stohlfutz's second oldest daughter. She was a mean-tempered, overweight woman who it was rumored ruled the household through threats and physical abuse. The couple's two portly children walked with their mother chattering away while Ben skulked along stoop-shouldered and bent behind them.

"Poor guy. I'd have left too if I'd have been matched with her. Ugh!" John said with a shiver.

"Me too," Eben said. "Could you imagine? How'd he ever get stuck with her anyway?"

"Poor bugger," Zachariah said watching them walk to their buggy. "He was supposed to be with Becca Yoder, one of our cousins, but they say he missed out on her when he ran. The Elders, Reverend Stohlfutz in particular, forced him to marry old miss cow patty there because no one else would have her and I mean, no one."

The boys laughed but quickly turned away when Ben stopped and gave them a long, cold stare. After a moment he turned to help his complaining wife and children into their buggy.

"Shhh..."

"So, are you both ready to turn sixteen?" John asked changing subjects. He'd celebrated his sixteenth birthday several weeks before and had always enjoyed lording what he considered his wise old age over his friends.

"Yep, my Father said he was going to give me a buggy and a horse," Zachariah answered proudly.

"Mine's coming up at the end of September. The twenty-ninth," Eben replied.

"Yes, that's right," John said snapping his fingers. "Boy, you and Josiah really are close in age aren't you."

"Yes, he was sixteen in November of last year."

"So he's only ten months older than you?"

Eben smiled. "Yes. But, he likes to remind me how old and superior he is to me. Kind of like you."

"Wow," John said. "Your mother had her hands full, walking into that and all."

"What do you mean?" Eben asked with a sideways look. The boys were always playfully digging at each other but sometimes it went too far. John and Zachariah always teased Eben about something having to do with his mother which infuriated him. No one spoke badly of his mother, not even his closest friends without paying for it.

"Walking into it? Why don't you come out and say it, John because I'm tired of you both talking about my mother! What do you mean?"

Zachariah quietly shushed John and looked at the ground.

"Um, nothing, Eben. I'm sorry."

Eben glared at John knowing his quick anger would get him in trouble in front of the church congregation and his parents.

"Anyway," John said. "Do you know, when you turn sixteen, um...you know."

"What?" Zachariah asked shooing a fly away from his face.

"You know, the thing, when you come of age. Um, since your fathers are both Elders..."

"No. What are you talking about, John, being baptized?"

"No, the other thing. It, um..."

Eben smiled and turned to Zachariah. "I think the heat's gotten to his brain. Just listen to him, blah, blah, blah."

Zachariah snorted. "Yeah, we all know, John. You turn sixteen and you can be baptized and marry. I think Eben's correct, the sun has gone to your head."

John scowled with anger. "That's not what I'm talking about you sheep lovers!"

"Well, what then?" Eben asked though his laughter.

"Nothing. You'll find out soon enough."

The boys lounged in the shade watching people ready their buggies and head for home. The heat was quickly becoming insufferable.

"Look at that will you," Zachariah said gesturing with his stick. "I'd like to beat the stuffing out of that little dung heap."

Thomas Stohlfutz snatched Katurah's teddy bear away and threw it into the Stohlfutz's buggy. Each time she tried to climb in to retrieve it Thomas would pull her down and push her away.

"You can't get in *our* buggy!" he cried mockingly. "It's for people. Not scrawny little rats like you!"

Katurah stood silently with tears welling up in her eyes. She tried climbing in to retrieve her bear again and again only to have Thomas throw her back each time.

"I have. So has Josiah," Eben replied. "We've thumped him pretty hard before too but he just won't learn."

Thomas continued his rant. "You're nothing but a dirty whore! Do you hear me, whore?"

All three boys groaned in unison.

"Oh, no, did he really say that?" John asked. "Because if he did, I'll teach him a lesson myself."

"Me too," Zachariah added. "Come on, let's have a little talk with him."

The boys began walking towards Thomas until Josiah suddenly appeared from behind a tree and enveloped Thomas in a choke hold. He dragged him away from the buggy and away from the groups of people standing outside the meeting hall. Seeing Eben and his friends approaching he removed his hat with his free hand and smiled. Thomas thrashed and choked clawing at Josiah's leg.

"Hey, boys. I'll take care of this. Eben, why don't you fetch Katurah's bear?"

Eben climbed into the buggy and retrieved the teddy bear. "Here you go."

Katurah snatched it from his hands and held it close.

"Thank you," she said softly.

"You're welcome," Eben replied. He and his friends turned to leave but he stopped and went back. "If Thomas ever gives you a hard time again, just let me or Josiah know about it. Okay?"

Katurah looked away trying to hide her face under her bonnet. "I will. Thank you again."

Eben nodded and walked back to his friends who had returned to the relative comfort of the shade tree.

"I feel sorry for her," John said as the boys watched Josiah drag Thomas further into the trees lining the parking lot where he began beating the boy's backside with a switch. "Reverend Buzzard Nose and that witch he's married to treat her bad enough, but then she has to deal with him too."

"Yeah," Eben said wiping the sweat from his forehead. "It's bad enough they make her walk behind the buggy. Besides, we've all heard what the Reverend does to her."

"I don't even like thinking about it," Zachariah answered. "It's disgusting and it's well…it's so wrong."

John spit on the ground and ran his boot through it. "I've heard the old lady knows about it too, and lets him do it. I've heard he even beats on the poor girl while he has his way with her."

Eben stole a quick glance at Katurah and shivered despite the heat.

Gideon approached the boys smiling.

"Well boys, how are you all doing?"

"Just fine, Mr. Wittmer." John and Zachariah answered.

The boys stood uncertainly for a moment taking great care not to look him in the eye. Eben carefully peeked out from under his hat to see if Josiah was still spanking Thomas but luckily for him, he'd seen Gideon approaching and made a run for it.

"What's this? You're not talking about something you shouldn't are you boys? Girls perhaps?" he asked with a smirk.

"No Father, it's not like that. We were talking about Katurah and how badly she gets treated by Thomas."

"Yes, I've noticed that as well. Young Thomas would most certainly benefit from some ah, guidance," Gideon said softly. "Your mother and I wanted to take her in after her parents died but Reverend Stohlfutz insisted on taking her."

The boys looked away.

"It's God's will she be with them and not us though the Reverend can be a bit of a disciplinarian I'm afraid. In spite of that, he and his wife do much for our Community. Anyway, what are you boys up to?"

"We're just talking about turning sixteen and what we'll be doing," Eben answered.

"Hmm, yes. I pray you all stay true to your faith and your families and make full lives here for yourselves. I believe God wishes for each of you to marry and become our next generation of leaders. We'll need you boys to think about being Elders when it's your turn."

"Yes, Mr. Wittmer," Zachariah said standing up straight. "That's my intention. I want to marry a good girl and work with my father in his cabinet shop."

Eben and John cautiously rolled their eyes. Zachariah loved to lay it on thickly but he stopped short of outright lying. He'd secretly told the boys he wanted to sneak into town to drink alcohol and hopefully, have sex with an English girl or two before he came back and took his baptism.

"Good for you Zachariah," Gideon answered with a wink to Eben and John.

"And, what of you John?"

"I plan to work with my father on the farm and marry. I'd like to have a lot of children. To be honest, I can't imagine anything better than spending my life here."

"Do you have any young lady in mind, John? Or, do you want the Elders to find you a match?"

"Well, Mr. Wittmer, I do fancy Hannah Burkholder and I believe she fancies me as well. We've talked about marriage."

"Good for you, young man, good for you. Her father serves as an Elder as you know. She's a good girl and comes from a good family."

"Yes, thank you, Mr. Wittmer."

Gideon put his hand on Eben's shoulder and smiled. "The Community needs you boys. Zachariah, I pray you and John find the next steps in your lives agreeable."

John stood up straight and gave Zachariah and Eben a snooty smirk.

"Well son, let's get everyone together and get headed home. We'll have to make sure the animals have plenty of water today."

"Yes Father," Eben answered.

Eben and Gideon said their goodbyes to John and Zachariah and stepped out into the hot sunlight.

"That Zachariah…" Gideon said quietly. "Doesn't have a pure thought in his head does he?"

Eben stifled a laugh. "You have no idea Father. He has big plans for next year."

"Hmm, I'm sure of it. His father…well, he had some hard choices to make. He was nearly twenty-five before he was allowed to be baptized. Come, get the buggy ready and we'll go home. You and I can make ice cream later this afternoon."

"Yes Father," Eben said pausing for a moment.

"What is it Eben? You want to ask me something?"

Several questions filled Eben's head but he was afraid to ask. What had John had been trying to say?

"Um, Father?"

"Yes?"

"What happens when a boy turns sixteen?"

Gideon smiled and continued walking. "Why? Has Zachariah put bad thoughts into that head of yours?"

"No, it seemed as though John were trying to tell us something would happen when we turn sixteen."

"What did he say?"

"Nothing. He just mumbled and finally told us to forget about it."

For a moment Gideon's face clouded over. He coughed quietly and looked down at Eben from under the brim of his hat. "Maybe your friend has gotten to know Miss Burkholder a little better than he should, eh? That could explain why he's already talking about marrying the girl."

Eben chuckled loudly. His father rarely spoke of such things and only ever did so in the barn or in the fields, certainly not around the women.

"It could be. He didn't act as though he were happy about it though. I mean, he seemed too serious."

Gideon winked at Eben and lowered his voice as they approached the rest of the family waiting at the wagon. "Maybe he found it to be a disappointment for some strange reason, although, I couldn't imagine why."

Eben smiled and climbed into the buggy with Isaac and his sisters. He immediately noticed Josiah was missing. Gideon did too.

"Where's Josiah?"

Mary shrugged her shoulders. "He said he had to use the outhouse."

The family waited for several more minutes before Gideon began losing his patience. "He went to the outhouse?"

"Yes, that's what he said," Mary replied. "He jumped down and said that's where he was going but that was fifteen minutes ago."

Gideon grumbled and adjusted his hat and turned in his seat trying to see where Josiah was. He wasn't in the mood to sit in the hot sun much longer. "I'm going to find him. He better have a painful stomach ache."

"Oh, Gideon, it's okay."

"No, it's not. We're sitting here boiling in our own sweat and he's out running around as usual! We have lunch to eat and chores to do!"

Just as Gideon jumped down from the wagon, Josiah appeared from behind the meeting hall out of breath and red-faced.

"What happened? Did you fall in?" Gideon barked.

Josiah quickly climbed into the back of the buggy and purposely fell into Eben and Isaac. "Sorry, Father. Must have had too many eggs for breakfast."

The girls squealed with revulsion and made awful faces at Josiah who sat fanning his hand in front of his nose. Eben and Isaac hooted with laughter.

"Josiah!"

"Sorry, Father. I'm just saying, nature called and wanted her eggs back, and she didn't want to wait. She wanted them right now! Whew!"

Gideon slapped the reigns gently on the horses and shook his head. "Is that really where you were, or were you doing something you shouldn't have been doing?"

"No, honestly Father, I was in the outhouse. Just ask Eben."

"Is that true Eben?"

Josiah squeezed Eben's arm tightly. Eben glared at him with fury. He knew if he told his father the truth Josiah wouldn't hesitate to retaliate and say something to get him in trouble. Begrudgingly, he decided to let it go for the time being. He wouldn't let it go without Josiah being indebted to him though.

"Um, yes, father. I saw him go out there when I was talking to John and Zachariah."

"Well, Josiah, since you seem to be ill, you can go to your room for the rest of the day once we're home."

Eben smiled wickedly.

Josiah sat up and looked at his parents with pleading eyes. "But, father, we're having roast beef, potatoes and carrots today! And honey cake! It's my favorite! Honestly, I feel fine now! I do! It's... passed!"

Both Mary and Gideon suppressed their laughter while Josiah continued to plead with them on his knees. Eben noticed a bit of paper money sticking out of his front pants pocket. Money was used sparingly in the Community and then, only by adults. Trading and working for goods and services was the usual way of doing business unless people were buying goods in the Community store or in town. For anyone not married, having money was forbidden. Seeing his brother staring at his pocket, Josiah quickly covered it with his hand and sat back down. He glowered at Eben slowly shaking his head back and forth.

"Not a word to anyone. Understood?" he whispered.

Eben shook his head angrily.

NIGHT MEETING

The night air was damp and heavy with humidity and clung to Eben's body as he made his way through the dark field. He stopped and drank deeply from the water bottle he'd remembered to fill with the cold well water from the pump at home earlier in the evening. Wiping his forehead on his sleeve he gazed up through the corn leaves and tassels at the cloudless sky above. It hadn't rained for weeks and much of the corn was beginning to turn a pale yellow. Eben continued walking through the hard dirt of the field cringing every time the dried out leaves crackled and crunched.

Reaching the edge of the field Eben again stopped and wiped his forehead on his now sopping wet shirtsleeve. He drank from the bottle again and crouched low watching for any sign of Wendy on the other side. It was a strange night just as the past few days had been; the intolerable heat and lack of wind had made the world a breathless, simmering oven which sapped the strength out of everyone. Gideon, a man who believed in hard work and no exceptions had even relaxed his strict rules allowing the family to do the chores early in the morning before sunrise and later in the day when the sun finally went down. The hottest parts of the day were spent inside reading and using hand-held fans to try and stay cool. To Eben, the heat coupled with the odd schedule left him tired and depressed for much of the time while he anxiously waited for nightfall.

He had waited several long hours sweating and turning in the bed wanting to make absolutely sure the rest of the family was asleep, most especially, Josiah.

"I'll be watching you tonight, Eben. If you sneak out I'll follow you so I can meet Miss Wendy."

Eben only frowned at his brother who laughed in his face; he knew Josiah wasn't lying. For four long hours Eben alternated his gaze from the tiny wind-up clock next to the bed and his brother. For the first two hours each time he rolled over, Josiah opened his eyes and mumbled.

"I'm still awake. What are you up to?"

"Be quiet, I'm trying to sleep."

"Are you, or are you waiting for me to fall asleep first?"

"Just stop, it's miserable enough in here."

"Yeah, thanks to you, Eben."

"You're impossible. Why don't you shut up?"

"Because, I don't have to," Josiah replied mockingly.

Finally after two A.M. Josiah couldn't fight his fatigue any longer and fell into a deep sleep. Eben fell in and out of consciousness for nearly another half-hour before slipping quietly out of bed. He struggled to pull his clothing over his sweaty body and didn't bother trying to tuck his shirt in. Luckily, the window in the bedroom was opened as far as it could go; it creaked and groaned loudly whenever anyone open or shut it.

Reaching out for the maple branch just above the window, Eben carefully pulled himself out and swung his legs over to the next branch. The rest was easy; he'd been climbing up and down this tree his entire life. Once on the ground, he waited in the shadows for a moment watching the window and the rest of the house. Hearing and seeing nothing, he darted through the farm-yard and plunged into the corn field.

Eben decided to run directly to the creek as he'd done before instead of waiting around to see if anyone would get up. Several times he stopped trying to catch his breath which came in long gasps. Guessing it was nearly three o'clock in the morning he didn't expect Wendy to still be waiting for him. Wiping his face on his sleeve, he continued on.

Reaching the tall weeds at the end of the field, he paused. Wendy's voice called out faintly.

"Eben? Is that you?"

"I'm here. Where are you?"

"I'm over here," she answered from somewhere ahead in the dark.

Eben stopped in front of the dry creek bed and gazed into the darkness on the other side trying to see where she was.

"Eben! I've been waiting for two hours. I'm glad you came!" Wendy exclaimed appearing from the shadows. Eben unconscious-ly slicked his hair back and stood grinning like a fool thinking about how beautiful she looked in the pale light of the moon.

"Hello, Wendy. I'm sorry I'm late. I had to wait for my father to go to sleep. And, my brother too."

"Oh, it's alright, I had the same problem. My aunt and uncle stay up late sometimes watching T.V. I skinned my knee climbing out of my bedroom window."

"I'm sorry. Are you okay?" Eben asked.

"I'm fine, nothing to worry about," she said holding her hand out. "Come with me, I want to show you something. Look," she said kneeling down at the base of an enormous old maple tree. "This tree is hollowed out on the inside. See?"

"I didn't know this was over here," Eben said squatting down and sticking his head inside the space.

"Of course you didn't. It faces away from your father's land and well, it's over *here*," Wendy said with a giggle. "Go on, go inside."

Wendy clicked on a small flashlight she carried illuminating the interior. Eben peered through the narrow opening and was amazed to discover how big and roomy it was.

"Isn't this neat?" Wendy said squeezing herself through the narrow opening. "Both of us can sit in here comfortably."

"It is. I can even stand straight up," Eben said following her in. "And look! It's almost as wide as my arms."

"Here, please sit," Wendy said. "I brought a blanket."

Eben sat on the blanket and smiled. Wendy beamed with pleasure.

"I love it! A secret place! No one would ever find us here."

"I like it," Eben replied. "It's really something. How did you find it?"

"I was sitting on the log over there this morning and the sunlight was shining in."

"It is fairly well hidden," Eben replied.

"You know, Eben, I was thinking, we could leave each other letters in here. Just in case one of us comes down here and the other one isn't around. If you want to that is."

"You know, that's a good idea, Wendy. The only problem is the raccoons and squirrels will eat the paper."

Wendy thought a moment and snapped her fingers. "I have an idea! I found a metal box in the old barn behind Uncle David's house the other day and he said I could have it. I'll leave it inside here the next time I come down. That will be our mailbox."

"Hey, you're pretty smart. That's a great idea."

"Thank you, Eben! I just, um, I hope you don't think I'm being too forward by asking you to write to me."

Eben smiled. "No, I don't think you are. I think you're nice."

"Good. That's settled then."

"So, tell me about yourself," she continued pulling the note-book from the bag always at her side. . "Tell me about your family."

"What do you want to know?"

"Everything. What do you like to do? What's your favorite food? What are your brothers and sisters names?"

Eben thought a moment and began telling Wendy about himself. She wrote furiously, obviously mesmerized by what he had to tell her.

"And, my brother, Josiah, well, he's a year older than me. He's the one who showed me this place when we were little," he said after nearly ten-minutes of nonstop talking.

"Does he have brownish-blonde hair like you? And he's a little taller than you are?"

"Yes, how did you know that?"

"I saw him down here one day last week but I didn't know who he was. He was wandering through the woods over on your side of the creek muttering something to himself. He kept looking over here and shaking his head. It was kind of strange."

"That's Josiah," Eben said. "He wants to leave the Community but he doesn't know anyone outside of here. On top of that, he I don't think he has the guts to run. He said something the other day about possibly having you drive him somewhere if he ever decides to go."

Wendy gave him a strange look. "Oh really? Why would I do that? I don't even know him!"

Eben shrugged his shoulders. "I don't know. He's always trying to take things away from me because he's the oldest. And, well, he knows how to talk to girls better than I do. He thinks everyone owes him a favor."

Wendy laughed and playfully touched Eben's leg causing him to jump as though he'd been burned. "Who says I'm some object he can just take from you? Besides, I think you do just fine. Talking to me that is."

"I do?" Eben asked with genuine surprise.

"Yes, I do," Wendy answered happily.

In the distance thunder boomed and echoed across the dark countryside. For a moment, their tiny space in the tree was illuminated by far-off flashes of lighting.

"Sounds like it's going to storm," Eben said leaning forward to peek outside. "The temperature is dropping too."

"I feel it," Wendy said leaning in close to Eben. The couple sat watching the storm slowly roll in.

"Eben, can I ask you something personal?"

"Sure. You can ask me anything."

"Well, um. No, I won't. It's stupid."

"Try me Wendy."

"You won't get mad at me?"

Eben smiled. "I don't think so. No, I won't."

"Okay. You promised," Wendy said.

She took a deep breath and turned to look at him with wide hopeful eyes. "I like you, as a friend that is."

Eben's mouth fell open in surprise. "You...do?"

"Yes, I think you're nice. You're certainly much nicer than 'English' boys. There's something, I don't know, uncomplicated and honest about you."

He laughed at her reference. "Thank you, I like you too, Wendy."

"Really? I mean, I hope you don't think I'm too forward!"

"Oh, no, don't worry," Eben said. "In a way, you remind me of my mother."

"I do? How?"

"You both have very pretty eyes and well, she likes me too."

Wendy's laughter filled the small space.

Lightning flickered in the western sky and was followed by a long crack of thunder just above the timber. Looking back at Wendy, Eben was surprised to see her face had suddenly changed from delight to one of fear.

"I hate the storms you have in Iowa."

"Why?" Eben asked. "It's just rain and a little noise."

Wendy grabbed ahold of Eben's hand tightly as a sharp crack of thunder rumbled nearby. "They just scare me and always have. I suppose it's because they're so big here and you can see them coming for miles. It's creepy."

"Well, some can be bad. A person just has to respect of the power some of them have," Eben said, remembering the tornado which had ripped through the Community several years before. It had torn a path of destruction through the farms and fields for nearly a mile before disappearing into the clouds. One family of seven Eben knew were killed when their house was picked up and shattered. He shivered remembering the thunderous sound of the funnel cloud and the debris flying in the air while the family ran to take shelter in the root cellar behind the back door of their house. Luckily, the storm had passed a mile to the east of their farm but it had still done some damage to the house, outbuildings and flattened most of the crops.

"How do you know? If they're going to be bad?"

"You don't. Sometimes they just pass by without doing much. But, a tornado roars like the devil once it gets started. Don't worry though, this is probably just a normal old summer storm."

"It doesn't sound like what I'd call normal," Wendy said inching closer to Eben.

Suddenly, an enormous clap of thunder exploded just over the tree shaking it like a small toy. Cold, damp air smelling of rain immediately whistled through the opening.

"What's going on, Eben?"

"This is a big one. Wendy, you need to go home now. Don't walk. Run as fast as you can. Okay?"

"Eben, I'm afraid."

"I am too. I have to get back up to the house. My father will be up now."

"Will you come back tomorrow?"

Eben shook his head and glanced at the sky. "I'll try, Wendy, I really will. I like your idea about writing. Let's do that and see what happens."

More thunder exploded in the sky shaking the ground and trees with its fury.

"We need to go, Wendy. Now!" Eben shouted squeezing through the opened with Wendy right behind him.

"I'll see you soon!" she shouted.

"I hope so!"

Eben turned and ran blindly through the timber hoping he wouldn't get caught in the open by the storm. His heart nearly leapt out of his chest when the lighting momentarily lit the sky: Josiah stood on the other side of the creek watching him intently.

JOSIAH'S PLAN

"Josiah! What are you doing?" Eben shouted. More lightning tore across the sky in spidery veins and was followed several seconds later by a series of more cracks and rolling rumbles. "Josiah!"

Rain began pelting Eben as he jumped across the creek and began running towards the corn field. In a flicker of lighting he was able to catch a glimpse of Josiah disappearing into the field just ahead. Eben strode out with anger consuming him. Mud bogged him down in and he swore as his foot came out of his shoe. The rain began coming across the field in sheets but he continued running trying to catch Josiah who had always been the faster of the two boys. The wind increased in intensity, howling and shrieking bringing with it heavier rain and more lighting. While he ran he could hear Josiah running and slogging through the mud somewhere to his right.

"Josiah! Damn you!"

Eben reached the barnyard and saw Josiah run into the barn. Running crazily through the rain and puddles in the driveway, he followed him and scurried back to the horse stalls where he fell heavily to the musty smelling floor. Josiah lay on his back in a pile of straw panting from fatigue.

"That's a pretty nice deal you have going on down there. I wish I could see her up close in the daylight."

Eben stared at him with a hatred he'd never felt towards anyone before. Rising to his hands and knees he fought to catch his breath. "What are you doing? Trying to get the best of me again?"

"I wanted to see for myself what you've gotten yourself into," Josiah wheezed. "Kind of a nice little hiding place you have."

"Darn you Josiah! I ought to beat your head…"

"Calm down, Eben. I'm not going to steal her from you if that's what you're thinking."

"What are you doing then? Trying to get the best of me again?"

"She's my ticket out. Since you're all friendly with her maybe you could convince her to help me."

"Why in the world would I help you? Why don't you just go on your own? No one's stopping you!"

"Come on, we're brothers. We've always been together, ever since we were little. I need some help. I have to get out of here. They're getting suspicious."

"Who is? What are you talking about?" Eben snapped.

"They are, The Ten. Father made me do something a couple of weeks ago I wish I wouldn't have done. If I don't have a quick way out far away from here I'll be stuck here forever," Josiah whispered. "I think they know I intend to leave."

Eben shook his head. "What are you talking about? The Ten?"

Josiah sat up and wiped his forehead with his wet shirt sleeve. "It's a secret group of Elders. They control things here. If you're selected to go to the Sanctuary it's all explained."

Eben's head swam from fatigue and from everything Wendy, and now Josiah, had told him. None of it made any sense.

"What's the Sanctuary? I don't understand, Josiah. What's going on?"

"What are you boys doing?" Gideon asked appearing out of the darkness. He stood silently glowering at Eben and Josiah while rainwater dripped off his hat in long, silent drops. Eben knew from the look on his face he was angry, and when he was angry someone always received a painful thrashing.

"Nothing father, just checking on the animals. I, um, couldn't sleep because of the heat and the storm. What are you doing out here?"

Gideon ignored him and let his hands fall at his sides. In his left hand he carried the thick razor strop which usually hung by the back door of the house.

"I came to see if Eben needed any help," Josiah said fearfully.

"Hmm, yes, they are acting strangely. Does everything look okay with them?" Gideon asked gazing at the animals.

"Yes, the horses are upset, so are the cows. They're all bunched up and making a racket."

"Probably that storm. It's really coming down, isn't it?" Josiah said hoping for a miracle.

"Yes, the lightning is impressive," Eben added trying to hide his shoeless foot from his father.

Gideon scowled and shook his head. His eyes turned back to the boys.

"Well, let's hope we don't get a washout. Remember a few years ago?" Josiah exclaimed anxiously.

Gideon paused before speaking. "So, tell me, where were the two of you?"

Eben panicked feeling his stomach immediately tense up. Josiah fidgeted began chewing on his fingernails, something he'd always done when he was nervous.

Outside the wind howled through the barnyard and trees. Hail began clattering on the roof of the barn. Both boys looked at the floor with dread evident on their faces.

"Neither one of you is going to answer me?"

"I was at the creek. Down where the timber is," Eben croaked.

Gideon swung the strop with frightening speed catching the side of Eben's head knocking him sideways into a heap.

"You're correct, this is quite a storm. God be praised, we'll get some rain and some relief from this heat wave."

Eben lay whimpering, tears filling his eyes. The left side of his face burned with pain. He knew this was only the beginning.

"And you?" Gideon asked turning towards Josiah.

"I was down there as well. Father, I..." Josiah's words were immediately cut off as the strop caught him in the face with a loud smack.

Outside the lighting flashed and the thunder roared continuously.

"It seems as though I've been much too lenient on this creek business," Gideon said standing over Eben. "Wouldn't you agree?"

Eben looked up only far enough to see his father's black dirty boots standing in front of him.

"Yes, Father.

Again, the strop came down heavily on his back this time. Eben howled in pain as Gideon struck him four more times. While he lay curled up in a ball crying he could hear Josiah bawling out as he too, was whipped.

"Why must you boys defy me? The other children certainly don't," Neither Eben, nor Josiah answered. "This Community has survived for generations because of trust. Trust in the Lord being the most important. This trust is then passed down to men and their wives who as parents must teach their children. If that trust is broken anywhere, everything we have and everything we stand for is for naught."

Neither boy dared move. Gideon continued.

"You both think the outside world is such a fun place, heh? It's full of sin and corruption. It's the devil's world out there. You boys are my sons. I'm an Elder and that means something here. People look up to us. We're the right hand of God here in the Community and our job is to protect everyone. If you defy me and don't trust me, well then, the rest of the Community sees that. When they see the sons of an Elder acting in sinful ways, they start to believe it's okay for them to become lax and not live by the word of God and by our rules. When that happens, our Community, our way of life breaks down and we all end up in the hands of Satan!"

"I can't wait to get out of here!" Josiah shouted pulling himself up from the floor. "I don't care who you are or what this damned Community means to you or anyone else. I hate it!"

Eben watched with terror in his eyes; no one had ever spoken to Gideon in such a way before. To his surprise, his father merely shook his head.

"No, Josiah, you're wrong. You took the Obligation, remember? Your hands were placed on the Holy Book when you did so. You drank from the Cup. You can't possibly leave."

"I don't care! None of it means a thing. None of it! It's all made up to scare people into submission!"

This time Gideon's expression changed to one of fear. "Josiah," he said calmly, "Remember what you swore to in your Obligation. It's not something to take lightly. You can't turn away, we won't let you."

Josiah fell to his knees and began sobbing. "I wish I wouldn't have!" He turned and grabbed Eben's shoulders shaking him back and forth. "Don't do it, Eben. Promise me you won't do it!"

Hearing a loud gasp behind them, Eben, Josiah and Gideon turned to see Mary standing in the doorway of the barn. She wore a shawl over her head which was soaked from the rain but the terrified look on her face was evident.

"No!" she screamed. "Not him too!"

Gideon turned and waved the strop at her. "Get out of here you damned woman! This is none of your concern!"

Instead of backing down, Mary stood her ground. "No, Gideon! I won't allow it! Did Josiah...? Is Eben next? Is he?"

"Mary, you can't meddle in this. Now, get back to the house!"

"I will not! You can't allow him to have them!"

"Nothing will happen if they don't cause trouble for themselves!" Gideon roared.

"And if they are stubborn? You know how they both are! What if they want to live their own lives? What if they just want to be free? Just as Ruth did!" Mary screamed.

"No! Don't you dare! We don't mention that name!"

Mary began sobbing. *"Just as Ruth and Dan did?"*

Gideon howled with rage and rushed from the barn into the stormy night. Mary ran to the boys and hugged them tightly.

"I love you boys, I always have. You're both mine no matter what, and I'll do whatever I can to protect you."

Eben clung to her wondering what was happening. What obligation had Josiah taken? What did it mean? Who was the 'he' his parents had mentioned? Wrapping an arm around Josiah, both boys tried to comfort their mother who was sobbing uncontrollably.

SECRETS

For the rest of the hot, miserable week Gideon rose well before dawn and took his tired, frightened boys out to milk cows and work in the fields. He never let them out of his sight. Eben was careful not to go down to the creek for three days but spent his time writing Wendy long, carefully worded letters late at night when no one else could see him. They were filled with stories about his life on the farm, his parents and siblings, the things he enjoyed such as mystery books and his mother's cooking, his love for the many animals on the farm and even what he envisioned his future to be, something he'd never given much thought to before. When he finally did manage to sneak down to the creek one afternoon while his father, Josiah and Isaac took the wagon to the lumber yard to buy shingles for the barn which been blown off by the storm, he was overjoyed to find several letters Wendy had left for him in their secret place in the tree. She wrote page after page about herself and her life in St. Louis, a huge, foreign place Eben had never heard of and couldn't even begin to imagine.

Eben had many questions for her and carefully wrote them down in his old notebooks from school. He took great care to hide the letters he wrote and the ones he received from Wendy in a hollowed out space in the hayloft. The thought of his father finding them and the ensuing punishments filled him with dread. If not for the other things happening around home with Josiah, Eben would have been happier than he'd ever been. But, since the night Gideon had beaten the boys his mind was often clouded with worry and fear for his brother. Each question seemed to lead to more. When Eben would question Josiah about the Obligation at night long after the rest of the family had gone to sleep he would become silent and turn away. But, Eben knew whatever it was, it clearly had Josiah frightened.

"Are you boys ready?" Gideon shouted impatiently. Isaac had hitched the horses to the wagon while Josiah and Eben had loaded their father's treasured carpentry tools passed down to him from his grandfather. Like most teenage boys, once the work was done they often disappeared finding other new, interesting things to capture their attention.

"Isaac! Josiah! I'm leaving without you!"

Eben watched Gideon sullenly while he mopped the floor in the milking parlor, one of the many jobs he shared with his brothers. Each morning the boys and Gideon arose at 5 A.M. and began the long, arduous job of milking cows. Normally, Eben didn't mind the work; he loved the cows. He'd helped his father with all of them from their birth and he and his siblings had named all of them. Yawning, Eben gently rested his still-bruised forehead on the end of the mop handle.

Feeling a presence, Eben lifted his head from the mop.

"Where are your brothers?" Gideon asked curtly.

Eben yawned again and shrugged his shoulders. "I don't know Father. I think Isaac is in the outhouse but I haven't seen Josiah since we milked this morning."

"Didn't he help Isaac load the wagon?"

"No," Eben replied suddenly thinking how odd it was now that he thought about it, Josiah had slipped away quietly. "No, he didn't."

Gideon frowned and rubbed his beard. "He didn't, eh? Where did he go?"

"I honestly don't know."

Gideon turned and stomped out of the milking parlor and out to the farmyard where the horses waited patiently.

"Isaac and Josiah!" he bellowed. At once, Isaac rounded the corner of the house hastily tucking his shirt back into his pants which had fallen down around his knees.

"I'm coming father!" he said taking two more steps before falling face first on the ground. Gideon scowled.

"Come son, get your shirt tucked in, grab your hat and get on the wagon. We're running late."

Isaac ran and climbed in taking his usual spot in the back.

"Where is Josiah?" Gideon asked the boy.

Isaac's eyes grew wide. He shrugged his shoulders and looked away. "I don't know, Father."

Gideon mumbled something under his breath and strode to the edge of the barn where he could see his fields all the way down to the creek and timber.

"Did either of you see where he went?" he asked coming back.

"No, Father," both boys responded. Gideon sighed deeply and thrust his jaw out. Eben watched as his head and shoulder slump down.

"I'm here!" Josiah appeared from behind the chicken coop carrying his shoes and shirt in his hands. He was dressed only in his denim pants and straw hat. Eben noticed he was dripping wet.

"Where have you been?" Gideon shouted.

"I was swimming down in the pond. After we got done milking I was hot so I went and jumped in."

Gideon frowned and crossed his arms. "Were you now?"

"Yes, I was. See?" Josiah exclaimed pointing to his soaking wet clothes.

"Hmm. Why didn't you help your brothers with the chores?"

Josiah shrugged his shoulders. "I don't know. I guess I didn't feel like it."

"Is that right?" Gideon said taking two giant steps towards the boy.

"Yes, that's right," Josiah replied standing up a little straighter and clenching his fists tightly.

Instead of striking Josiah, as was normal for shirking work or mouthing back, Gideon only grunted.

"Get dressed and get yourself in the wagon then. The rest of the men are expecting us. Hurry, we're late as it is."

Josiah gave him a derisive smile and climbed into the back of the wagon where he rung out his wet shirt.

"Go ahead and sit up front with Father," he said to Isaac, who stared at him with open-mouthed surprise.

"You never let anyone sit up there when you work with Father," Isaac replied. "Ever."

Josiah laughed and gestured with his head. "Go ahead. I'm not sitting next to him."

While Isaac jumped to the front seat Gideon looked back turned to Eben with a pointed finger. "Do you remember what we talked about?"

Eben nodded angrily blushing deeply. He too, was growing tired of the constant barrage of notices from his father to mind himself.

"You're to help your mother and the girls. When they're ready, bring them on over. Do you understand me?"

"Yes, Father."

"Good. Go, finish your chores and then report to her. If you dare go down to the creek again I'll beat you so hard you won't walk for a month. Do what's expected, not what you want."

Eben nodded and kicked at the gravel driveway. "Yes, Father. I will."

"Go on then," Gideon said turning and climbing up to the seat of the wagon. "We'll expect you in a couple of hours."

Watching the wagon slowly pull out of the driveway made Eben even angrier than he'd been before. Now, here he was, stuck at home with the women and all of Josiah and Isaac's chores to do on top of everything else. In the back of the wagon, Josiah made several rude gestures.

"Darn you, Josiah," Eben muttered shaking a fist at his brother. "I'd like to kick you in the privates so hard you'd talk like a girl."

Eben watched them pull out of the driveway and begin the five-mile trip to the raising. He was happy to have seen Josiah acting more like himself today. He'd even smiled, something he hadn't done in a week.

Quickly finishing his work in the milking parlor, Eben climbed into the hay mow and flopped into the pungent hay. He continued to watch his father and brothers meander down the road. They were off to spend the day helping the Linnenbaugh family with a barn raising, something all males in the Community volunteered to do. Normally, he would have gone along to help but he had been given an unusual job of taking his mother and sisters over later to prepare lunch for the men. Eben closed his eyes and blushed deeply at the thought knowing the other boys his age, John and Zachariah especially, would tease him unmercilessly for being left behind to take care of the women. This was his father's way of punishing him and the shame it created in Eben burned in his chest.

Once the sound of the horse's hooves crunching along the gravel road faded Eben bounded through the hay and jumped to the main floor below landing with a thud. He ducked down behind the larger wagon where he could watch the house through the barn door. Lydia and Rebecca, his two youngest sisters played in the yard while Miriam stayed inside helping their mother prepare food for the men.

"The heck with this. I'm going to do what I want today Father. A few minutes won't hurt," he said working his way out the back of the barn. With a quick look back at the house, he ducked into the weeds lining the cattle yard and sprinted to the edge of the cornfield. With one last look towards the house he slipped into the corn which at nearly ten-feet tall would shield him from his mother and sisters. Within minutes, he arrived at the creek sweating and out of breath. To his surprise and relief, Wendy sat on her favorite log which over-looked Gideon's fields. She was reading a book and smiling. Eben felt a quiver between his legs while he secretly watched her.

"Hi, Wendy," he said approaching her.

"Hey you," Wendy chirped closing the book in her lap. Next to her on the log was her ever-present camera and notebook.

Eben slid next to her. He immediately noticed something different in Wendy's expression.

"What's the matter? You look sad or something," Eben said.

"Oh, I'm not sad. I just, I've just been thinking."

"Like what?"

Wendy turned towards Eben and put her hand on his shoulder. "Eben, Josiah was down here this morning. I talked to him."

Eben immediately became angry. "Is that right? What was he doing down here?"

"We had a nice talk. He seems nice."

"Oh?"

"Yes, Eben, I think he is. He said some awfully nice things about you."

"He did? I don't believe you. He never says nice things about anyone but himself," Eben snorted.

Wendy stood up and frowned. "Is that how you're going to be today? Because if you are, I'll just walk back to Uncle David's house and help my Aunt Shelly in the garden."

Eben pouted and thrust his lower jaw out just as his father did when he was angry. With a loud, huff, Wendy began stomping away through the underbrush.

For a moment, Eben didn't care if she left or not. After all, she was part of the reason he and Josiah were in trouble.

Rubbing his forehead, he turned to watch her walk. "Oh, I don't understand girls at all."

Wendy reached the heavier trees and foliage and disappeared. Eben suddenly felt a pang of regret. He wondered if she'd come back.

"Wendy! Wait! Please? I'm sorry!"

Wendy reappeared with her arms crossed and sighed deeply. "Are you going to be nice?"

"You're starting to sound like my Father," Eben replied sullenly.

"He does sound rather, um, controlling," Wendy said returning to sit next to Eben on the log. "Your brother said he beat the two of you the last time we were here together."

"He did. See?" Eben raised the side of his face into the sunlight. "He got us good too."

Wendy touched the faded bruise tenderly. "I can't believe he does that to you."

"Oh, it's okay. I guess I'm used to it."

"But why would he beat you? My parents have never hit me."

Eben shrugged his shoulders. "That's the way it is here. Spare the rod, spoil the child as the adults all like to say."

"Once is too much if you ask me," Wendy said. "But why would he do it just because you boys come down here? I mean, what's so bad about it here? It's so beautiful and quiet."

"I don't know. Ever since we were little he's told all of my brothers and sisters never to come down here. He says things about something evil being here, sin and all of that."

Wendy sat back and thought for a moment. Suddenly, she snapped her fingers and pointed at Eben. "That's interesting. It sounds like he has something to hide, a secret perhaps."

"I never thought about it I guess."

"He tells you not to come down here but yet, you and Josiah do. What about the other children?"

Eben smiled. "No, never. They're all straight-laced rules followers. They're never in trouble."

"Well, that tells me a lot about you and your brother then," Wendy said smiling.

"What's that?"

"You're both stubborn and headstrong. I think you do it unconsciously, you know, to defy your father and all of the strict rules the Community has."

Eben nodded in agreement. She was correct: Eben and Josiah had always gotten in trouble for doing exactly what their parents had told them not to do. It wasn't something they always did purposely either, it just seemed to happen.

Eben looked up at the sun which was now high in the sky. "Oh, no."

"What's the matter?"

"I have to get back up to the house to help my mother. We're going to a barn raising over at the Linnenbaugh's today.

Wendy looked at Eben with surprise. "A barn raising? Really? Oh, Eben, I'd love to come and watch!"

Eben shifted uncomfortably on the log. "I wish you could too, but you're not allowed."

"But why? I've heard about them before and have always wanted to see one. I could take photos too! Is it true the men can build an entire barn in a day or two?"

"Well, yes, they can, but you can't go Wendy, and you sure as heck can't take photographs. Remember what we talked about?"

"Oh, Eben! You're no fun!"

"I'm sorry. Only members of the Community are allowed there. They never let English watch. Not ever."

Wendy again crossed her arms and scowled. "That's not fair. It would be fun though."

"It would," Eben said. "I wish I could introduce you to everyone."

"You do?" Wendy asked with a smile creeping into the corners of her mouth.

"Yes."

"What would you tell them?"

"I'd hold your hand and say, "Everyone, this is my friend, Wendy," And then, they'd all stare at us like we were some strange creatures that had crawled out of a hole in the ground."

"You're sweet. Would they really stare and all?"

"Oh, yes. Community kids aren't allowed to be with English kids. Not at all."

"But you'd like that? You wouldn't mind?"

"Of course I'd like it, Wendy. I like you very much," Eben said gazing into Wendy's eyes. He felt his stomach quiver from excitement. He never imagined he'd ever say that to a girl but he had.

Wendy smiled and brushed a strand of hair out of her face. "I feel the same way."

"You know," she continued. "Do you remember how I said you unconsciously do what you're not supposed to do?"

"Yes."

"Being seen with me would cause you a lot of trouble, wouldn't it?"

Eben shook his head. "I hate to think how much."

BARN RAISING

Eben sprinted through the steamy cornfield hoping he hadn't stayed with Wendy too long. Judging from the position of the sun in the sky, he knew it was probably close to ten o'clock. Well past time for the horses to have been hitched to the buggy and the food for the barn raising loaded.

"Please don't let it be past ten. Please..." he said to himself as he ran. He reached the edge of the field and continued running instead of stopping to watch for anyone as he usually did. Once he burst out of the corn breathless and sweaty, he came face to face with his mother who stood glaring at him with her hands planted firmly on her hips. Her right hand gripped a long green stick she'd picked up in the yard.

"Oh, no..."

"Oh, no is right Eben John!" she shouted. He knew he was in for it now; she'd called him by his middle name. "And where have you been?"

Eben shifted on his feet not knowing what to say. Instead, he chewed on his lower lip and stared at the ground. Mary took several large steps towards him and grabbed him by the ear and began swatting his backside with the stick.

"Down at the creek again?" she asked pulling on his ear. Eben thought for a moment she might tear it off.

"Yes, ma'am."

"Well now, that's just dandy! Dandy! Didn't you get in enough trouble for that a few days ago?"

"Yes, ma'am."

Mary stared at Eben with the most awful look he'd ever seen; her mouth was screwed into a tight frown and her squinted eyes sparkled as though they were on fire. He noticed she was on the verge of crying.

"Then why? Why do you keep going down there?"

"I don't know."

"I don't know is not an answer! Tell me!" she cried swatting him with the stick again.

Eben took a deep breath not sure what he should say next. Deciding to take his chances, he shrugged. "Do you want the truth?"

Mary pulled harder on his ear. "That would be nice for a change. Yes, I do!"

"Mother, the reason I go down there is because I met a girl down there. Her name is Wendy Harrison."

For a moment, she loosened her grip on his ear. "You did what? A girl?"

"Yes, Mother."

"Who's girl? Who are her parents, and why would they allow her to run along the creek bottom with a boy?"

"She's um, English and she's staying with her aunt and uncle and..."

"Eben!"

Eben winced from the pain in his ear. Mary was pulling harder on it now. "Mother, you're going to rip it off!"

"Why should you care? You don't use either one of them anyway!"

"I'm sorry, Mother."

"You met an English girl? Oh, Eben, I can't believe it. You're in enough trouble with your father the way it is, but if he knew about this…well, he'd explode."

The thought of Gideon suddenly exploding caused Eben to smile ever so slightly. "I'm sorry."

"Don't tell me you're sorry. You know the rules here. You cannot see an English girl under any circumstances. If someone were to see you with her the Elders could make things hard for you. Besides, you know how I feel about you boys seeing girls without your father and I there to supervise. It's not acceptable."

"But, all we do is talk. She's so different from the girls here. She's interesting. We don't do what you think."

Mary sighed with disgust and began dragging Eben along with a firm grip on his arm. "I was young once too, so don't tell me you don't do anything. She's English! Those girls have no morals, none!"

Eben staggered along behind his mother trying to explain things the best he could but it wasn't going well. "Mother, honestly, I haven't ever touched her. We talk, that's all."

"Hmmfff!" Mary replied. "Those girls out there, all they want to do is bed a good Community boy so they can brag about it to all of their friends. Oh, Eben, what have you done?"

"Mother, I…" Eben tried in vain to explain. He could hear her crying while she continued beating him on the backside with the stick. Once they reached the edge of the barn, Mary threw the stick into the weeds and wiped her face on her apron.

"You will hitch up the horses and meet the girls and me by the back door."

"Yes, Mother," Eben scampered into the barn and got the horses and buggy ready faster than he'd ever done so before. With a loud click and a slap on the reins he tore out of the barn and stopped at the back door where Mary and the girls waited. Jumping down, they quickly loaded the food and dishes. Eben helped Miriam, Rebecca and Lydia climb in, then hiked himself into the front seat where he took his mother's hand and pulled her up. With another loud click and a crack of the reins, they tore off down the gravel road towards the Linnenbaugh's.

For the first mile Eben sat sullenly on the front seat of the buggy loosely hanging on to the reins as the horses trotted along the road. Next to him on the bench, Mary sat with a scowl on her face. His ear burned from the punishment it had received and Eben knew he would soon forget about it entirely once his father found out where he'd been.

"Mama, where was Eben?" Rebecca asked from the back seat.

"He was in the milking parlor finishing up his chores sweetie," Mary answered.

"No he wasn't, we looked there."

"He must have been up in the loft getting hay when you looked. He was in the milking parlor when I found him just now."

"No, he wasn't."

"Well, Rebecca, you must have just missed him because he was in the milking parlor mopping the floor when I found him."

Eben looked at Mary out of the corner of his eyes. If any one of the girls knew anything he was done for but, he was fairly sure of the day's outcome anyway. None of them could keep a secret for long, especially Rebecca who was the tattletale in the family.

"Mama?"

"Yes, Rebecca."

"Why are your eyes wet? Have you been crying?" Eben felt himself stiffen knowing his sister would immediately run to their father once they arrived at the barn raising to tell him that Mary had been crying. The day was quickly looking as though it would become one of pain and suffering.

"No, sweetie, I just got some pepper in my eyes when we were cooking. I'm just fine."

"Why's Eben's ear so red and puffy?"

Mary turned and smiled. "Enough questions Rebecca. Why don't you girls sing us a song? How about, *How Great Thou Art*? I love to hear you three sing it."

In the back the girls laughed and chattered with delight. They enjoyed singing just as much as they liked getting praise from their mother, something Mary never tired of doing for her children. Eben whistled quietly along with them and was thankful Mary had suggested they sing to distract Rebecca's constant questioning.

O Lord my God, When I in awesome wonder,
Consider all the worlds Thy Hands have made;
I see the stars, I hear the rolling thunder,
Thy power throughout the universe displayed.

Once they reached the chorus, Mary and Eben joined in.

Then sings my soul, My Savior God, to Thee,
How great Thou art, How great Thou art.
Then sings my soul, My Savior God, to Thee,
How great Thou art, How great Thou art!

After nearly an hour of pushing the horses along at a half-trot and several more songs, Eben and the girls finally reached the Linnenbaugh's home. The road was lined for nearly half a mile on both sides with the buggies, wagons and horses which had brought everyone in the Community together for the day. Eben knew the day would be insufferably long while he waited for the beating that was surely to come once the family returned home and his father discovered he'd been at the creek again.

"Come," Mary commanded once Eben had helped her down from the wagon. "Get the girls down, then help us carry the food."

"Yes, Mother," Eben answered dejectedly. He'd already noticed John and Zachariah over with the men pointing at him and taunting him with laughter. Holding out his arms, the girls jumped to the ground one by one. Eben climbed back into the buggy and began handing the crocks full of hot food down to his mother and the girls. Once the buggy was unloaded, he slowly climbed down and gathered up the last two crocks the girls hadn't been able to carry.

"Hey, Eben!" a voice called. Eben looked up to see John snickering while Zachariah held his hands up to his chest to imitate jiggling breasts. "Looking good today! Where's your bonnet?"

Instantly angry, Eben opened his mouth to reply but Mary stepped in front of him. "Don't you dare say a word to him. If you drop my potatoes you're going to be in for it."

"I thought I was already."

Mary held a finger up in his face. "Don't talk."

Eben nodded and trudged up the wide lawn to place the crocks on the long tables overflowing with food. All around him, people laughed and visited happily all oblivious to the anguish he felt. For a moment he stood watching the men swarm over the skeleton of the new barn busily sawing, hammering and drilling the freshly cut, sweet-scented wood. He saw his father too, perched high on a beam driving nails with his hammer. Gideon was an excellent carpenter and enjoyed barn raisings a great deal. He particularly enjoyed teaching younger men the craft of building. Eben felt his chest tighten watching his father working and smiling with other boys and not him.

Feeling a presence close by, Eben looked up to see Katurah walking across the lawn in front of him. She looked up at him and quickly turned away.

"Eben, come help us set the tables then I want a word with you alone," Mary said but stopped when she caught sight of Katurah. "My, she's a pretty girl. Don't you think?"

"Um, yes Mother. She is."

"It's too bad she has to live with the Stohlfutz's," Mary said spitting the name out of her mouth. "Such horrendous people they are. You know, I don't believe I've ever seen her smile before."

"She does sometimes."

"Really? Do you think she might fancy you?"

Eben blushed. "I don't know, I've never thought about it before."

"Maybe you should. I think Katurah would be a much better choice than some wild harlot running around in the timber."

"Mother! She's not a harlot; she's just not a Community girl."

"We've discussed that. Now, come with me," Mary said walking towards the buggy. "Come, over here where your father can't see us."

Eben obeyed and stepped behind the buggy with Mary. He knew from the look on her face that she had something important to say to him.

"I'm not telling your father about where you were this morning."

Eben felt a wave of relief rush through his body. "Thank you, Mother. I'm so sorry I…"

"No. You listen to me. I understand your desire to do your own thing. You and Josiah certainly always have but you can't go there. Not ever."

"But why? Father has told us that for as long as I can remember but it doesn't make sense. What's so bad about it?"

Mary looked deeply into Eben's eyes. "Something bad happened there a long time ago. Something horrible that your father can't get out of his mind."

"What?"

Mary sighed and peeked around the buggy. "He had a brother named Dan who was a year older than he was."

"Father had an older brother? I thought his only brother was Uncle Jacob."

"No, Dan was the oldest. And Eben, you can't let on that you know anything about what I'm telling you. Don't even tell Josiah. Promise me?"

"Um, yes. I promise."

"Dan, Jacob and your father used to play down in the timber by the creek when they were boys. One year, the creek was full of water and wide, not like it is this year. It was a hot day and once they were done with their chores they decided to go swimming."

"What happened?" Eben asked wide-eyed.

"Dan got pulled under by the current. He…he got trapped in the branches of a submerged tree and couldn't get free. By the time your father and Jacob realized what was happening, Dan had drowned."

Eben stared at his mother. He'd never heard of Dan before and to hear how he had died, especially in a place Eben loved so much, was disheartening. "Oh, Mother, I didn't know."

Mary hugged Eben and kissed him on the cheek. "That's why your father doesn't want any of you children to go there. He's haunted by Dan's death and the other part is he doesn't want any of you to drown down there either. It took them two days to find Dan's body and when they did he was bloated from the water and the summer heat. Your father still has nightmares about it all."

Eben could kind of understand his father's point now but he still didn't feel badly about being angry at him. "I'm sorry Mother. I wish I'd have known."

"You couldn't have. He won't talk about it with anyone. Not even me."

"What about Jacob?" Eben asked. "Is that why he and Father don't speak to each other?"

"As far as I know, yes. Jacob and his family are here, but he and Gideon won't as much as acknowledge one another."

"Remember, don't mention a word of what I told you to anyone. It will upset your father."

"Yes, ma'am."

"And don't go down there anymore. If you must run and, Lord willing, do whatever it is you've decided you're going to do, then find somewhere else. Okay?"

"Okay, I promise," Eben replied hugging his mother. He wondered how he'd be able to keep his word.

REVELATION

"Did you finish your chores this morning?" Gideon asked tucking a napkin into his collar. The entire Community was seated in a large square of tables in the Linnenbaugh's alfalfa pasture enjoying an enormous lunch. Everything one could imagine was laid out in heaping, steaming piles on more tables: Fried chicken, steak, lamb, mashed potatoes, green beans cooked with bacon, casseroles, vegetables, cakes, cookies and pies of every kind were laid out.

"Most of them," Eben replied taking a drink of lemonade. "I didn't have time to clean out the chicken coop before mother came to get me."

"You can finish once we're home," Gideon continued. "You and Josiah both have been getting lazy. It's time that all stopped."

Josiah grunted and continued tearing his way through his overflowing plate. "Yeah, yeah," he said under his breath when Gideon turned to speak to the man next to him. "Having fun with the girls today?" he asked.

"No. This is the worst day of my life. Everybody's making fun of me."

"They should. You look like a fool over here doing the women's work."

"Shut up!" Eben hissed. "What else am I supposed to do? Tell him no?"

Josiah laughed shoveling green beans into his mouth. "Why not? It's been working for me lately."

Eben scowled and stabbed at his food. Josiah was correct: For the past week he'd decided he wasn't going to do any more work than he had to. Some mornings he didn't even get up with Eben and Isaac to help milk and other days he simply disappeared. And, much to everyone's surprise, Gideon let him get away with it.

"Why does he?" Eben asked. "What makes you so special?"

Josiah shrugged. "I don't know. Maybe he thinks that if he doesn't punish me I'll decide to stick around and be a good little Community fool like everyone here."

"I've wondered that too. What are you going to do? You can't keep thumbing your nose at him. He'll take only so much."

"I'm still trying to figure it all out but I might have a way."

Eben knew he was talking about Wendy. It made perfect sense; she lived in the world Josiah desperately wanted to live in and knew how everything worked. He hoped if Josiah was going to actually go through with his plan he did it soon. The tension in the family was bound to lead to quite a bit of trouble if something didn't change.

Eben looked around carefully and leaned in close to Josiah. "I've been thinking, what if I talked to Wendy about um, what you want to do? There might be a way she could help somehow you know, since she knows me a little bit better than you."

Josiah stopped chewing and also looked around the table at his family and neighbors who were chattering away. "I talked to her about it this morning."

"Yeah, I know," Eben replied. Even though he was fairly certain Josiah's visit with Wendy had been purely innocent, he still burned with jealousy.

"You do? Were you down there again?"

"Yes, right after you, father and Isaac left. Mother caught me."

Josiah laughed and sawed into a piece of beef. "Wow, Eben, you have a lot of guts. What did she do?"

"She about ripped my ear off and she thrashed me with a stick."

Josiah tilted his head back and laughed loudly causing everyone around him to stop and stare. Loud, boisterous outbursts were frowned upon at all times, especially at the dinner table even though they were at a barn raising. "I'd have given a dollar to see that!"

"It wasn't anything to laugh about. You know how she can be."

"So, you're ear hurts, your backside hurts and your pride is hurt by having to help the women today. You should have stayed in bed this morning."

"You're funny Josiah."

"Anyway, father told us on the way over here that he's putting an end to the creek business."

Eben stopped and stared at his brother. "How's he going to do that?"

"I don't know. He didn't say but you can bet it won't be good."

For a moment Eben considered telling Josiah what Mary had shared with him earlier but decided to do as she had asked and kept it to himself. He still didn't know what he was going to do about it all. Now, Gideon was involved. A sense of gloom settled over him.

"So, what did you and Wendy talk about?"

"Nothing much. I just introduced myself. Asked her some questions about the English world, you know, where to get a job, how to live and all of that."

Eben looked around the table carefully and leaned in close to Josiah.

"So, do you really want me to help you?"

"Do what?"

"Find a way to leave. It would be much easier for you with Wendy's help."

"You'd do that for me?"

"Of course, even though you make me madder than a hornet you're still my brother. You can't stay around here, Father will beat you to death one of these days the way you two have been going at it."

Josiah laughed and bit off a piece of bread. "Yes, you're probably right. I have some money. I know you saw it."

"Yes, I can't believe you stole from the church. You're just asking for it aren't you?"

"Where else would I get any?" Josiah shrugged. "Besides, I didn't take all of it. Just a few dollars here and there. Heck, I've been doing it for quite a while too and old buzzard nose and his herd of idiots haven't caught me yet."

"You and I both know he will eventually. So, will you go if I can arrange something with her?"

"Yes. Eben, I've never wanted to stay here. There's too much in the world out there to see and do. There's nothing but farming and church here. And, getting married when you're sixteen or seventeen and having a big flock of children. No, it's not what I want. You know that."

"Yeah, I do. Just make sure you do it as soon."

Josiah smiled. "I'll come back and see you. Maybe we can meet at the creek in the middle of the night."

"Yeah, that wouldn't be a good idea. If you decide to go, don't come back."

Both boys went back to their food each lost in their own thoughts. A peculiar feeling of happiness began to well up inside Eben the more he thought about Josiah leaving. For as long as he could remember, Josiah had always picked on him and made his life generally unpleasant. No matter what Eben did, Josiah had always tried to best him using any means possible; fists, his mouth, telling lies to their parents or outright sabotage. Eben burned with anger remembering a time when Josiah had purposely unlatched the gate to the hog lot after Eben had done chores allowing all of the pigs to escape into the fields. Gideon had beaten him good for it while Josiah sat back and laughed. There were too many other instances to count. In a way, part of him felt guilty about celebrating because they were brothers and brothers are supposed to love one another and take care of each other. But, in the past year Josiah's indecision and his disrespect towards Gideon had made everyone in the family, Eben especially, miserable. If he wanted to go, so be it.

A smile crossed Eben's face thinking about life without Josiah there to taunt him constantly. Sure, there would be more chores to do but he'd be the oldest. He'd get the entire bed to himself for the first time in his life too. When his time came to be baptized and marry he'd eventually inherit what would have been Josiah's share of everything. Instead of splitting the land three ways, Gideon would give half to Eben and the other half to Isaac once he came of age. Yes, he thought to himself, it might work out rather well after all.

BREAKING POINT

"Oh, I'm stuffed!" Josiah exclaimed pushing is plate away. He'd gone back for seconds on the main meal and had devoured three pieces of pie. "That peach pie is awfully good, Eben. You should get a piece before it's all gone."

After thinking about Josiah and his plans Eben didn't have much of an appetite left. Instead, he looked at the food left on his plate wishing he could get up and run to the creek. All around him people were finishing lunch while they talked and laughed. Gideon and Isaac joined the men and began making their way back to the barn, the women and girls were starting the long, tedious job of cleaning up.

"Look at that arrogant ass," Josiah said with a nod referring to Jonah Stohlfutz, the Reverend's oldest son. "He's been standing around old buzzard nose all morning acting important. He hasn't done as much as lift a finger to help us. And look who he has with him."

Jonah, nearly thirty, was married and so far, he and his wife were childless. He approached the Wittmer family with a condescending smile on his face. Josiah and Eben, along with almost everyone else in the Community, despised him. His youngest brother,

Thomas, who Josiah had beaten up the week before walked behind him with a smile plastered across his ugly face.

"Hello, Josiah. Eben," Jonah said.

"Jonah, what a terrible surprise," Josiah said smartly. "What do you want? Need some advice on how to make friends?"

Jonah smiled weakly and shook his head. He ran the sawmill, one of several businesses his father owned, and was known throughout the Community as a man who had never done a lick of work in his life. Instead, he rarely showed up at the business and never helped the men with the tough work. Most days when he did show up he stayed hidden in the office where he kept the books while making his employees miserable with taunts and threats. And worse yet in the eyes of most residents in the area, the Reverend had already decided he would succeed him as pastor of the church when the time came.

"Thank you, no. I would like to have a word with you about what you did to Thomas last Sunday though."

Josiah frowned and put his elbows on the table. "Whatever are you talking about, Jonah?"

"You know darn well what I'm talking about!" Jonah said loudly leaning in close to Josiah and Eben.

Josiah turned to Eben and shrugged his shoulders. "Do you know what he's talking about? I sure don't." Eben crossed his arms and stared back at Jonah as menacingly as possible.

"You attacked my little brother you big, oversized brute! His stomach and neck are all bruised up not to mention the bruises you left on his backside from the switch."

"I never touched him. I did see him fall out of the buggy though. Ask anyone, the boy trips over his own feet all the time."

"I have. It seems that John and Zachariah suddenly don't know anything either, but I know you did it. You hurt Thomas and I'll see to it you're punished."

Josiah smiled and stood. "Thomas is a liar, just like you are and just like that pig sucking father of yours is too with all of that religious nonsense he shovels."

Jonah howled with rage and took several steps towards Josiah. With a table separating them, Jonah began shaking a fist while he threatened Josiah.

"I'd like to tear you apart Josiah, but we all know I won't fight."

"Yeah, you won't fight because you still have your momma's tit in your mouth."

Eben, and everyone else within earshot gasped. Josiah had crossed a line.

In one swift move, Jonah vaulted over the table. Just as he landed on his feet Josiah punched him squarely in the face causing his nose to erupt with a spray of blood. While he looked at the sticky redness on his hands with surprise, Josiah attacked with a vengeance throwing several more punches. Jonah, who wasn't a small man, astonished everyone by hitting Josiah back. Soon, the two were rolling on the ground while they yelled and hit one another. Thomas tried jumping in to help Jonah at one point but Eben grabbed ahold of him and held him back.

"Let them sort it out or I'll beat you to a pulp," he said shoving the boy who quickly retreated to find his father.

Josiah, who had spent his entire life fighting with Eben and being whipped by Gideon, rapidly got the best of Jonah who began begging for mercy. Instead of letting him go, Josiah sat on top of him and began beating his head on the ground. By this time, virtually the entire Community had gathered to watch much to Eben's concern. He tried to pull Josiah off but was swatted away.

"Josiah! Stop it! Let him go!"

Almost immediately, Gideon broke through the crowd and jerked Josiah from atop Jonah.

"What are you doing?" he shouted shaking the boy like a rag doll.

Josiah merely smiled and wiped a trickle of blood from his lip. "He started it."

Gideon threw him to the ground and stood over him shaking. "I can't believe you! Fighting! At a barn raising in front of the entire Community! What in God's name is wrong with you?"

Josiah spit blood on the ground and glared up at his father who was red-faced and clenching his fists. Despite there being nearly four-hundred people standing in a circle around them, not a sound could be heard other than the wind rustling through the corn fields. Jonah's wife pushed her way out of the crowd and knelt over her husband crying. Reverend Stohlfutz came forward and also knelt by Jonah's side for a moment where he spoke a few hushed words with his son. He then stood, and walked over to Gideon and Josiah with a malicious look on his face.

"The boy will be alright. He wishes to forgive your son," he said to Gideon who lowered his eyes in shame.

"Do you hear that Josiah?" Gideon asked not looking at him. Josiah said nothing. "Do you?" he roared.

Josiah stood and dusted himself off. "No, what's wrong with all of you?! Everybody knows Jonah and his father are crooked, immoral thieves and sinners, stealing from every one of us, not doing a lick of work on their own, and God himself only knows what goes on in that house of theirs with poor Katurah there! What's wrong with you that everyone turns a blind eye? Am I the only one who will stand up to the evil in our midst? To them?"

Not a single person made a sound except for Stohlfutz who laughed and shook his head.

Josiah frowned at everyone for a long time. "I think," he said slowly, trying to find the right words. "I think all of you can go to hell. Every single one of you." He turned and began running, pushing people out of his way until he reached the edge of the corn field where he turned and looked back.

"Josiah!" Eben shouted. "Josiah!"

But Josiah didn't stop. He ran into the tall corn and disappeared.

CAPTURE

E ben and Mary sat at the kitchen table staring into barely touched glasses of lemonade now warm and stale. A sputtering kerosene lantern on the center of the table threw long shadows across the walls of the room adding to their feelings of unhappiness. Outside, a gentle summer breeze blew through the windows bringing with it the rich, earthy smell of the fields.

After arriving home from the barn raising earlier in the afternoon she sent Isaac and the girls outside to play while Eben helped her bring in and clean up the food and dishes they'd hurriedly thrown into the buggy. With the silent, judgmental eyes of their neighbors upon them there was no point in staying any longer after Josiah's outburst.

"What do you think he'll do?" Mary asked.

"I don't know, Mother. He's in for it now if he comes back."

"He is," she said sadly. "Why does he have to be so difficult? Why?"

"I honestly don't know. If he has any sense he's already miles from here."

"Yes, you're right, Eben. I know how he is. He could have left anytime he wanted but he had to go and do this! Oh, Josiah, why!"

Mary had done her best not to cry in front of the children but once they were home she retreated to her bedroom for nearly an hour while Eben and Isaac took care of the horses and finished cleaning out the chicken coop. For good measure, he split enough firewood to last a week while he watched the girls play in the yard. The work was good for him and allowed him a few moments to try and make sense of everything that had happened during the day.

During the trip home he'd begun to formulate a plan in case Josiah was stupid enough to come back. It seemed simple enough: Convince Wendy to help by having her uncle drive him into town and perhaps loan him some more money or even help find him a job. Even if she didn't, Eben was convinced that he'd drag Josiah kicking and screaming to the creek and throw him across if need be with a swift kick in the pants for good measure. All that mattered now was getting Josiah out of the Community if he hadn't already done it for himself.

There were two things that would make this simple plan fail; if Josiah came back Eben knew he'd most likely be shunned by the Elders making it virtually impossible for him to get out of the house. Gideon, he knew, would go to extreme measures to make certain the boy stayed put because of the mysterious Obligation Josiah had taken. Besides, if he were indeed shunned no one, not even Mary, Eben or the other children would be allowed to speak to him. He would exist as nothing more than a ghost.

The other problem was Gideon. Once he'd recovered from the shock and embarrassment of what had happened he'd grown angrier than Eben had ever seen him before. Without even bothering to collect his tools he stomped to his wagon and whipped the horses into a sprint hoping to head off Josiah. And worse, much to

Eben and Mary's horror, Leroy Fisher and his Sentinels left right behind him after a short whispered conversation with Stohlfutz. Presumably, they had orders to help Gideon hunt down Josiah and bring him back.

Eben absently spun a finger around the rim of the glass trying to make sense of the day. He knew what he wanted to say but he was unsure of how his mother would react. Would she do anything to save Josiah or would she go along with whatever Gideon told her? He didn't know for certain. Community women he knew, were expected to do whatever their husbands told them to do even if they knew they were wrong.

"Mother?"

"Yes, Eben," she replied not looking up from the table.

"If I could find a way to get Josiah out of here would you...?"

Mary sniffled and wiped tears from her eyes. "Yes."

"Would you tell father if you knew I was going to help him?"

As he said this her lower lip began trembling. Tears once again began streaming down her face in long silvery streaks. "I think," she began in a barely audible voice, "that you should do what you need to do without having to tell me."

Eben nodded and continued playing with the glass. So, she was afraid of Gideon too. He'd known it all along but never wanted to admit to himself that his father could be anything other than the loving, God fearing man he wanted everyone to think he was. Though Eben had never seen him hit her before, he knew the occasional bruises she had on her face some mornings didn't come from running into a door in the night as she always claimed.

Leaving his mother alone, Eben walked slowly up the steps to his room careful not to wake Isaac or the girls. Sitting at the desk the boys shared, he lit a candle and retrieved an old school notebook and pencil from the drawer. After chewing on the eraser for several moments, he began writing.

Dear Wendy,

As I promised, I'm writing you another letter. I hope to see you at the creek to ask you this in person because this is the most important thing I've ever had to do in my life.

As you know, my brother Josiah is in trouble. He has to leave the Community for good. The problem is, he got himself involved in something I can't explain and this something has tied him to this place. I don't know what it is or what he did, but he took some sort of secret Obligation which seems to be as binding as being baptized is here if not more so. Once a person has done it, they can never leave. If they try, the Sentinels come after them and punish them.

To make a long story short, he's running now and I hope my father and the Sentinels have not found him. I pray he's far from here, possibly in town and safe for the time being. I know we've only talked a couple of times but you seem like a good person to me, one who has a good soul. I mentioned this to you last week and don't know how else to say it, but would you help Josiah escape if for some reason he comes back or is dragged back? Maybe you've seen him tonight, maybe not. I hope you have and he's done this for himself. He has to get out of here and go far away from our father and the others. There's no coming back for him now.

Wendy, I'm begging you, will you and your uncle please help me help him?

Eben

Eben stared at the words on the page hoping it would be enough. If not, he knew he'd simply have to find another way.

Squinting at the clock next to his bed, he could see that it was nearly midnight. With a quick puff, he blew out the candle and returned to the kitchen where Mary still sat with her face in her hands. Picking up his shoes from beside the door, he shoved his feet into them and pushed the screen door open. Mary looked up to see the folded paper in his hand and the familiar determined look on his face he'd always had. She'd seen it many times during his lifetime and knew he'd made up his mind to do something no matter what the consequences would be. Without saying anything, she turned and put her face back into her hands.

Eben didn't know whether or not his father would return but curiously, he no longer cared if he came home to find him gone. Running the same path through the corn field brought the same nicks and cuts on his face and hands from the rough leaves but he continued on ignoring the pain. At one point, a group of crow clattered in all directions cawing and crying out as he disturbed their peace.

The creek and timber spread-out before him in the bluish light of a full moon when he emerged from the field. Dim, flickering spots of yellow light from fireflies hovered peacefully in the air. Other than a light bit of wind blowing through the tops of the trees, the night was completely silent and still. Eben crossed the creek and headed directly to the hollowed out tree where he hoped Wendy might be waiting for him.

"Wendy?" he called softly. "Are you here?"

Hearing no response, he peered into the darkness of the opening and silently mumbled to himself for not having the sense to bring a lantern along.

"Wendy?"

Eben held the letter, now damp from the humidity and from his perspiring hands between his teeth and crawled into the hollow. Feeling around blindly he found the box on the blanket Wendy had left the week before and deposited the letter inside. He knew Wendy came here nearly every day but he wanted to make absolutely certain she'd find what he'd written as soon as possible. Squirming back through the opening, he pulled out a red handkerchief out of his back pocket and tied it to a low hanging branch.

Deciding he'd done as much as he could for the time being, Eben left the timber and slowly walked back to the house. His mind was filled with many questions, especially why he was doing what he was to help Josiah. He'd never helped him before and never even given it much thought. Why was it so difficult for him to simply leave as he wished? Eben knew Stohlfutz and the Church preached total obedience to God and the Community. In addition, parents were expected to exercise complete control over their children and to raise them as the Church directed. Everything was controlled from what clothing people could wear, what food they could eat, whom they could marry, when to worship and even, what to name the multitudes of children they were expected to have. What Eben didn't know and couldn't possibly understand was that after generations of this conditioning, indecisive children grew into vacillating, fearful adults whose dependence on the church was absolute.

Eben approached the house glad of what he'd done but a bit fearful too. The light of the lantern still flickered through the kitchen windows telling him his mother was still sitting at the table thinking perhaps the same things he was. At least Gideon hadn't returned home yet, something he was grateful for.

Just as he thought this, Eben could hear the clatter of hoof beats on the road. Soon, the dark shape of a wagon pulled into the driveway followed by another. He caught a glimpse of Gideon's familiar shape hopping down from the first wagon to quickly walk back to the second. Eben ran to the orchard where he slid in behind an apple tree to watch. Four men climbed down from the first wagon and gathered around Gideon exchanging a few muted words. Two of them separated from the group, dropped the tail gate and pulled a form out of the back dropping it heavily on the ground. The men laughed and kicked at it. Mary walked out of the house and halfway to the drive tentatively holding the lantern.

Gideon immediately brushed past her and held the door for the four men who picked up the bundle they'd unloaded and began carrying it towards the house.

"No!" Mary screamed. "Leave him alone! Leave him alone!"

Eben's skin crawled hearing his mother's screams of anguish piercing the night.

SHUNNED

Josiah sat alone on the porch swing which hung on the front side of the house. Around his ankle was a clamp attached to chain which Gideon had wisely wrapped around a porch column with a strange looking lock he'd found somewhere. Cursing under his breath, Josiah pushed his right foot against the floor sending the swing off at an awkward angle. Eben watched him from around the corner for several minutes unsure if he should talk to him. It had been four days since the Sentinels had brought him back bloody and bruised to deliver him to Gideon. After lying in bed recovering for the first two days, he now spent his time alone, chained down and sitting in the swing staring off into the endless corn and bean fields with his treasured pocket knife and the stick he'd whittled down to nothing as his only companions.

"Hey, what are you doing?" Eben asked, approaching cautiously.

"Nothing," Josiah muttered.

He never raised his eyes to look at his brother but only continued staring off into the distance.

"Do you mind if I sit down?"

"Be my guest," Josiah said stopping the motion of the swing long enough for Eben to sit. The boys sat in silence for several minutes watching the carefree birds in the birdhouse go about their daily lives in a flurry of feathers and chirps.

"So, has Father said anything to you?" Eben asked.

"Nope. Except for the other day when told me I have been officially shunned by the Community."

Eben gasped. For all he knew, being shunned was the worst thing that could happen to a member of the Community. From now on, Josiah had no rights but it meant he had to attend church services where he would be seated at the front of the meeting hall with Samuel and the Bible holders. In addition, he couldn't participate in any Community events such as barn raisings, weddings, funerals, family reunions or anything else but like church, he would be forced to attend and stand alone doing nothing but observing life going on without him. Other than these outings which were mandatory for all Community members, he couldn't leave the family home for any reason. Eben knew some punishments such as this one could sometimes last for years until the Elders decided the person in question had suffered enough and if they had done enough penance. Their mother had suffered through the Community's strange punishment system but she had only been admonished which was not much better than actual shunning.

"My gosh, Josiah, you had your chance and you blew it. How did they find you anyway?" Eben asked with a hint of exasperation in his voice. He was so angry with his brother he couldn't stand it. "Tell me, how could a young, healthy person like you get caught by fat Leroy and his pigs?

"I don't know. I thought I was doing a fairly good job of it but they caught me when I tried getting across the river bottom up by the Weber's place. Heck, I walked right to them."

"They must have been tracking you the entire time. Didn't you look around at all?"

"Sure I did. I hid in the fields most of the day trying to wait father out. Somehow they knew I was coming back here."

"What? Why would you do that? Are you stupid?"

Josiah stiffened and grew red-faced. "No, you idiot. I had to come back for my money. Then I was going to go north and west away from here towards Wellman. I figured they'd think that would be the last thing I'd do, going right through the center of the Community."

"Well isn't that great! It's not like you haven't had plenty of chances to go. Now you're chained up to the porch like a dog."

"You can shut up, Eben! The timing hasn't been right. I..."

"Yeah, yeah. Always an excuse with you, Josiah. I'm sick of it!"

"Darn it all, Eben. Do you think you've always been the one he counted on to be the good son and be baptized right away? All of this," he said waving an arm in the air, "do you honestly believe this is going to be yours someday? You and your dreams of your little Community wife given to you by the Elders and all of your damned perfect little Community children living on forever out here in perfect harmony with God and all of the rest of that stuff they love to shove down our throats."

"You don't know how I feel," Eben retorted. He felt his fists tighten. "You don't know at all."

Josiah twisted in the swing to face Eben. His eyes were nothing more than slits. "Don't I? I've always been in trouble with father because of one thing or another. I hate him because he's never let me do any of the things I've wanted to do. You, on the other hand, have never gotten it as bad as I have."

"What? Me? You're crazy! I'm in trouble just as much as you are! Both of us, we've always been at the end of his razor strop."

Josiah pursed his lips and gazed at the birds. "It's always been strange. Even when we were little, it's like there was something secret going on. Father has always acted like you and I were a burden to him somehow, like we didn't belong for some reason."

"I think you're just trying to find any old reason to justify the things you've done. You didn't have to steal the money. You didn't have to beat up Jonah. You've brought it upon yourself!"

"Yes, I did! I can't let him or the rest of the sheep in this Community tell me how to live my life! Haven't you ever noticed? You and I are different from Isaac and the girls and what's more, father treats them entirely different from how he treats us. We're outcasts in our own home!"

"That's because they're still little," Eben said, but not quite believing it either. Josiah did have a point. Gideon was hard on Josiah and Eben, sometimes too hard. Eben remembered a time when he was seven or eight and had forgotten to tightly close the gate on the chicken coop one night after feeding the chickens. Virtually every one of the forty birds were slaughtered by hungry foxes during the night. Eben shivered remembering the bloody feathers and the torn chicken corpses inside of the coop the next morning when Gideon had dragged him out of bed to see it. The awful beating he'd received as a result still remained fresh in his memory, even after nine years. More recently, Isaac, had tried to light a lantern and had nearly burned the house down while the rest of the family slept upstairs. Eben shook his head remembering the three pitiful smacks he'd been given with the razor strop for his misdeed. If Josiah or Eben would have done the same thing they would have been beaten senseless.

"Is this what you really want, Eben? The farm? The Community telling you what to do for the rest of your life?"

"I don't want to talk about it."

Josiah reached over and grabbed Eben by the arm. "I guarantee, you won't get the farm, the animals or anything else around here. Father will send you over to work for Jonah like he was going to do with me. Either there or somewhere else, but you won't get any of this."

Eben stared at him. "What do you mean he was going to send you to work for Jonah?"

Josiah shook his head angrily. "He told me I hadn't earned the right to work on *his* family land and *my* place was in that awful sawmill instead."

"That's a bunch of bull."

"No, it's not! He told me a couple of weeks ago after he made me take the Obligation. Why do you think I want to get out of this place so badly now?"

"Why didn't you tell me?" Eben asked incredulously. "Does mother know?"

"Of course mother knows. She said something about how it was probably for the best. You know how she goes along with whatever he tells her. Besides, what good would it have done for you to know? You'll be shipped off to work for someone else soon enough. I think he's saving it all for Isaac and the men the girls will marry someday."

In a fit of rage, Eben jumped to his feet sending the swing zigzagging wildly. He intended to hit Josiah. "You're a liar and a troublemaker!"

"What's going on here?" Gideon rumbled. "Eben, you come over here right now. You're not to be speaking with him."

Eben glared at Josiah who made it a point to turn away from both of them.

"Come, help me with the chores. Mother will have lunch ready shortly."

"Yes, Father," Eben said furiously. He turned to look at Josiah but he continued to watch the birds and push the swing.

THE TREE

After lunch, Eben and Isaac wearily tramped to the edge of the sorghum field north of the house with hoes slung over their shoulders. It was another hot and utterly still afternoon which seemed to suck the breath right out of them.

"I hate walking fields," Isaac whined. "Father always makes us do this when it's hotter than the blazes out too."

"I know," Eben replied bending over to pull up a clump of grass. "I don't know what he's doing. He said he had to wait for someone."

"Who?"

"I don't know. Maybe the Beiler's want to buy some of our calves."

"I hope they don't take the one with the big white spot on his muzzle," Isaac said digging at a weed. "I named him Pete and I want to keep him."

Eben smiled at his younger brother from under his hat. "I don't think they will, father knows you like him."

The boys began wading through the dense sorghum stopping to dig up foxtail, milkweed and broadleaf weeds which never seemed to stop growing in the fertile Iowa dirt. Seeing a four-foot tall this-tle, Eben pulled an ancient machete from his belt and hacked it down to the ground before digging up the extensive root system.

"Who's that?" Isaac asked pointing towards the house.

Eben turned and squinted his eyes in the bright sunshine. He immediately felt his stomach tighten up. "Reverend Stohlfutz and Jonah are here."

"What?" Isaac asked. "Why?"

"Yep, it's them alright," Eben answered eyeing his brother who watched fearfully. "You can bet it's not good whatever they want."

The boys continued watching to see Gideon quickly stride across the barnyard to meet his guests holding his hat in his hands. Eben could only feel disgust to see his father groveling in front of Stohlfutz just as everyone else did. Within minutes, another wagon containing four men pulled in beside them.

"Who's that?" Isaac asked. "Who are the other four men?"

"It looks like the men who work for Stohlfutz in the lumber mill. You know, Levi Hirsch, Paul and Oliver Bochy, and Caleb Hollman."

Eben and Isaac squatted down amongst the thick plants while their father continued to visit.

"Why are they here?"

Eben suddenly felt a shiver run through his body as a thought struck him. "Maybe they're going to cut down the timber."

"Naw, they wouldn't do that. Would they?"

"I don't know. Father's been doing some strange things lately."

"Yeah, because Josiah talks back to him."

Soon, it became apparent what the men were doing. Levi climbed high into the tree and began cutting out branches with a hand saw he carried. Caleb, also short and agile worked the op-posite side while the burly Bochy brothers made quick work of the branches falling to the ground.

"What in the name of God?" Eben roared not quite believing what he was seeing. "No! That's our tree! They can't do that!"

It pained him to see the enormous and majestic tree being butchered. He remembered his father telling him and his sibling's stories about their great-great grandfather planting it sometime in the 1890's. Now it would be turned into boards for houses and furniture.

Hearing Eben's outburst from the field, Gideon turned to glare at him while with his hands on his hips in a show of triumph.

THE GRANARY

The next morning, Eben and Isaac gazed at the interior of the old granary with less than enthusiastic looks on their faces. Neither could believe what they were expected to do.

"It shouldn't take more than a few hours," Gideon said, picking up a bucket and rummaging around to see what was in it. "It needs to be done. All of the scrap lumber and fence material can go in the back of the barn where Betsy used to be. All of the old nails, you can dump in one bucket. The paint, well, throw it out because it's all been frozen at one time or another. If it looks like trash or is rotten, haul it out and we'll take it down to the burn pile later."

Both boys groaned. Cleaning out the granary was the last thing they wanted to do. They had already been up since five milking cows and thrown more hay down from the hay mow and the morning was rapidly heating up. Now this.

Gideon continued looking at the interior and concrete floor of the shed intently. Reaching down to pick up a 1 x 4 lying haphazardly in the mess, he used it to push against a board at the top of the wall. It pushed out several inches with a squeak.

"That won't do at all," he mumbled turning his attention to the boys.

"Eben, while Isaac's taking care of the things he can manage I want you to go around and check each board to make sure they're nailed down."

Eben nodded and shifted uncomfortably on his feet.

"And, while you're at it, put an extra couple of nails in each stud. I want this building buttoned up and tight."

"Yes, Father."

"Okay then, Eben, you're in charge. No messing around."

"But Father, it will take days to clean all of this out," Isaac complained.

"No, if you keep after it, it should only take today. I have some things to attend to but I'll be around home and that means I'll be checking up on you boys regularly."

"Yes Father," the boys muttered.

Gideon nodded and disappeared around the corner.

"This is just great!" Eben said throwing a board against the wall once he was sure his father was out of earshot. "It's ninety degrees outside and we're supposed to clean this stupid building out!"

Isaac watched his brother silently waiting for him to give the word to begin working. Finally, Eben sighed and threw his hands up in resignation.

"Come on, let's get started," he said reaching down to pick up some scraps of lumber. "Let's haul out this pile first then you can work on the smaller things back there."

After helping Isaac, Eben retrieved a nail pouch, and handful of number sixteen nails, a hammer and a short ladder from the barn. Cleaning the granary and putting extra nails in every board didn't make any sense. It merely seemed as though Gideon was just looking for any old job for the boys to do no matter how ridiculous on top of their regular chores and other work around the farm. He knew the likely cause for the additional work however.

"Crazy old man. Heaven forbid if anyone has any fun around here," Eben muttered softly to himself. He was standing on the top rung of the ladder stretching as far as he could to drive a nail in the loose board Gideon had discovered. "I'll go down to the creek if I want to. You'll see."

Driving nails through the ancient oak boards was tough going. Unless he hit the nail squarely on the head each time it would bend and crumple forcing him to pull it out and start again. After ruining the seventh nail, Eben exploded with anger.

"Darn it!" he shouted drawing the hammer back behind his head intending to smash it into the bent nail. Instead of hitting the nail, he hit his thumb instead.

"Owww!" he screamed dropping the hammer and pulling the injured thumb into his right hand. In a split second, the ladder wobbled, Eben lost his balance and felt himself falling. In desperation, he reached out and somehow grabbed the loose board. It held for a moment, then pulled completely free of the framing sending him crashing down into the weeds. He lay there for several minutes wanting to scream and throw things but the shade was nice and relatively cool.

"Are you okay?" Isaac asked peeking around the corner. Eben looked up to see him watching intently with a smirk on his face.

"I'm fine!"

"Did you fall?"

"What do you think?"

Isaac shrieked with laughter and disappeared.

Eben stood and brushed himself while trying to shake the pain out of his left hand. Bending the thumb hurt but at least it wasn't broken as far as he could tell. With a sigh, he righted the ladder and retrieved the hammer from where it had landed in the cattle yard. With the board on his shoulder, Eben carefully climbed the rungs and tacked one end on. It swayed and squeaked in a light breeze mocking him.

"Stupid board."

Instead of nailing the rest of it securely, Eben hammered it back into place and carefully drove a nail into each end without bothering to sink the heads in. Since it was on the back of the granary facing away from the main barnyard, he didn't figure Gideon would bother checking it as long as he could see that it wasn't hanging loose.

An hour later, the work was progressing slowly. Eben finished his nailing job and returned to help Isaac. They silently went about carrying items out and throwing them in different piles outside the door which they would move later on once Gideon returned to look through it. Stepping over several wooden boxes filled with nails, screws, bolts and other odds and ends, Eben spied a pile of old rope, musty and frayed from age which had been thrown haphazardly in the back corner.

He knelt and wrapped his arms around the pile to begin pulling but it weighed more than he'd originally thought.

"Hey, Isaac. Come help me drag this out."

"What?"

"This rope back here."

Isaac wrapped his arms around of the opposite side and after a fair amount of grunting and groaning, they finally managed to pull it through the door.

"Where does it go?" Isaac asked breathlessly.

"I don't know. Let's just throw it off to the side here for now."

The boys dragged the pile around the corner and dropped it.

"Boy, I don't want to move that again. I'm all itchy now," Isaac said scratching his arms. "And it stinks."

"Yeah, me too. Let's get a drink and rinse ourselves off. I need to run some water over my thumb."

"Why, does it hurt?"

"Isaac!"

Isaac laughed and ducked Eben's halfhearted attempt to swat him. "Good, I need to visit the outhouse too."

The boys trudged across the sweltering barnyard to the well.

As they walked, Eben stared at the ugly stump where the tree had once stood. The memory of Stohlfutz's men cutting it down as though it were a rotten old tree in a barn lot angered him. He believed Gideon had done it partly out of spite along with his desire to keep the boys in. Either way, it was a waste and was something Eben didn't know if he could ever forgive. The yard looked barren and unnatural without it there looking over the house as it had done for over one hundred years.

"You first," Eben said pumping the handle. Isaac fell to his hands and knees allowing the cool water to cascade over his blonde curls.

"Feel good?"

"Yeah," Isaac replied turning his face to fill his mouth with water. Once was finished, they switched places. Gideon appeared from the barn.

"There you boys are. Finished already?"

"Not yet, Father. We thought we'd take a quick break."

"Very well. Hurry up and get back to it. We have feed to grind."

Eben made a quick visit to the outhouse and returned to the granary where Isaac was busy dragging a roll of wire through the door.

"I'm tired. I wish father would let Josiah out so he could work."

"I do too," Eben replied helping pull the wire. "I think he's trying to work us to death."

"I'm ready for school to start. Only two more weeks!"

Eben hadn't thought about school for much of the summer and now with his last year approaching, he felt oddly indifferent about going back. It was the last thing on his mind. "Wow, I hadn't thought about it at all. Why, do you want to go? I thought you hated school."

"It's better than doing this," Isaac replied. "I'm ready for recess. I wish father would let us have recess twice a day."

Eben laughed, for the first time in weeks it seemed. "You're nuts if you think he's going to allow that!"

Isaac smiled, obviously pleased with himself. "Maybe, you never know."

Gideon leaned in the doorway and stood with his hands hanging on his suspenders. "Looks good in here boys. Really good."

"Thank you Father," they replied in unison. Gideon walked around the interior of the space pushing on boards here and there and tapping the lower sections with his foot. Eben wondered why cleaning had taken on so much importance.

"Hmm. Yes. This will work perfectly," Gideon mumbled. "A drain in the floor and it has an opening for air in the roof. Yes... Did you get it all nailed down, Eben?"

"Yes, Father. Those old boards are tough," Eben replied holding his thumb up. It was swollen and beginning to turn a remarkable shade of purple.

"They are indeed," Gideon answered brusquely. He stopped and looked up at the board which caused Eben so much grief. "Did you fasten that one down really well?"

"Yes, Father."

"Good."

He continued looking around stopping occasionally to push on the walls.

"What are you going to do out here?" Isaac asked. "Are we getting more animals?"

Gideon shook his head knowing Isaac's love for all types of critters. "No, I'm sorry son. No more animals. I think we have enough for now."

"What are you going to do out here then?" Isaac persisted. "I was hoping I could put my rabbits in here."

"Oh, nothing much. This has been in need of a good cleaning for years and I thought it would be a good job for today."

Eben scowled and examined his swollen thumb.

"Well boys, let's go finish our chores. We can quit early tonight."

Isaac whooped for joy and ran out at Gideon's side. Eben waited for a moment and took a long hard look around the granary. It was sturdily built of native Iowa oak with walls nearly eight-inches thick and had been constructed by his great-grandfather. For many years it was a granary, then a horse barn, then goats, and finally, a place to simply store junk. With one heavy oak door which latched from the outside, the structure was stout and built to keep out hungry wild animals while holding in tons of corn. Why would his father want to have it cleaned out? It was always the junk building in Eben's memory and never anything else. Stepping out into the fading afternoon sunlight, a thought creeped into his head about what his father intended to do with it. Yes, Josiah had to leave, and soon. Gideon was going to lock him in it.

PLANS

E ben lay bathed in sweat on the sofa his mother had fixed into a bed for him in the stifling heat hanging in the downstairs of the house. Next to him on the other makeshift bed on the floor, Isaac lay sprawled out stripped down to nothing but his undershorts. Neither was comfortable nor happy with the new arrangement. With Josiah still locked in the boy's bedroom upstairs alone, Eben and Isaac were forced to sleep in the living room until their father decided what he was going to do with him. He was now virtually a prisoner in the house and wasn't allowed outside unless accompanied by Gideon or Mary on his three times daily visits to the outhouse. Otherwise, he didn't do chores or do anything else around the house except sit chained to the front porch all day with a Bible as his only companion. Eben prayed he'd eventually figure out a way to get him out, but the opportunity hadn't presented itself yet.

Pulling the sheet to his face, Eben wiped his sweaty face on it and sighed. He thought about everything that had happened so far during this long, miserable summer and suddenly wished none of it ever would have happened. After not being able to get out and down to see Wendy for nearly a week, he'd begun to wonder if everything might have been better if he'd never met her. Getting Josiah out and on his way was up to him now but he hadn't figured out what had to happen yet.

With a yawn, Eben stretched and walked softly to the kitchen doing his best not to step on the places he knew creaked. Reaching the back door, he quickly stepped out into the humid night and headed to the well. Filling the bucket, he raised it drinking deeply and looked up at the stars weaving across the inky black sky.

"Eben!"

Eben jumped from the strange whisper coming from somewhere in the shadows across the barnyard. Setting the bucket down he stared ahead to where the noise had come from feeling his heart thumping.

"Eben! Come over here!

"Who's there?"

"It's me! Wendy!"

"Wendy?" he whispered.

"Yes. It's me. Hurry up!"

With a quick look glance back into the house to be sure his father hadn't heard him and was watching from an upstairs window, Eben headed towards her voice. No matter what he'd been doing for the past week, whether it be milking cows or going to the outhouse, he'd had the strange sensation of being watched. For a brief second, he considered walking back into the house and locking the door but he quickly cast his doubts aside.

Once away from the house, he ran across the gravel drive on his bare feet not minding the pain from the sharp rocks.

"I'm over here, next to the barn," she whispered. Approaching the shadows he stopped trying to guess where she was until a hand suddenly reached out and grabbed ahold of his arm.

"Come on. Let's go back behind there so no one hears us," Wendy said pulling him along through the weeds. Rounding the corner, she turned and smiled broadly.

"Hi."

"Wendy, I left a letter for you but then I wasn't able to get back down to the tree and..." Eben responded breathlessly. "Things have been so crazy here and my father...I'm sorry I haven't been able to see you."

"I know, but it's okay now. I've been watching for quite a while. He's turned this place into a prison."

"Yes, he cut down our tree. Josiah's locked in the bedroom...I think he's going to lock him in the old granary building."

Wendy sat down with her back to the shed and pulled Eben down to her side.

"I read your letter then you didn't come back or respond. It's been driving me crazy wondering what's happened."

"I know, I haven't been able to stand it either," Eben said. "Josiah has to get out of here as soon as possible."

"I'm glad you finally came out. I've been up here the past several nights looking for you," Wendy said. "Your father almost caught me the other night. I spooked your chickens and he came out prowling around."

"You were? Up here by the house?"

"I hid in the sweet corn in the garden. He wasn't more than two feet away from me."

Eben shook his head thinking of Wendy in her strange clothing with her equally strange buckled shoes hiding in the weeds from his large, angry father. She had to be fearless, he thought to himself. Or crazy. Gideon had extraordinary eyesight and hearing.

"I just came out for a drink. I didn't know you were up here."

"Well, from what you wrote I knew you were serious. I want to help."

"You do? I'm glad."

"I have some money I can give your brother and I'll give him a ride up to Iowa City. Aunt Shelley lets me take her car sometimes so I can do some shopping or go to the library."

"Why Iowa City?"

"There's a bus station there. Surely he doesn't want to run away ten miles to Kamron does he?"

Eben frowned knowing Wendy was correct. "No, you're right. It's too close. If my father wanted to bring him back badly enough he'd be able to find him there. I'm trusting you on all of this because you live out there and you know how it works. My biggest question is, where is he going to go? I mean, he doesn't know anyone, where's he going to live? Find a job?"

"I did some research on the internet and found a group who helps people who escape from um, groups kind of like the Community."

"Internet? What's that?"

"Oh it's, well, it's hard to explain but it has a lot of information about everything."

"So, what's this group? What do they do?"

"It's called the Deer River Center and they help people who live in places like this. You know, find them jobs, and teach them how to live in the outside world, talk to them about what they went through and all. Actually, therapy is a big part of what they do. It looks like a perfect place for Josiah to go. He'd be safe with them."

Eben sat listening to the crickets chirping in the darkness. He'd spent the last week wracking his brain trying to come up with ways he could help Josiah but he simply didn't know what to do other than escort him to the creek and wave goodbye. Writing to Wendy had been a good idea after all.

"What's he have to do?" Eben asked. "Anything special?"

"Have him meet me at Uncle David's and I'll take care of the rest. I'll buy him a bus ticket and put him on the right bus so all he has to do is sit back and enjoy the ride. Someone from the Center will be waiting for him when he gets there."

"Where is it?"

"Greencastle, Indiana."

Eben knew Indiana was located in the United States but wasn't exactly sure where. Several subjects such as geography and science were banned in the Community school as were maps of any kind. The three 'R's', reading, writing and arithmetic, constituted the majority of the curriculum along with a sizable dose of religious instruction.

"Wow, I don't know what to say, Wendy. Thank you. It's all so... much. Maybe Josiah can finally have the life he's always talked about."

Wendy grinned and took Eben's hand. "I have to tell you this and I hope it doesn't make you angry, but I called talked to the man who runs it and spoke with him. He told me to mention the name Elizabeth Beiler to you."

Eben looked at Wendy with open-mouthed surprise. "What? How could he know her?"

"She showed up in Kamron last summer and luckily, the Methodist minister there found her hiding in his garden shed. He reached out to her and did an internet search like I did. It led him to the Deer River Center and a few days later, he took her out there."

"I know Elizabeth. She's my age and well, I always had a crush on her. But then one day, she just disappeared."

"She's there, in Indiana. The man, Todd, said she's doing wonderfully, has a job, she's finishing school and wants to go to college someday."

Shaking his head in amazement, Eben discovered to his surprise that he was smiling from a strange mixture of happiness and discovery tingling throughout his stomach and chest. So, someone got out and found a way to live in the world despite what Stohlfutz and Gideon claimed. If a person managed to leave the Community for good without being caught their names were never mentioned again as though they'd never existed. But no one ever knew what happened to them, this was the mystery. If Elizabeth would have been brought back just as Samuel or Ben had, or everyone else who'd he'd seen being punished in church for as long as he could remember, every person in the Community would know it.

"Eben, I want to ask you one more thing."

"Okay."

"If Josiah goes through with this, have you ever thought about going with him?"

Again, Eben was caught by surprise. "What?"

Wendy gently placed both of her hands on Eben's face. "Why don't you go with Josiah?"

"I don't know...I've never thought about it. I've always believed that my place was here and..."

"Now listen to me, Eben. I don't want you to do something you don't want to do. We're talking about your life here and I want you to do what's best for you. It has to be your decision. But, I think you should seriously consider it. You'd be happier," Wendy said.

"Really? Do you think so?"

"I do. There's some kind of despair hanging over you and your brother that I can't figure out, something deep and dark hidden inside the two of you that makes you fight against your father and the Community and all of their rules."

Eben was surprised by Wendy's assessment of him.

"Do what your heart tells you to do Eben. I can't do it for you."

"I will. Wow, I have a lot to think about. Thanks, Wendy, I can't tell you how much I appreciate what you're doing."

Wendy's smile radiated in the faint, bluish moonlight of the evening. "You're very welcome. Tell Josiah to come straight to Uncle David's property. All he has to do is go directly south from the hollowed out tree through the timber. There's an old farm building set back from the house. Tell him to wait for me in there but don't let David or Shelley see him. I'll be looking for him."

"I'll tell him. This is going to work isn't it?"

"Yes, once he crosses the creek he's home free."

"I can't believe this is happening. It's exciting but it's scary too," Eben said amazed by just how quickly events were unfolding.

"New things always are. Now, I better get back. It's getting close to dawn."

"Thanks Wendy, thank you so much."

Wendy hugged Eben tightly. "I'll see you soon."

SIMMERING

The rest of the night crept agonizingly along for Eben who sat in his mother's chair contemplating everything Wendy had told him. To his surprise, he was quivering with excitement.

Rising to his feet, he crossed the room and touched Isaac's arm to see if he were asleep. The boy didn't move in his uncomfortable bed and continued snoring gently.

"At least you can sleep little brother. You're lucky, you don't have any worries in the world."

Eben gazed at him for several moments continuing to think about helping Josiah out and on his way as soon as possible. Closing his eyes tightly, he brought his hands together.

"God, I don't like asking for favors but, please give me the strength to help Josiah in whatever he does. If he stays, please let him find a way to live his life in peace. If he goes, allow him to get far away from here, keep him safe and help him find his way. That's all I ask Lord, please help him find his place in life whatever it is."

The emotions bubbling throughout Eben caused him to tear up. He normally didn't cry but there was something about knowing Josiah was leaving. Would he ever see him again? Would he be okay? Eben sighed and wiped his eyes, then crossed the living room to lean on a window sill. Just outside the open window he could hear the eerie, raspy call of a barn owl calling out from somewhere in the trees lining the front of the house. Immediately, goosebumps dotted his arms: The sound always unnerved him. It reminded him of the whispered ghost stories he'd heard as a child which told of spirits wandering the darkest places of the Community hunting down victims for the Crow Man.

Shaking his head, Eben returned to the chair. After visiting with John and Zachariah at church two weeks before he couldn't stop thinking about it. The Crow Man was surely just a myth as everyone said, but was it? What had really happened to Ben Isler? He wouldn't tell and no one dared ask him. Would it happen to Josiah if he weren't careful just like the other day when the Sentinels caught him? No, Eben thought, Josiah was going to get away cleanly, thanks to Wendy's willingness to help. The creek was three-quarters of a mile from the house and David Robinson's house was another half mile beyond. It seemed easy enough.

After an hour of fidgeting, Eben finally got up and headed to the barn to begin the day's milking well before Gideon came down to wake him and Isaac. It would be better he knew, to keep busy until the entire plan could be set in motion. Finally, Gideon and Isaac appeared yawning, their faces drawn and heavy from their restless sleep.

"What this?" Gideon asked stepping into the parlor where Eben was busy milking Jenny, Isaac's favorite cow. "What are you up to so early?"

"I couldn't sleep because of the heat so I decided to get started."

"Well, I'm proud Eben. That's very good of you."

"Yes Father, thank you."

"Well," Gideon said stretching and yawning widely, "Let's get to it."

The day seemed to last for an eternity while Eben waited for night to come when Gideon would hopefully lock Josiah in the granary. He'd watched Isaac and Gideon carry lumber out there where they'd spent a good portion of the afternoon sawing and hammering away. Eben didn't dare go and see what they were building but guessed it was either a bunk or they were reinforcing the interior walls. Instead, his time was spent scraping dried clots of paint off the barn in preparation for the painting he was expected to do. In his mind it was yet another meaningless chore Gideon had dreamed up for him to do. Josiah spent his day as he'd spent every other day since being brought back by the Sentinels: Sitting on the porch swing chained to the post.

Once supper was finished, Eben hauled in water for baths without the usual grumbling and complaining. As he made the countless trips between the well and the house he could see Josiah at the window watching. It was a pitiful existence for the carefree soul who was Josiah: He was always brought in before supper and taken up to the boys' room where Gideon locked him in with a plate of food and a bucket of water. His meals were always taken alone and were always taken to him by their father. Breakfast and lunch were given to him on the porch swing and in the bedroom if it rained. When he was allowed to use the outhouse Gideon led him along as though he were a dog on a leash, then it was right back to be locked up. No one, not even Mary was allowed to even interact with him in any way. Eben wondered how much longer it would go on

"You've done well the past few days Eben," Gideon said testing the bathwater with his big toe. "It's good to see you working and being mindful. I believe my prayers have been working."

"Yes, Father, thank you. I was wrong thinking I could disobey you." Eben replied hoping that being agreeable would temper his father's displeasure for the time being.

"Hmm, good, very good. Now, once I'm finished it's your turn then Isaac can go. I'll need to bring your brother down to bathe as well. He's beginning to smell."

With a curt nod, Eben fled the room leaving Gideon to his bath. Neither one of his parents called Josiah by his name anymore. He was simply, "your brother" or "him". Isaac and the girls had caught on to this quickly too making guarded jokes and comments which infuriated Eben. The entire situation was ridiculous and made him wonder how Josiah felt about it all. Despite always giving everyone the impression he was tough and didn't care about anything, Eben knew it had to be tearing him apart.

Eben entered the living room where the children were busy playing games or reading. Mary sat quietly in her chair staring out at the trees rustling in the evening breeze absently fingering the knitting needles in her lap

"Hey Eben, how about a game of checkers?" Isaac asked holding out the box containing the set.

"No thanks, not tonight. I have a headache."

"Are you sure?"

"Yeah, I'm sure. Maybe tomorrow okay?"

"Okay," he replied. "I'll practice so I can beat you."

Eben smiled weakly watching the boy set up the board to play.

After the initial rush of excitement after talking to Wendy, Eben's confidence had begun to waver throughout the day. He went through every conceivable scenario he could think of for helping Josiah get to David Robinson's and on his way to Indiana. One idea was to simply sneak out during the night, retrieve the long wooden ladder from its storage place in the barn and lean it up to the bedroom window. Another plan he formulated was to saw through the bottom of the post on the front porch allowing the chain to slip through allowing Josiah to make a run for it. Other outlandish plans crossed his mind such as sneaking into his parent's room in the night and stealing the key Gideon used on the lock or telling his brother to simply knock their father on the head with a log. None except the ladder idea he knew, would work and even then, it was questionable; the ladder was heavy and required two people to move it around. He could drag it to the house but the way Gideon had been watching him lately it was a sure way to get caught. His only option was to hope he was correct in assuming that his father was going to lock Josiah in the granary. All he had to do was run out some night, pull the pin up out of the latch and tell Josiah about the plan he and Wendy had come up with. Then hopefully, he'd go.

But, Eben was also troubled by what would happen to him once Josiah was gone. If Gideon knew he was involved in any way the granary would be his prison instead. In addition, the beating he'd receive would be far worse than anything his father had ever doled out before. Perhaps Wendy was right, maybe he should leave with Josiah and be done with what he was quickly learning to be the truth about the Community. Trying to navigate the strange English world would be better if the two of them were together and besides, maybe, just maybe, Elizabeth would be interested in him.

"Your turn," Gideon said appearing from behind the sheet used to close off the kitchen from the rest of the house during bath time.

Eben, then Isaac, scrubbed themselves in the rapidly cooling water leaving it clouded and gray from grime and soap. Once they pulled on their nightshirts, Mary came in and put her hand in the water swishing it around.

"Why don't you give me a few minutes and I can heat up some clean water for him?" she said sticking her head out of the kitchen. Gideon stopped halfway up the stairs on his way to retrieve Josiah.

"No," he replied. "He'll have to make do. We're not going out of our way to accommodate the boy."

Mary frowned. "No matter how badly you want to punish him, he's still our son and I think he should have a clean, hot bath!"

Gideon stomped back down steps down the stairs to stand over Mary. Isaac and the girls scampered out of his way scattering their books and checkers across the floor. Eben took several hesitant steps towards her ready to fight his father if need be. He was quickly growing tired of the shouting and bullying which seemed to be getting worse as the summer wore on.

"No! He's lucky he's getting a bath at all!" Gideon shouted pointing a finger in her face. "As far as I'm concerned he can go without but he's smelling up the house!"

Mary stifled a sob and shook her head forcefully. "When is all of this going to end? When? He's just a boy!"

"You know when! When the Council decides!"

"When the Council decides? You're his father! Just for once, can't you show him some compassion?"

"You watch yourself woman," Gideon growled leaning in close to her. "You should know as well as anyone, no to defy me and not to challenge the Council."

Without another word, he abruptly turned and disappeared up the stairs. Mary sniffled and fell into her chair crying quietly. Eben went to her side and gently rubbed her shoulder wishing he could tell her about his plans. At least she might have some kind of hope to look forward to. She responded by squeezing his hand tightly.

"Come now," he said to Isaac and the girls. "Back to what you were doing."

Isaac scooted around the floor picking up the checkers; Miriam, Rebecca and Lydia retrieved their books but none of them could concentrate any longer. Gideon appeared again following closely behind Josiah.

"All of you, look away," Gideon ordered.

Eben felt his face flush from anger. Instead of looking away, he stared directly at Josiah. What he saw astonished him: Just a week into his captivity, his once healthy, well-tanned face had become strained and ashen. Large, dark circles outlined his eyes which seemed to be devoid of any sort of life. A frown replaced the mischievous smirk he'd always had. And worse in Eben's mind, he looked like as though he'd simply given up. Just as he pulled the sheet back to enter the kitchen, he and Eben locked eyes for just a moment. Eben bowed his head slightly hoping Josiah might some-how understand that he still had hope.

While Josiah bathed, Eben heard his father mumble some-thing unintelligible before the screen door banged shut. After a moment, he could hear Gideon walking across the porch where he began jingling the chain. Leaning back to carefully peek out the window, Eben watched him unwrap it from the post.

Sitting on the floor next to his mother, Eben smiled ever so faintly to himself and squeezed her hand again. Gideon was finally going to take Josiah out to the granary.

JAILBREAK

E ben's stomach churned from a mixture of nervousness and excitement as he lay in his bed for the first time in nearly two weeks. He should have been overjoyed at the prospect of finally having it all to himself but he wasn't. It was strange without Josiah there kicking in his sleep, breathing noisily through his mouth and mumbling in his sleep. Instead of lying in the middle and stretching out as he'd always imagined he'd do if he ever had a bed to himself, Eben kept to the side.

Sighing, he turned to look at the clock on the night table. It read close to two A.M.; nearly four hours since the family had finally gone to bed leaving him alone to brood over what he was going to do. Other than the occasional creaks and groans typical of the old house, no one stirred upstairs. Perhaps, Eben thought, Gideon felt he could rest now that he'd dealt with Josiah. Still, he waited and stared at the blurry hands on the clock in the darkness. If he and Wendy's plan to send Josiah to Indiana was to work, he knew he had to be especially careful and he also knew the plan had to unfold soon.

Earlier in the evening, Gideon had indeed taken Josiah to the granary just as Eben had guessed he'd do. Given nothing more than a blanket, a wooden bucket of water and another bucket for personal needs, it was anyone's guess how long he'd be locked in. No one, not even Mary had spoken to him nor did she or the children speak to Gideon once he returned to sit in his chair and read his Bible as though nothing had happened. Despite growing up around the man and knowing all too well his wildly varying moods, Eben was infuriated by his father's complete lack of empathy. It was as though he'd locked up one of the cows instead of his son.

Strangely, Eben didn't feel badly about being angry with his father. Too many beatings and too many years of watching him abuse his wife and boys had taken their toll leaving him feeling hollow inside. Family didn't seem to be as important as the Council of Elders, the Community, the Church and Reverend Stohlfutz were in Gideon's mind. He eagerly went along with all of it without worrying about what it all meant for his family. Maybe, Eben thought, going with Josiah wasn't such a bad idea after all. With a deep sigh, he flopped back to his left side trying to get comfortable wondering if Gideon would even miss them. Still, doubts about going nagged at him. Who would look after Isaac and the girls? Who would look after Mary? Without Josiah there to pick on, would Gideon turn the full effect of his displeasure against Eben? If Josiah had been telling the truth about going to work in the sawmill, Eben knew his future would be bleak at best.

"Out of the frying pan and into the fire," he said softly. The thought of having to work for Jonah made him shiver.

Another hour passed with the only sound being the wind whispering through the gently swaying curtains above the window. Eben tossed and turned, tense with anticipation until finally deciding to make a run for the granary. He wished there had been some way he could have let Josiah know of the plot but it was impossible for anyone in the family to come into contact with him anymore.

Eben crept down the steps and began running once he'd slipped through the back door. Upon reaching the granary he fumbled with the heavy latch trying to pull it open but stopped: Gideon had used the lock from the porch to secure the door. There wasn't much time to try and pick it and beating it with a hammer would make too much noise.

"Hey, Josiah! Wake up!" he hissed.

"Eben? What are you doing out here?"

"I've come to let you out."

"You what? Father put the lock from the porch on the door."

"I saw it."

"What are you going to do?"

Eben's mind raced until he suddenly remembered he hadn't nailed the top board down completely a few days previously.

The boards lining the granary were placed horizontally with a half-inch gap between each to allow air to circulate through the grain the building was designed to hold. It allowed just enough room for Eben to grab ahold with his fingers and climb to the top.

"Slide the bunk over and see if you can reach up here," he commanded. "When you do, start pushing on this board I'm pulling on but make it quick!"

Josiah did as he was told and began hitting the board with the heel of his hand. "It's not coming loose."

"Keep working on it, it's starting to move."

Slowly, agonizingly, the boys worked the end until it finally popped free. Eben carefully slid over and pulled it out far enough for Josiah to slip through. His hands and fingers burned with pain but he ignored it. All that mattered now was getting Josiah out and on his way as quickly as possible.

"Hurry up, climb through there," Eben grunted through clenched teeth. "I can't hang on much longer."

Josiah fumbled around in the darkness trying to pull himself up. "I can't do it."

"Yes you can! Hurry!"

Josiah continued scrabbling and clawing before managing to swing a leg up and through the opening. Next, he eased his torso through the opening finally swinging himself out and to drop to the ground with a thud. Eben slowly eased the board back into position and fell to his brother's side.

"What are you doing? Are you crazy?" Josiah asked breathlessly.

"Listen to me, I worked it all out with Wendy. All you have to do is get over to David Robinson's and hide in a building behind the house. Don't let David or his wife see you. Wendy will take you to Iowa City and put you on a bus."

"What? Where will I go?"

"There's a place in Indiana she knows about where you'll be safe. They'll help you find a job or go to school, whatever you want to do. It sounds like they help people from places like the Community. Elizabeth is there."

Josiah looked at him with surprise. "Elizabeth Beiler? Really?"

"Yes, she's there. You have to go."

"What about my money? I'll need to get it."

Eben silently cursed himself for not remembering to grab it from the bottom drawer of the desk where Josiah had hidden it. "No! Forget the money! If you go up there father will catch you. Wendy's already told me she'll give you what you need and pay for the bus ticket."

Josiah peeked around the corner towards the house and looked back upon Eben with hesitation apparent on his face. "Well, I don't know, maybe I should just stay here and accept my punishment. I don't have any clothes and…"

Eben grabbed him by the shoulders and slammed him into the wall of the granary. "You simpleton! This is your big chance to get out of here like you've always talked about. What? Do you want to be shunned for the rest of your life and locked up in here? Do you want to work in the sawmill for Jonah and the Reverend? Go! You can have a life now!"

"Yeah, um, well, you're right I guess."

"You know I am!"

Josiah looked away with the most mournful look on his face Eben had ever seen. "Eben, I don't know…"

"Don't know what? What's the matter with you?"

"I'm…I'm afraid. That's why I never left before."

Eben's anger suddenly evaporated as he looked upon Josiah. He now looked helpless and fragile in the light of the moon. "I know, and it's okay."

"Is it?"

"Yes, you've never lived anywhere else or done anything other than live on this farm. Heck, I'm scared too. For you, for me, for Isaac and the girls, for mother. If you don't want to leave then I'll help you get back inside the granary and we'll forget any of this ever happened. If you want to get out of here, this is the time. Tell me, Josiah, do you really think you'd be happy staying?"

Josiah shook his head and sniffled. "No."

"Then go!"

"You're right. But what about you? What's going to happen to you when father finds out I'm gone?"

Eben shrugged his shoulders. "I don't know and I don't care. What matters to me is seeing you get on your way and knowing you'll live a good life free of beatings, Sentinels, Stohlfutz's and all the rest of it."

"I, I'm worried I won't, you know…know how to act or anything else."

Eben crossed his arms and scowled. "Well, if it's so bad out there you could always come back. I'm sure father would like that."

A smile crept across Josiah's face. "Boy, wouldn't that be stupid."

Eben laughed halfheartedly. "What's the worst thing they could do? Lock you in a granary?"

"Yeah, I guess you're right."

Both boys sat in the grass listening to several coyotes yipping somewhere out in the night.

"So, what are you going to do?" Eben asked.

Josiah sighed deeply and grinned. "I'm going to do it."

Eben choked a bit before tears began streaking down his face. He didn't try to stop them either. Looking up, he was surprised to see Josiah fighting them back as well.

"I'm going to miss you little brother."

"And I'm going to miss you. Be safe okay?"

"Yeah, I will. Maybe I'll write to you once I'm settled. You know, I could send them to Wendy and she could forward them to the Robinson's and maybe they could hide them in the hollowed out tree down there."

Eben wiped his eyes on his hands. "It's a good idea, I like it."

Without another word, he crushed Josiah with a hug, the first time he'd ever done so. "Remember what I told you? Don't stop until you get to the Robinson's and don't ever come back here. Promise me you won't."

"I won't."

Finally, the two separated and regarded one another.

"Take care of yourself," Josiah said. "If you ever go back down to the creek look inside the tree. I'll leave something there for you."

"I will," Eben replied wiping his eyes on his shirtsleeve.

Josiah jumped the fence into the cattle lot and crossed down the draw behind the barn just as a cloud drifted over the moon hiding him completely. Eben stared into the darkness but he was gone. With a sigh, he turned to begin making his way back to the house but stopped and looked back just as the cloud passed. There at the edge of the field, he could see Josiah clearly in the moonlight for just a moment. Seeing Eben, he waved before another cloud crossed the moon, then disappeared.

WAITING

The next day, Eben yawned and rested his head against Jenny's side as he squeezed and pulled on her teats. The milk squirted into the bucket beneath her in a rhythmic swish swish lulling him to sleep. All he could think about was Josiah and if everything had gone according to plan, Eben knew he should be hiding in the Robinson's old farm building waiting for Wendy to find him sometime during the day and then, he'd be on his way. Instead of being excited the knowledge of it all made him feel sick. The tension building during the past few weeks left him exhausted and fearful of what his father would do once he discovered what had happened. Eben knew that's just what he was going to have to face and hoped it would all be over sooner than later.

"Good morning, Eben," Gideon said walking into the milking parlor with Isaac.

Eben immediately tensed up at the sound of his father's voice but continued milking without looking up. "Good morning, Father."

"Back at it early again, eh?"

"Yes, Father."

"Well, well. You've been doing a good job lately and I'm thankful."

He must not have discovered Josiah's missing yet. Eben thought. *Act as though nothing's out of the ordinary.*

Gideon and Isaac guided the next two cows into the parlor and began their work. It wasn't unusual for the morning milking to go by in silence since it was so early in the day but today it drove Eben nearly mad with worry.

Half an hour passed and still neither boy nor Gideon had spoken. Eben's mind began racing wondering if his father was allowing the tension to build up before unleashing his anger as he sometimes did. When he finally spoke, Eben nearly fainted.

"Later this morning I'm going to run over to buy some hardware and a new screen door for the kitchen. It's been beaten up lately and can't be repaired any longer. We also need more paint for the barn and outbuildings once we've used up what we have. Eben, I'd like you to come along with me," Gideon said breaking the silence.

Eben froze gripping the udders tightly until Jenny showed her displeasure by mooing loudly and leaning hard against him. "Um, yes Father, it sounds like fun."

"We've all been through a lot the past few weeks and it would do you some good to get out for a few hours."

"Thank you, Father."

Once the rest of the cows were milked, Eben and Isaac began the long arduous chore of cleaning the parlor from ceiling to floor.

"You boys get finished up in here and I'll go and start throwing hay down," Gideon said. "I asked Mother to make us a nice big breakfast this morning so once you're done we'll go in and eat. She's making the bacon and cheese potato casserole we all like."

"Yes!" Isaac shouted. "I can't wait!"

Eben forced himself to smile knowing he'd be lucky to choke even a mouthful of food down. It would be a matter of minutes before Gideon discovered Josiah was missing and what happened after was anyone's guess. He swallowed hard knowing he'd done the right thing and mentally prepared himself for the trouble that was coming.

With a nod, Gideon walked out leaving the boys to their cleaning.

"Come on, Eben, hurry! Let's get done so we can eat!" Isaac cried as ran with buckets in hand to the water pump just outside the door next to the barn.

Eben followed him and held the buckets while Isaac pumped keeping an eye on his father the entire time. Sure enough, he headed directly to the granary and began digging in his pocket for the key. Eben's stomach churned.

"Hey Isaac, bring those in when you get them filled up. I'll finish sweeping everything out," he said nervously stepping around the corner to watch the inevitable explosion. His heart pounded so hard it felt as though it were about to leap out of his chest. The side door where the cows were funneled into the parlor still sat open facing the corn field and creek. The long leaves blowing gently in the morning wind beckoned to Eben telling him to run and join Josiah at David Robinson's. For a moment, Eben considered doing just that but put it out of his head. If he were to run Gideon would certainly follow him and then it would all be over. No, he thought, stay and deal with whatever was going to happen and give Josiah a chance to get away cleanly.

Isaac burst through the door sloshing water with each hurried step.

"Hey! I thought you were going to sweep!" he said setting the buckets down.

"I will, just give me a minute, okay?"

"Come on, Eben, hurry up!"

"Yeah, yeah, just a second Isaac!"

Eben steeled himself and carefully peered around the corner fairly certain he was going to see Gideon stomping back to the parlor to begin beating him in earnest. What he watched unfold surprised him: his father stood in the open doorway of the granary with his hands on his hips shaking his head from Instead of coming back to punish Eben, he closed the door and disappeared inside the barn. Eben waited with sweat pouring down his face and back wondering if he was retrieving something he could use as a weapon but he didn't come back out. After another torturous few moments, Eben gasped when he saw him throwing hay down for the animals.

"Well, okay," he mumbled and began sweeping the floor while Isaac shoveled manure out the open door at the back. "Please God, give me the strength to face the today and the next few days."

Despite his worry, the boys made quick work of the cleaning.

"You both about done? I'm starving."

Eben looked up from his mop and was surprised to see Gideon leaning casually on the door frame.

"We're just finishing up," he said.

"Good. It's going to be hot again today. The more we can get done this morning the better."

"Yes, it feels like it."

"Come boys, let's wash up and have some breakfast."

"Yoo hoo!" Isaac shouted. "Pancakes and eggs and breakfast casserole!"

Gideon smiled watching Isaac bolt across the driveway making a beeline towards the other water pump by the house singing happily to himself as he went. Eben hesitated wondered if he'd just been waiting for Isaac to leave before pouncing.

"Are you coming?" Gideon asked.

"Um, yes. Let me put the mops and buckets away and I'll be right along."

Gideon smiled again. "I'm surprised you didn't try to beat your brother to the house. Mother's casserole is your favorite."

"Oh, I'm just tired this morning," Eben said returning the mops and buckets to their place in the corner. "But I'll be right along."

"I'll see you in the house."

Eben waited a moment before following his father cautiously from a distance all the while trying to guess what he was up to. He didn't seem to be angry or even surprised that Josiah wasn't in the granary, he simply walked along with the same long legged, purposeful stride he'd always had. He hadn't yelled and he hadn't punished Eben. What was going on?

As he walked, Eben took a careful glance down to the creek and timber wondering how Josiah was doing and if he was finally on his way to Indiana. His father's behavior was baffling but the longer he stayed around the farm the more time Josiah had to get farther and farther away. Hopefully, the plan was going smoothly and the worry he was experiencing would soon go away. Looking back, he was horrified to see Gideon watching him.

"Not thinking about going back down there are you?"

"Um, no. I'm just looking around."

"Hmm, that's all behind us now. We all need to look forward from now on."

"Yes, Father, I believe we do."

"Good, very good."

UNCERTAINTY

The day passed uneventfully into night and still Gideon did and said nothing. During breakfast Eben was even more surprised to see his mother in seemingly good spirits for a change. Perhaps she knew what had transpired during the night and knew Josiah had finally made it out though he couldn't imagine how. It was all very strange and despite not being punished, Eben still felt on edge. Part of him wondered if his parent's had simply given up on Josiah and his absence was something they saw as a blessing in disguise. If this were indeed the case, so be it.

Instead of going to the hardware and lumber store as promised, Gideon, Eben and Isaac spent the rest of the morning and afternoon scraping and painting the barn to use up the paint on hand before buying more. To stay cool despite the oppressive heat, they followed the shade around the structure as the sun crossed the sky; the morning was spent on the west side and by afternoon they'd worked around to the east. Eben watched the creek the entire time from his tenuous perch high on the ladder hoping to get a glimpse of Wendy's bright red hair and colorful clothing but she was nowhere to be seen. He couldn't wait to talk to her to hear that Josiah had indeed gotten on the bus and left. Not knowing what was going on and unsure of when he'd actually see her again drove him crazy with anticipation.

After yet another hot, sleepless night, Gideon and Eben rode next to each other in the wagon on their way to the lumber yard the next morning. Barn swallows and sparrows darted in and out of the tall grass and weeds in the ditches as they slowly trundled along the dusty road.

"So tell me, do you want to go back to school this fall?" Gideon asked.

"Yes, Father, I think so."

"Perhaps you could do something else instead. Have you considered that? Learning a trade maybe? Most of your friends are already working. John's father told me he isn't going back."

Eben looked up at a red tailed hawk slowly circling above riding what little wisps of wind there were higher up. He had no idea what he was going to do but according to Josiah, his future was already planned out just as his had been. Maybe that was the reason behind the trip to the lumber yard.

"John's not going back to school?"

"No, he isn't. He's asked to be baptized next week and I hear he's going to ask for Hannah's hand once she's of age in a few months."

"Really? What's he going to do?"

"Farm with his father," Gideon said. "He needs the help Lord knows with all of the girls they have."

"I can't believe it. He said he was going back to school the last time I talked to him."

"Hmm, well, sometimes things change," Gideon replied. "Eben, I've never told you this before but I think it's time."

"What Father?"

"You've never done anything except help me on the farm. I think it would be wise for you to work for someone else for a few years just to experience something different."

Eben felt his chest seize up as the words came out of his father's mouth. He knew whatever his father was going to say wouldn't be good. Ahead of the wagon, the red tailed hawk suddenly rocketed out of the air to pounce on a rabbit or mouse in the ditch.

Gideon continued: "Someday, the farm might belong to you and Isaac and you'll need to know many things in order to make it work. My father sent me to work for Moses Roth for a few years for two reasons: So I'd learn to work for someone else and so I'd learn a trade other than farming. It's the best thing he ever did for me. I've worked it all out with the Reverend and Jonah. You'll be starting with them next week full time."

"But Father! I don't want to work for Stohlfutz! Why...?"

Gideon abruptly turned on the seat and glared at Eben with stony eyes. "Your brother must have told you all about it eh? First of all, you don't have any say in the matter. Secondly, the Stohlfutz's were kind enough to offer as a favor to me. You are going!"

"Is it because you don't want me to have the farm someday? So you can save it all for Isaac?"

Gideon gave Eben an evasive look. "What are you talking about?"

"You know! You've always been hard on Josiah and I and it seems like we're a burden to you! Isaac never gets punished like we always have. You go easy on him and he's going to get it all!"

"What? That's because he's still a child and yes, he'll get his share but you'll get yours too!"

"Is that right? He's never been punished like we have been. Even when we were his age and younger you thrashed us pretty hard!"

"I'll tell you why that is!" Gideon roared jerking the reins back bringing the wagon to an abrupt stop in the middle of the road. "You boys are the most temperamental, difficult children I've ever met. Always running your mouths! Always insisting on doing what you want, not following the rules! Of course I'm hard on you! I was trying to make men out of you both!"

"By beating the stuffing out of us?"

"Yes! How else were you going to learn? Talking and gentleness certainly work," Gideon protested. "You've heard me tell you why many times. It's in the Bible: *He that spareth his rod hateth his son: but he that loveth him chasteneth him betimes.* Proverbs 13:24."

Eben crossed his arms and scowled with anger. Yes, he thought to himself, Wendy was correct: He should have left with Josiah when he had the chance. The more he thought about it all, the angrier he became, so much in fact, that jumping from the wagon and running away seemed like a good idea in spite of being miles from the borders of the Community.

Gideon shook his head and sighed deeply. "And I thought this was going to be a fine day. Good heavens, Eben, I honestly don't know what's gotten into you but it's going to stop now! I'm doing what's best for you!"

The rest of the trip to the lumber yard went by in an uncomfortable silence. Eben couldn't understand why his father seemed to be so loyal to Reverend Stohlfutz despite knowing the man well. Most people he knew couldn't stand the old buzzard and saw him for what he really was; a mean, judgmental hypocrite who use his lofty position and his Sentinels for his own nefarious purposes. Tonight, Eben knew for certain now, he'd make his way to the Robinson's farm and join Josiah in Indiana. There was no way he'd ever work for Stohlfutz and it seemed as though things with his father had reached an impasse.

The wagon rumbled down a gradual incline to the lumber yard which sat next to the Stohlfutz's expansive lumber mill on a relatively straight section of the meandering West Fork River. Eben sighed with disgust when he saw the crowd of men and boys who with a little time on their hands until fall harvest, were buying materials for repairs and various building projects or bringing in logs to sell. He didn't feel like being sociable with anyone today.

"Have you cooled off yet? Because if you haven't, you can just sit here while I go inside," Gideon said climbing down to tie the horses to the hitching pole in front. His cheerful outlook from the past couple of days was gone, replaced with the same cold detachment Eben knew all too well.

"I'll stay here," Eben answered smartly.

"Fine."

He watched his father stop and visit with several other men on his way to the door still burning with resentment. Josiah was gone and Eben was being sent to work for the most hated man in the Community but to see Gideon smiling and carrying on as though nothing were going on made him want to scream.

The mid-morning sun bore down on Eben as he sat contemplating his own escape. He wasn't particularly worried nor did he believe his father would miss him now that his big secret was out. He'd been in and out of the house so many times during the summer nights that getting out one more time should be a piece of cake. All he had to do was get through the rest of the day without losing control of himself otherwise Gideon might just lock him in the granary. Eben then thought about his mother and how she'd react to him leaving and this caused him to catch his breath. What would happen to her? How would she deal with losing two of her sons in one week? For a moment Eben considered telling her but quickly put the notion out of his head. For all he knew, she was either totally committed to whatever Gideon said and did or she was so afraid of him she had no choice but to go along. Better he leave quietly and be done with it.

Hearing a horse snort nearby, Eben looked up to see two of the last people he ever wanted to see: Leroy Fisher and Arlen Kopp.

Leroy rode a beautiful four-year old tan-colored saddlebred horse named Daisy which looked as though she'd already been abused considerably in her short life. Hairless, white masses of scar tissue lined her sides where spurs had been ground into her flesh, her eyes looked weary and lifeless. Though still a strong animal with a fine pedigree, Eben knew Leroy had a way of killing off every horse he'd ever had, usually by running or whipping them to death. A smirk slowly crossed his face thinking about how nice it would be to see her throw fat Leroy off on his head.

With a grunt, Leroy heaved himself down out of the saddle and approached Eben while hiking up the leather chaps the Sentinels all wore. Arlen followed close behind him chewing on a long blade of grass.

"What are you doing?"

"What's it look like I'm doing? I'm sitting here waiting for my father," Eben replied.

Leroy grunted and wiped his nose on the back of his hand. "Are you now? He's in there?"

"Yep."

"Huh, I'm surprised he lets you out of his sight," Leroy said putting a foot up on a wheel to lean close to Eben. He stank of sour sweat and bad breath. "Didn't work too well with that brother of yours did it? Heck, he couldn't keep him in line and look what he did. Up and ran off."

The mention of Josiah running away caught Eben completely by surprise. How could Leroy possibly know?

"That father of yours," Leroy continued with an evil smile snaking through his dirty beard, "just thinks he's something now doesn't he? Mister big important Elder, sucking up to the Reverend like a little puppy looking for a tit. You know what I think? I think he's a little too big for his britches. He ain't anybody special like he thinks he is."

"Yeah? Why don't you shut up Leroy, you fat disgusting pile of hog filth," Eben retorted. He was angry with his father, an anger which bordered on hatred but Leroy was someone he wouldn't ever allow to bad mouth family.

"Who do you think you are boy?" Leroy countered poking a heavy wooden club into Eben's chest. "You can't talk to me that way! I think you forget who you're dealing with!"

"Go to hell you fat loser."

With a howl, Leroy jerked Eben down from the seat and slapped him. Instead of curling up in a ball and taking it just as his brain was screaming at him to do, Eben recovered from the blow and hit Leroy back as hard as he could catching him in the nose. Leroy fell to the ground with a thump and screamed through bloody fingers once he realized someone was fighting back for a change. Knowing he was in for it no matter what, Eben charged landing a flurry of punches as he closed in, rolling Leroy onto his back. Just as Eben pulled back his fist to strike him again, Arlen jumped into the fray hitting Eben from behind with his club. Suddenly, everything went sideways. Eben lurched drunkenly the opposite direction falling painfully into the side of the wagon. Before he could react, both men were on him like wild dogs, screaming, kicking and hitting.

"Yeah! That damned brother of yours thought he could get away didn't he? Gideon Wittke's first born and a Levite to boot! Sure showed him up didn't he?" Leroy bawled. "You're going to pay the price he did you little skunk!"

"My brother's fine!" Eben managed to croak. "He's free! He got away!"

Leroy stopped hitting and grabbed Eben by the shirt to pull his bloodied face close to his. "No, he didn't get away. I caught the little bastard and I dragged him back kicking and screaming to get what he deserves. He's never leaving the Community! Never!"

Eben could only stare on with horror as more blows came through the haze before he spiraled away into blackness.

A MURDER OF CROWS

E ben crept along the edge of the cornfield his eyes wide and straining to see through the veil of darkness surrounding him. He stepped cautiously and waited, then stepped again. The endless rows of corn made strange shadows in the darkness causing him to jump every time the night wind shivered through the long leaves. Squatting down amongst the weeds, he prayed Josiah wouldn't stop running.

Moving to the edge of the timber, a strange sense of foreboding suddenly came over him causing goosebumps to prickle his arms and scalp. Something, or someone was there just to his right moving slowly and deliberately as though it knew exactly where it was going. Eben wiped sweat from his face and eyes waiting and watching, still struggling to see but there was nothing. The dry pop of a stick being broken shattered the silence. Closer to his left, a rustling sound and several muted footsteps thumped along, then stopped. The longer he waited the more frightened he became. There seemed to be several small noises all around him now and it seemed as though they were coming directly towards him. Eben took a shaking breath telling himself the sounds were probably just raccoons or possums out on their nightly excursions looking for food, or deer browsing through the thick underbrush looking for green shoots.

A fearful, bloodcurdling scream suddenly pierced the darkness echoing madly off the trees. Eben ran to the edge of the creek but was thrown back as though there were an invisible barrier of some sort there. No matter how hard he struggled, he couldn't move forward and he couldn't go back. Several dark shapes loomed out of the darkness and descended on the spot where the scream had come from.

"Josiah!" he screamed. "Run!"

The flickering light of a torch suddenly illuminated the timber in a ghostly glow. It was held by a man, or a creature of some sort wearing a strange black cloak which dragged on the ground at its feet. Eben caught his breath and cried in terror as it turned to face him with black piercing eyes set in a grotesque face of a crow. The creature pointed and shouted something at him at him in a wicked cackle and turned to two other creatures dressed exactly like the first. They held Josiah's arms and with a muted command from the first creature, forced him down to his knees.

The creature holding the torch raised his arms high and began waving them in circles while he chanted something unintelligible. One crow, then another and another flew out of the trees and descended upon Josiah. He cried out fearfully as more crows joined in creating a whirlwind of black feathers and shrieking calls. They picked and tore at him with their long curved beaks until he was covered in open bloody sores.

"Help me Eben! Please, help me!"

Eben cried out until he was hoarse still fighting to tear himself loose from whatever was holding him in place. No matter how hard he tried, he still couldn't move. The creatures turned to watch him as Josiah was devoured.

"Josiah! No!"

"Eben...!"

Eben awoke screaming and thrashing. His breaths came in short, labored gasps as he sat up in bed. Feeling sick, he leaned over the side of the bed and vomited in a large bowl held by his mother. His head throbbed with pain.

"Josiah," he sobbed. "What's happening to you?"

Mary reached over and gently wiped Eben's face with a cool cloth. "My sweet boy," she choked through her tears.

Eben gripped her arm tightly. "Mother, I had a dream. It was so bad...Josiah was being held down by men with crows heads. They called other crows out of the trees and they...they killed him."

"Yes," she said. "I know. You were calling out to him."

The two sat quietly for several minutes. Mary continued to wipe Eben's face and cry quietly to herself. Outside the wind wailed through the trees on the other side of the house causing several branches to rattle and scratch on the roof. Despite the perspiration running down his face Eben shivered. He thought he'd die from the pain in his head.

"Mother?"

Mary shushed him. "You need to rest. You have a big bump on your head and your face..."

Memories of the beating he'd received and what Leroy had told him were slowly coming back to through a waves of pain. Cold, terrible fear crept into his mind as it all began to make sense.

"Mother," he whispered. "Josiah tried to run away but I think they caught him. The Sentinels."

Mary raised a finger to her mouth and looked fearfully at the door. "You need to rest, Eben. Don't say a word about that to anyone. Do you understand me? Promise me!"

Eben forced himself to sit up and was shocked by just how sad and lifeless her face seemed to be. It looked as though she'd aged years in the last week.

"What's going on Mother? I helped Josiah get out of the granary two nights ago. I had a plan for him to get away from here but…"

"How is the boy?" Gideon asked from the doorway.

Mary jumped from the sound of his voice and turned away. "He's fine except for the bumps on his head and he's scared out of his wits."

"Hmm," Gideon grumbled. Taking several steps into the room, he stood at Eben's bedside and stared down at him. "You need to rest. What you heard today and your dream…well, you need to get it out of your head."

Mary cried out and covered her face with her hands. She began crying uncontrollably.

"Where's Josiah?" Eben asked.

Gideon continued to stare at him. "Rest. You and I will discuss things when you're feeling better."

THE DISAPPEARED

"You need to eat," Mary said holding a spoonful of soup in front of Eben's mouth.

Shaking his head, he gently pushed the spoon away. "I'm sorry Mother, I'm just not hungry."

"But you haven't eaten since yesterday at breakfast. Come, it will make you feel better."

Eben smiled weakly at her trying his best to make her believe everything was okay. Throughout the long day he'd been allowed to stay in bed recovering from the beating Leroy and Arlen had inflicted upon him but he couldn't rest. An overwhelming sense of dread permeated his every thought remembering what Leroy had said to him the day before. Had he really caught Josiah? And if so, where was he and what had they done with him? The thought of the Sentinels having him hidden away somewhere was almost too much to contemplate. Whatever they intended to do to him, or were doing, he knew it couldn't be good.

"Mother, I need to ask you something."

Mary set the bowl on the tray with the other uneaten food she'd brought up and walked to the window to stare out at the setting sun. "I know what you want to ask but I can't tell you anything. Please don't."

"Do you know where Josiah is?"

"No," she said softly. "But I know he didn't get away like you and I thought he had."

"How do you know?"

Before answering, she went to the door of the bedroom and carefully peeked out before returning to sit on the edge of the bed beside Eben. Downstairs they could hear Isaac and the girls chattering good-naturedly while playing their after supper games.

"Because I know your father all too well after being married to him for so long," she whispered. "At first, I knew he wasn't angry about Josiah being gone which told me he knows the Sentinels caught him. If he'd gotten away cleanly, he'd be madder than a hornet."

Eben nodded knowing she was right. "The other morning you seemed happy. Did you think he'd made it?"

"Yes, I did but when you boys were out painting the barn one of the Sentinels brought a message for your father."

"I didn't see it. What did it say?"

Mary shrugged her shoulders and sniffled. "I don't know. There was no writing on the outside and it had a wax seal holding it together. Very official looking. He read it when you and Isaac were washing up for supper and threw it in the fire as soon as he was done."

"If they caught Josiah where would he be?" he asked taking her hand. "You have to tell me everything you know. Mother, please."

With an eye towards the door, she pursed her lips in frustration. "You don't understand, these men your father deals with are evil. If you push them any more than you already have it could be bad for you. Please don't!"

Eben stared at her with surprise. "Mother! I'm going to find Josiah and once I do, we're both getting out of here but you have to help me."

"No," she said abruptly standing. "Leave it alone and don't tell me any more of this nonsense. I can't stand the thought of losing you as well. It's just too much!"

"Mother...!"

"No, Eben, stop it! I won't allow him to have you too!"

"What? Who?"

Instead of answering, Mary turned and ran from the room. Eben struggled to his feet intending to follow her but the sound of her bedroom door slamming stopped him in his tracks. He considered knocking on her door to try and question her further but the sight of Gideon at the bottom of the steps made him recoil in fear.

"Everything okay up there?" he asked.

"Yes, Father, she's just upset about me getting in the fight yesterday."

Gideon watched him suspiciously. "Okay then. Are you feeling better?"

"Yes, I think so."

"Good. Get some rest. I expect you to attend church with us on Sunday. Three more days of rest should allow you plenty of time to heal."

Eben could only nod in agreement. Returning to his bedroom, he leaned on the windowsill and stared out into the coming night. If only he could find a way to get in touch with Wendy again he'd know what was going on and hopefully, she might have some suggestions to help as she'd done before.

Yes, he thought rubbing his swollen eye, *I'll go down to the creek tonight and see if she's there. She'll have a good idea of what to do.*

THE BROTHERHOOD
OF LEVITES

F our hours later, Eben slowly awoke to the strange sensation of someone walking into his room. He opened his eyes slowly to see the pale light of a lantern throwing odd shadows against the walls.

"Josiah?" he asked, immediately sitting upright in bed.

"Shhh," Gideon said sitting gently on the side of the bed. "It's me."

"What are you doing Father?"

"You need to get dressed. You and I have somewhere to go."

An icy knot of fear settled in Eben's heart and slowly crept throughout his body. "What? It's nearly midnight. Where are we going?"

Gideon looked over to Isaac who was sleeping soundly in his bed on the other side of the room. "Just get dressed quietly and come downstairs. I'll be waiting for you outside in the buggy."

"But what are we doing?"

"Just come."

Gideon silently made his way to the door and headed downstairs. Eben watched the flickering light disappear leaving him in darkness. He wondered why his father had awoken him in the middle of the night. Where could they possibly be going? Deciding it was best not to provoke him any more than he had too, Eben quickly dressed and walked out to the buggy and climbed in.

The buggy clattered on down the deserted road passing darkened farms along the way. Eben and Gideon rode in silence for a time but Eben had many questions gnawing at him.

"Father?" he asked tentatively.

"Yes?"

"Where are we going?"

Gideon stared straight ahead showing no emotion. "I think you'll discover the answer to your questions very soon. For now, you need to trust me."

"Yes, Father."

After another half hour of silence Eben drummed up the courage to ask the question he had to know the answer to. "Father, do you know where Josiah is?"

"Enough about him!" Gideon replied slamming his hand down on the seat. "The boy made the decision to turn his back on his faith and his family. I've prayed hard over this and I can't find any answers. Faith takes hard work and commitment Eben, something your brother didn't have in him. He was tempted by an evil of great power and it overtook him. He chose to go down a dark path. He chose not to live amongst us. He made a commitment to the Lord and he broke it. I fear God's displeasure with him."

"Yes, but...do you know where he is?"

"No! He's gone and he's not coming back! End of story!"

"How do you know he's not coming back?"

Gideon gave Eben a cold stare in the pale light of the lantern hanging on the front of the buggy. "He's gone, son, he left us for good. He won't ever be coming back to the Community even if he wants to."

Eben eyed him suspiciously. Gideon lived in a world in which there was right and there was wrong with no middle ground or drama to confuse things. On the few occasions when he intentionally withheld information or simply lied it was obvious to everyone in the family, except for the girls who were too young to know the difference yet, that he was hiding something. This, Eben knew, was one of those times.

Eben wondered if what had happened to Josiah was about to happen to him too. For a moment he considered jumping from the buggy and running away from his father but he stopped. If "they" knew what Josiah's every move had been, wouldn't they surely be able to track him down? He and his father were in the middle of the Community and the possibility of running thirty-miles without being caught was virtually impossible. He knew too, that he'd have to stay around to find Josiah because no one else would anymore.

As they continued on, Eben wondered if he might being taken to the same place where Josiah was presumably being held. It would make sense especially since he was certain his father knew he was the one who'd let Josiah out of the granary to begin with. And, with them out of the way, Gideon's plan to leave the farm to Isaac when he was ready would be easy. Deciding it would be better to know for sure what was going on before rushing headlong into a situation he was still unsure of, Eben sat still and silent feeling his stomach churn. Thinking back to the conversation he'd had earlier with his mother made him want to cry but he held in it the best he could. She seemed to know what was going on but yet she did nothing.

"So Father, where are we going?"

"It's not what you're thinking. It's one of the most important things a young man can do for our Community. You're about to become a man above men."

"What do you mean?"

Gideon laughed gently. "No one's going to hurt you. This is just a simple get-together. You'll be a new Eben soon."

Eben leaned his still sore head against the side of the buggy feeling the shiver run through his body again. He didn't know what to believe anymore.

After several more miles of silence, Gideon pulled the buggy onto a narrow lane Eben had never noticed before. The two continued on for nearly two miles finally coming to the top of a towering rise named Founder's Hill, the highest point in the Community. It had never been farmed or built on as far as Eben knew and its crest was topped with a grove of native black oak trees which were visible for miles. Strangely however, buggy's, wagons and horses filled a neatly kept yard surrounding a long building hidden in amongst the trees. Eben looked around fearfully seeing several dark shapes milling about the grounds and entering the front door. To his surprise and horror, the silhouettes of hundreds of crows perched on tree branches and along the eves of the building silently watching the proceedings.

"What is this place?"

"The Sanctuary."

"What is it? I never knew this was out here."

"This is the most holy place in our Community, Eben," Gideon said softly. "This is where our men are made, the foundations upon everything we have and believe in. This hill looks over every part of the Community for miles and miles. This is where our faith is confirmed under the tenets of Heaven. No man is ever closer to God than he is here."

Eben sat mesmerized. He'd never heard his father speak in such a way before.

"Only men who have made their Obligation are allowed here. This is sacred ground and tonight is something for you to take seriously."

"What's going to happen?"

Gideon smiled. "You'll find out soon enough. You'll be fine, trust me."

The urge to run began screaming at Eben. Josiah had mentioned something about the Obligation several weeks before in the barn the night their father had beaten them for being at the creek. This must have been what he was talking about.

"Father?"

"Yes?"

"Does anyone…ever refuse to do whatever this is?"

"No, never."

Eben's shivering became worse. He tried to swallow but couldn't.

"Come, let's go in. It looks like everyone's here," Gideon said climbing down from the buggy. He walked to Eben's side and waited.

"Come now. It's okay," he said holding out his hand.

Eben paused a moment before jumping down. Gideon smiled and put his arm around his shoulders. They slowly made their way to the front of the building where a lantern hung above the doors. Eben looked up to see the words above with what looked like a painting of a crow beneath them.

Praise the LORD, you his angels, you mighty ones who do his bidding, who obey his word.

Above the sign along the entire length of the roof more crows gathered to stare down at their visitors. Eben wondered why they were so bold and yet none made a sound. They just watched.

Soon, all of the men in the yard disappeared inside the building and shut the door leaving Gideon and Eben alone. Gideon waited, then stepped forward and knocked three times. From inside the building someone knocked once, paused, then knocked two more times in quick succession which was answered in reverse by Gideon.

The doors of the building slowly opened inwards to reveal a man he knew well: It was his friend John's father, Abraham, and he was dressed in a black robe fastened at the waist with a piece of rope. With a slight nod to Gideon, he stepped forward and placed his hands upon Eben's shoulders. "And so comes the sojourner, a simple man lost in the wilderness whose heart has been tempted by false Gods, those detestable deceivers of man, those peddlers of flesh, gold and possessions, his soul has been torn from his one true path, that of light and righteousness."

Two other men also dressed in the same robes came from inside the foyer and stood on either side of Eben and Gideon.

"There is wonder and joy this day the Lord hath made," Gideon and the two men on either side of them said.

"Open the inner gate for he hath come to beg for the mercies of the Lord, the one true God, the Creator of all Mankind."

Another set of doors were slowly opened from the inside revealing a wide anteroom of some sort. Robed men stood silently on either side of the door watching. Gideon approached a single door and knocked, waited for the reply from the inside, and proceeded on when it opened. Eben followed him inside to the cavernous interior of the building where many more men in robes lined the walls watching him. Abraham turned and spoke again.

"What is your name my weary traveler?"

Gideon nudged him gently. "Tell him," he whispered.

"Eben John Wittke."

"What is it you seek here?"

Gideon raised his hand and quietly shushed Eben. "He comes to you starving and sick, yesterday a child, tomorrow a man, once lost in the wilderness, now found, once tempted, now of free mind and spirit, let it be known today and forever more, this is God's will, for he comes before us with an open heart prepared to do the bidding of the Lord. Oh, Watcher of the Wall, help him learn the ways of the Levites, those guardians of the faith."

Eben stared at his father trying to make sense of what was going on. He'd heard rumors about a strange group of men who watched over the Community for most of his life but didn't believe any of it until now. He suddenly knew what his friend John had been trying to tell him.

"Are you prepared to follow the Word given man by our Lord God on High and live a life of humble obedience to Him and your Community?" Abraham asked.

With affirmation from his father, Eben responded weakly. "I am."

"Will you, your soul cleansed by your own repentance and found worthy by the Ten and your Brother Levites, protect yourself, your neighbors and your family from the outside world where the Creator has been forgotten, his temples burned to ashes, His Word carried away on the wind and his people enslaved by that ugly beast of fire and damnation?"

"I will."

With this, Abraham lit a candle and lit a lantern held by the man next to him. This continued around the room until it was bathed in yellow, flickering light which gave the men's faces an unearthly glow. Eben gasped at the sight and felt another shiver run down his spine.

"Come then, for what you seek you shall find, for there is joy in the heart of the Lord!"

Eben was led to the center of the room where an ancient looking Bible lay on a simple wooden altar at knee height. Two hands pushed him gently to his knees, then reached around him and placed his hands on an old brittle piece of parchment lying on top of the Bible. As he did this, the men in the room put their lanterns on a rail of some sort which formed a circle around the altar. They then took the hand of the man next to him and bowed their heads as if in prayer. Eben recoiled in fear when a strange looking creature wearing a large mask resembling the head of a monstrous crow shuffled forward and stood in front of him. It was the creature from his dream. After raising his hands high above the strange head, he placed them on top of Eben's.

"A Levite protects the house of the Lord from corruption and worldly ideas. Stand true to the Word of God and do not waver. Protect the innocent flock from following lies, false ideas and unholy doctrine. Protect and cling tightly to the Word, find strength in the Lord's house and His Ways. You must keep the people from stumbling off the narrow path laid out before them. Keep the Lord's sheep safe until He comes back again to save mankind from its ultimate demise."

"God is great, God is righteous," The men responded together.

"Do you believe in the Holy Trinity?"

"I do," Eben replied.

"Do you swear on your life to live by the word of God, to live a humble, pious life of a man born of his Community, to protect it from within and without, to see that no man, woman, nor beast be seized by the creature of fire and led unto sinful fields outside the walls constructed and guarded by the Brotherhood of Levites, to act as an instrument of the Lord here on Earth for all of your days?"

Eben wavered for a moment wondering if he should simply refuse to go along with any more of it. He was more frightened than he'd ever been before. Behind him, his father gently squeezed his shoulder.

"I...do."

"Repeat after me."

Eben listened and repeated the words recited to him. "For he who betrays the work of the Brotherhood also betrays the Word of God and that of his Holy Kingdom, the penalty of such an act is death at the hands of a Brother Levite who wielding the instrument of pure faith, shall empty your blood upon the ground, your body left to rot and corrupt, buried deep in a lonely place which none will ever know. With these words, I, Eben John Wittke do solemnly and faithfully swear, to live accordingly with the rules of the Community, to guard the wall with vigilance at all times, to hand myself over to my Brother Levites, bearing in mind the penalties of my Obligation. This I swear and promise, for the rest of my mortal life."

The large room was silent except for the wind blowing through the trees outside and the ceaseless noise of the crows which had suddenly begun in earnest. The man turned and nodded to the other men standing in the circle. A silvery glint of perfectly polished steel forced Eben to blink as they pulled long knives from belts fastened around their robes. He stared on with horror unable to move wondering if they were going to gut him like a hog until Abraham approached one of them with a wooden cup. The man lifted the sleeve of his robe and nicked his wrist with the tip of the blade allowing a trickle of blood to run down his arm and into the cup. Once satisfied with the amount of blood, Abraham then approached each man who repeated the strange ritual. After taking Gideon's blood, two sets of hands forced Eben's arms across the Bible and parchment and held him fast. Gideon stepped forward and cut him in the same place and held his wrist up to allow his blood to mingle with that of the others. With the two men still holding him down, the man in the mask held the cup up for all to see.

"I say unto thee oh great Lord God in Heaven, let he who drinketh from the cup share in the bond of Brotherhood for all time."

Gideon gently pulled Eben's head back and whispered into his ear. "You have to drink. Just one swallow, that's all."

Eben retched at the thought of drinking blood but before he had a chance to reply, Gideon forced his mouth open allowing the man in the mask to pour it into his mouth. Warm, slippery, coppery-tasting, it slid down clinging to his throat as it went down. Eben tried to scream and spit it out but his father held his mouth closed. After a moment, Abraham approached and held out a plain glass and a handkerchief.

"Water," he murmured.

Eben took the glass with shaking hands and gulped the contents down trying his best not to vomit on the Bible.

After wiping his mouth and handing the glass back to Abraham, the man in the mask extended his hands towards Eben.

"Let him stand."

With the help from Gideon and one of the men standing with Eben, they helped him to his feet and stood uncertainly for a moment as blood rushed back into his aching legs.

"Welcome Brother Eben," the man said removing his mask. It was Reverend Stohlfutz. He smiled and was handed a neatly folded black robe by his son Jonah. "This is the garb of a Brother Levite which you will wear with great pride when in attendance at our holy gatherings. It is made of a simple cloth befitting a new man such as yourself who has chosen to protect his Community, his faith and his Brethren from those outside our blessed walls. It signifies your commitment to the glory of the Lord and your desire to live a humble, virtuous life of hard work and happiness."

Stohlfutz held the robe out and helped Eben into it. One by one, each of the men in attendance shuffled by and greeted him the same way. Once they had finished, they retrieved their lanterns and took their places on either side of the room waiting silently. Stohlfutz walked to the front where he carefully placed the Bible on an ancient looking wooden altar with the image of a crow carved into the wood on the front. After a short prayer, the meeting began to break up and the men gathered around a table to bandage the cuts on their wrists. Once they were done, each carefully folded their robes and put them in a row of storage shelves in the anteroom. With low voices echoing off the walls of the building, they began shuffling out into the night.

"Congratulations, Eben," a voice said. It was his friend John. He also wore a black robe and stood smiling in front of his friend.

"Um, thanks, John."

"Does it all make sense now?" John asked with a wide smile.

"Yes, it does. I had no idea what you were talking about a few weeks ago."

"Well, now you know. I hope you take all of this to heart, Eben. It's truly wonderful to be given the opportunity to serve the Community. I couldn't be happier."

Eben frowned not knowing how to respond. Everything had happened so quickly; he still wasn't sure of what was going on but he did know what the Obligation was. It was troubling however; the strange ceremony was downright bizarre.

"Thanks, John. Yes, it's a great thing indeed."

Several other men stopped to chat with Eben and Gideon as they made their way out of the building. Eben took it all in with wonder, amazement and fear: He knew them all. They were his friends and neighbors, people in church, even his schoolmaster, Mr. Evans, was a member of the strange society. But what did it all really mean? Eben wondered what he'd done and thought of Josiah. This had to have been what had made it so hard for him to leave.

"Are you ready to go home?" Gideon asked as they walked through the darkness towards their buggy.

"Yes, Father, I believe so," Eben replied.

"Good, since your still a bit bruised up you can sleep in. Isaac and I can manage the milking this morning."

"Thank you."

Gideon turned the buggy out onto the road to begin the long trip home. He and Eben rode in silence for several miles.

"Why were so many crows out there? It was strange."

"They've been here since the very first settlers of our church came here in 1849. The hill, where the Sanctuary is, was the first place they came to. That's why we call it Founder's Hill. God led our people there and showed them the lands he'd prepared for them, all of the land of the Community can be seen from there. Hundreds of crows lived in the grove of oaks which have never been touched. We believe it's sacred. When the settlers came, the crows didn't fly away, didn't steal their grain or attack them. They watched over our people and warned them when the non-believers came with their guns and fire to take our land. It was seen as a sign from God that they were blessed. God sent the crows to watch over them, and now us."

Eben sat back trying to take it all in. It was strange, but it was fascinating too. He'd always seen crows as dirty scavengers who made too much noise.

Gideon continued. "This was supposed to be for Josiah, but since he decided to turn his back on us I had to bring you in to take his place."

"So, Josiah did the same thing? This was the Obligation he tried telling me about?"

"Yes. He was the oldest, and only the oldest son of a member in good standing can take the Obligation. It's their birthright. The others, those who aren't the oldest son, have to be invited to join."

"You mean not every man is a member of...it?"

Gideon laughed gently. "No, this a very select group of men. It's called the Brotherhood of the Levites and you can't talk about it to anyone. Not ever. Only other men you know are part of the group are allowed to speak of the Brotherhood to one another. What we say and do is secret Eben. I can't stress that enough. Remember the words in the Obligation. They are serious business to us. You should feel good about it, it's quite an honor. Harvey, the black-smith is one of our members and he'll be making your knife. You should have it in a few weeks."

But Eben didn't feel good about it. If the words were indeed meant literally it meant Josiah was in bigger trouble than he'd thought.

"What if I'd refused?"

"What?" Gideon asked with a surprised look on his face.

"What if I'd refused to do it? Perhaps I don't want any part of it, Father."

Gideon's eyes flashed wickedly in the light of the lantern.

"You were chosen by the Ten, our leadership council, not just me. There's no going back for you, Eben! You are a Brother Levite now and your place is here!"

"So I had no choice? Why?"

Gideon jerked back on the reins bringing the buggy to halt. "That's right! You are a servant of the Lord and you will do what is necessary to defend Him and the Community! The Sentinels can't ever lay a hand on you again, Eben. None of them are allowed to be members of the Brotherhood nor can they do anything to a Brother. Our place is above them and everyone else!"

Eben glared at his father. "What about Josiah? He took the Obligation but yet Leroy told me he caught him the night he ran away. What are they doing to him?"

"They aren't doing anything to him," Gideon said softly. Eben immediately knew he was hiding something by the way he averted his eyes when he answered.

He knows.

"What? Why would Leroy tell me that? I think there's more going on than you're willing to tell me!"

"Because he's a bad man, Eben! He hates me because of my position in the Community! It's his way of trying to get back at me the only way he can. But he can't now since you're one of us. You're untouchable!"

Eben exhaled sharply and crossed his arms in defiance.

"If you turn your back on us you'll suffer the consequences of your Obligation," Gideon continued. "Damn you, why must you be so difficult? I'm trying to protect you!"

"I don't need your protection and I don't need this nonsense," Eben replied throwing his hands up in frustration.

"You can't! You're one of us now whether you like it or not."

QUESTIONS

E ben leaned on the side of the house trying to catch his breath
while he waited for his sister Miriam to come hold the screen
door open. The morning air was heavy and wet meaning it would
be another hot miserable day. He hadn't slept at all since visiting
the Sanctuary the night before and knew he had some hard choices to make.

Staring out at the fields, Eben was now certain Josiah was being
held against his will somewhere in the Community. No matter how
he tried to look at the situation what little clues he'd been able to
piece together pointed in this direction. But where was he? This
alone was seemingly an impossible task. The Community was just
too large a place for him to look in every farm house, building and
field. But what if he wasn't on a farm? The Sanctuary perhaps? It
made the most sense. Down along the river perhaps? The heavily
timbered banks of the West Fork River meandered for miles and
miles throughout the Community and there were places there so
remote he guessed no one had ever explored them before. And
worse, Eben knew the search would require him to have a horse

along with the freedom to come and go as he pleased, neither of which Gideon would consent to. Even if by some miracle he would agree, it would take years to look everywhere and by then, who knew what would have become of his brother? The only way forward now was to get out and find Wendy as soon as possible with his only hope being she might have some ideas he hadn't thought of yet.

"Hurry up Miriam!" he called impatiently.

Miriam, a pretty girl of twelve finally came to the door wearing a stained apron over her simple blue dress. Holding the screen door open she scowled at her brother with tired eyes.

"Make enough noise when you came in last night Eben? You scared the daylights out of us girls stomping up the stairs."

Eben lifted the buckets of water he'd brought from the well and pushed past his sister.

"Shut up Miriam," he hissed. "I think I'm getting sick."

Miriam shot him a dirty look. "You're not sick. You're just trying to get out of doing your chores again."

"Yeah, yeah," he muttered. *And I'm never going to do them again either.*

Carrying the water into the house he poured them into the large copper vat on the stovetop and paused to wipe his face on his shirtsleeve.

"Is this enough water?" he asked his mother who was busy kneading bread dough out on the opposite side of the kitchen.

Mary wiped her hands on her apron stepped around and peeked into the vat on her tip toes.

"Go fetch two more and leave them outside the door. When you come back I need you to help me bring some things up from the cellar."

"Yes, Mother."

Eben took his time walking out to the well hoping the more time he spent hauling laundry water in meant less time helping his father. Leaning on the pump he sighed deeply and wiped his forehead while gazing down to the timber and creek. It was so close but Gideon, he knew, was in the barn always watching, always waiting for a chance to pounce. He wondered if Wendy were there now staring up at the house wondering if she'd ever see him again.

"My gosh, I have to get out of here as soon as possible."

With a large sigh, Eben finished filling the buckets and hauled them into the house.

"Set those by the door and come help me," Mary commanded impatiently. Eben followed her down the narrow steps into the dank airless cellar beneath the house where the family stored hundreds of mason jars filled with vegetables and fruits Mary and the girls put up every fall. Once Eben reached the bottom of the steps, Mary pulled the heavy wooden trap door down behind her and lit a lantern.

"Where's your father?" she asked in a barely audible whisper.

"Outside in the cattle shed."

"Good. Now, you listen to me. You have to be careful. Your father and the others, they made you take the Obligation early hoping you'd conform. That's when it all starts."

"You know about that?"

"Yes. Josiah told me about it. My guess is, they made you do it so you wouldn't cause them any trouble. They made Josiah do it too hoping he'd be frightened and conform to their rules but it only made him fight back even more."

Eben stared at his mother in the soft iridescent light not sure of what to say. Her face was bathed in fear.

"What's wrong, Mother?"

"You listen to me Eben. I love you more than anything in the world and I always have. Ever since you and Josiah were little. You're my boys."

"I know Mother and I love you too. What are you getting at?"

"Nothing...Have you decided what you're going to do?"

Eben stared at her with surprise unsure of what he should share with her. "I've been thinking about it, yes."

Mary wiped silvery streaks of tears from her face and continued: "I know how you are my sweet boy. You and Josiah are so stubborn and so set in your ways. I understand you so much better than your father ever did. Those things aren't acceptable here and they have a way of dealing with people like you."

She looked at the floor and began sobbing quietly. Eben reached out and pulled her close to him.

"If you're going to leave and I think you are," she cried, "then swear to me, don't go down to the creek, go a different way."

"Mother, I'm sorry to say this but I don't know if I can trust you. You didn't want me to say anything about it the other night but now all of the sudden you want to talk about it."

Mary grabbed Eben by the face and shook him angrily. "You can trust me! I'm trying to help you but if I know anything he'll get it out of me!"

Eben flushed with anger thinking back to all of the times Gideon slapped, threatened and badgered her while he and the other children stood helplessly by too afraid of their father to do anything. Yes, if he told her anything he'd get it out of her. He knew he had to be careful.

"I'm telling you not to go down to the creek because your father has Sentinels hiding down there. Did you see the wildflowers upstairs on the table?"

"Yes," Eben replied. He hadn't given the flowers much thought because it was normal for his mother and the girls to pick them throughout the summer.

"I had to know something, anything, so we went out yesterday evening before I talked to you. We walked down the fence line almost to the creek. There was a man down there, a Sentinel. The girls didn't see him but I did."

"How do you know it was a Sentinel?"

Mary exhaled sharply. "I know what they look like and so do you. The leather chaps, the clubs they all carry and the way he walked. They're all the same. He was hiding in the timber on this side of the creek but I saw him plain as day. And where there's one, there's always another. The other one must have been hidden somewhere else down there. That's why you can't go that way, if you do, they'll catch you just like they did Josiah."

Eben took a deep breath. Now the picture was becoming much clearer and it also explained why Wendy hadn't snuck up to the house since before Josiah left. He gently placed a hand on her cheek trying to act as confident as possible. "Okay, I'm not going to tell you anything because I know what Father does to you. But, you're going to have to prepare yourself for some changes."

"I've known for a long time this day would come. Do what you have to do Eben and remember, you've always been the one I could count on to do the right thing. You're a good boy and you have a good heart."

Eben felt his stomach churn as though he'd be sick but he was absolutely committed now. There was no way back for him anymore.

RUNNING

The afternoon dragged on in misery for the Wittmer family as they sat in the shade of the oak and maple trees surrounding the house trying to find a way to stay cool. Eben, along with his father, Isaac and sisters nearly passed out as they pumped water for the animals throughout the long hottest parts of the day. Now, as the sun was beginning to set the skies turned a strange orange yellow color while the tiny wisps of wind which had fortified the family during the afternoon stopped blowing. The air surrounding the house and fields was completely still and filled only with the singing of cicadas and crickets.

"I pray it storms tonight," Gideon said to his family. "We need some rain. The fields are dry as a bone."

Eben took this in with interest as he gazed at the long clouds streaking across the sky. It did look as though a storm were coming in. Yes, it would be the perfect cover for him to escape.

"So, Eben. Did John tell you about the calves they've lost?"

"Yes, Father," he said trying to act as normal as possible. "He said they've lost a few over on the Yoder's."

"Yes…I don't know why they keep cattle over there. There's little shade and little grass. Besides, the creek bank is too steep for them to get much water. It's no wonder they've lost some. The creek barely has any water left in it anyway."

Eben felt himself trembling from anticipation and turned away so Gideon couldn't see his face.

"What is it?" Gideon asked wiping his brow.

"Um, nothing."

"I can see it in your eyes Eben. You want to ask me something?"

Gideon turned to Isaac and held out his empty glass. "Isaac, get some more lemonade for us will you? Take your time son."

Isaac collected the empty glasses and walked into the house.

"Well?" Gideon asked.

"I know the Sentinels caught Josiah and I know he's somewhere in the Community," Eben whispered.

Gideon's face never changed but remained as calm as ever. Looking back to the other side of the porch where his Mary and the girls sat singing songs he turned back to Eben.

"We're not talking about it," he murmured from under the brim of his hat.

Eben kicked at the peeling paint on the porch and looked hard at his father. "Why not? I think it's time you started telling me what's going on. After all, I'm a Brother Levite now."

Gideon stood and motioned with his head for Eben to follow. "Come with me. We need to check on the animals."

Eben followed his father uneasily wondering if his mother had told him about their visit in the cellar. If she had it was all over and he knew the rest of his life would be one of misery.

As soon as they were around the corner and out of sight of the house, Gideon grabbed Eben by the shoulders.

"You listen to me son. Josiah's gone, I don't know where he is. This girl down there, at the creek, she was playing a game with you boys."

Eben pulled himself free of his father's grip. "No, you know as well as I do, Josiah wanted to leave for years but he didn't know how he was going to survive out there. She had nothing to do with him leaving. I was the one who got him out of the granary and I was the one who planned it all out for him."

"Is that right?"

"Yes, Father, it is."

"Hmm," was all Gideon could manage before barely composing himself. "There have always been girls down there tempting the young men of our Community. They tempt our young men and lead them astray when they should be following the laws of God and our Community. These girls, they're sent from the devil!"

"Come now Father, they're not sent from the devil! Wendy certainly wasn't. You and the rest of the Council and the Brotherhood just don't want anyone to leave here. I think you're all afraid you'll lose control if anyone sees how good it might be out there."

"No, Eben, there is much you know nothing about. Anna, Sarah...whatever their names are, these girls, those from the outside are all the same. It's been this way since our forefathers came here. They want to take our young people away and tempt them with their cars and their money, their pursuit of pleasure and possessions, their alcohol and their pornography. It's all a trick to turn us away from the Lord. Satan takes many forms in order that this Community falls apart!"

"Maybe people should be allowed to make up their own minds instead of having it forced upon them!" Eben cried.

"And what would happen then? I'll tell you! Chaos! Disorder! Our way of life here would collapse and then we'd have nothing! Our society functions because we must do everything for the common good of the Community no matter how unpleasant or hard it may be. God chose us! We all have to work together so that one day we may ascend to the glory of Heaven!"

"The common good huh!" Eben spat the words out as though they were poison and threw his hands in the air. For as long as he could remember the words 'common good' and the 'glory of Heaven' were used to justify everything. The Sentinels stole and beat people for the common good. No one was allowed to choose their marriage partner because the common good dictated they be matched with suitable partners. The common good forced them to work in the fields, hog lots and sawmill, it denied them an education and it denied people of their happiness. Eben was sick of it.

"You don't understand do you? Let me give you an example, Eben. When I was a boy it was the same as it is now. My brothers and I used to go down there until my father put a stop to it one day just as I've tried to do. Something evil lurks down along the creek, something we can't control."

Eben stared at his father with disgust. "I know you went there too! Dan drowned down there."

"That's not entirely the truth," Gideon said elusively. "There's more to it all."

"Really? What?"

"I'll tell you what!" Gideon shouted. "Dan became charmed by the English and he made plans to leave just as Josiah did. He said he would never come back because his temptation got the best of him! Dan wasn't supposed to leave. He was the oldest, he was to be an Elder on the Council, he was supposed to inherit all of this! He was expected to be much, much more and he threw it all away! It shamed my father into his grave. For the rest of his life people whispered and laughed behind his back. He was removed as Head Elder because the rest of them reasoned that if he couldn't control his own son how could he lead the Community? Do you want the same thing to happen to me? To our family?"

Eben felt an ice-cold shiver go through his body despite the heat of the day. What was he talking about? His father turned his back to him and stared in the direction of the creek.

"I will not permit you or anyone else in this family to defy me nor will I allow any of you to defy God any longer! Do you understand me boy? You're a Brother Levite and I suggest you shut your mouth and live your life the way it's intended! Do you think you can do that?"

"Yes, Father. I'll do whatever you ask," Eben lied through clenched teeth. His entire body was shaking with anger. If the conversation continued he knew he'd find himself locked in the granary, or worse, beaten so badly he'd wish he was dead. No, better to head things off now so his plans for later would work.

Gideon spat on the dusty ground and pointed a finger menacingly at Eben. "You see that you do. It's time you forget about all of your childish desires and that brother of yours. Neither will do you any good from now on."

Wait. Eben kept repeating to himself. *Wait for tonight.*

FLIGHT

Hours later after the family had retired for the night, Eben sat on the edge of his bed wide awake shaking with excitement. He knew everything which had happened during the hot, dry summer had led up to this moment. Glancing over at Isaac who was sound asleep, he swallowed hard trying to control his quivering stomach. Hot rivulets of sweat ran down his back and dripped from his forehead. He was afraid.

Mary hadn't said a word to him the rest of the afternoon and evening but the quick glances she shot him through her teary eyes reinforced his resolve to go and do what he had to do. By the time everyone drifted off to bed she'd hugged and kissed him as she always did. But Eben knew from the expression on her face that she was overwhelmed with grief.

Eben knew his father would probably be sleeping lightly again. Slipping out of bed, he took his pillow case stuffed some clothes in it along with the money Josiah had stolen from the church and hidden in a desk shelf. Grabbing his pillows and an armful of more clothes, he quickly jammed them in his bed and covered it all with a sheet to look as though he were still in it.

"God, please protect me and help me find Josiah," he prayed before creeping down the steps. Halfway down he stopped cold: Gideon lay sleeping on the couch. Eben stiffened, not quite sure if he could get across to the back door without waking him.

"Eben."

He turned to see his mother standing at the top of the stairs in her nightgown gesturing to him to join her in her bedroom. Once he was inside, she closed the door and took him by the hand.

"Go down and hide in the kitchen. I left the back door open so don't let the screen door bang. I'll make him come back upstairs to bed. I left one of your father's leather canteens sitting by the well, make sure you take it. Then, you get going," she whispered. "And Eben, I love you."

"I love you too, Mother," Eben said choking back tears.

"Take care of yourself. You have to promise me you will."

Eben nodded and hugged her tightly. "I'll come back to get you and the kids someday."

"Yes, I know you will. Be safe my sweet boy," Eben thought he'd burst when she kissed him on the forehead. "Go now."

Eben did as he was told and tread softly to the kitchen watching his sleeping father the entire time. He hid on the edge of the cupboard next to the screen door and waited. In the living room he could hear his mother waking Gideon who grumbled.

"Is Eben in bed?" he asked.

"Yes, I just checked."

"Good. This couch isn't very comfortable to sleep on."

Eben waited until he heard his parent's bedroom door shut, slipped out into the night and ran.

Instead of going straight into the cornfield, Eben skirted the side of the house making sure to grab the canteen and ran through the orchard away from the timber and creek. He continued through the sorghum field, across the pasture and on through the neighbor's field until he reached the east-west road which he knew was two miles from home. With two hours until sunrise at five-thirty, he jogged on the shoulder of the road looking over his shoulder every few steps in case his father or anyone else for that matter, was coming after him. After another two-miles, he slowed to a quick walk and kept going.

Once the sun began peeking over the horizon, Eben hauled himself over a field fence and pushed his way into a cornfield, sweaty, tired and tense. Once he was in nearly a quarter of a mile, he came to a wide, grassy waterway dissecting the field and flopped down at the edge of the corn. The water in the canteen was hot and odd tasting but it was wet. While he rested, a crow landed just a few feet in front of him and began cawing. After the strange ceremony at the Sanctuary two nights before, Eben didn't care if he ever saw a crow again. He'd never cared for them much to begin with but now they possessed a certain malice he couldn't get out of his head.

"Go away you stupid crow," Eben muttered. "Go back to the Sanctuary with all of your noisy little friends and leave me alone." The bird persisted and continued making its racket.

"Shoo, darn you!"

Eben found a rock sitting next to him in the soil and threw it at the crow. It jumped a few feet and hovered just above him and landed where it had been and began cawing once more. This time Eben jumped up and ran at the bird.

"Go away!" he shouted stomped towards it. Finally, it clattered away into the early morning sunshine leaving him alone. Eben walked back to where his satchel and pillow case lay, removed a sandwich and eased himself down on the rough dry ground. Knowing he had to act quickly to find Josiah, he ate in silence mulling over his plan. By his estimates, Eben guessed he was around seven or eight miles from home which meant the narrow country bridge crossing the creek further upstream was another five miles away. He'd been going over several ideas in his mind since talking to his mother the morning before and one made more sense than the rest: Cross over to the English side at the bridge and make his way back along the creek bottom until he reached Robinson's farm where he prayed Wendy would still be. Gazing up at the morning sun, he sighed, gathered up his meagre possessions and continued slogging down the waterway

After a long hard day of pushing himself forward, Eben crept to the edge of another field and looked up and down the empty road sighing with relief. There was the bridge a mere fifty feet away. He was almost there. And to his complete surprise, the Sentinels weren't guarding it for the time being. There were piles of fresh horse droppings all over the road leading up to the bridge indicating they'd been there sometime during the day but for now, no one was around. The worst part was, he knew he had no choice but to use the bridge because this was where the creek and the West Fork River intersected making it too wide to swim and the banks too steep to climb for several miles.

Eben hesitated and continued looking up and down the road while carefully scrutinizing the cornfields for anything out of the ordinary. It could be a trap, he thought to himself. He'd come too far to get caught now. If he were caught, he knew he'd probably never see his mother, Josiah or Wendy again. Several times during the day he'd come close: The first was when he came to the end of the first field he was in. As he squatted in the corn waiting to cross the road to another field, the Hansaker boys appeared out of nowhere looking for a lost cow. Thankfully, one of them called out to the animal just as Eben was going to stand and jump the fence. Instead, he froze and watched as they walked within feet of him and continued on their way. The second time he nearly fainted from fear. Around noon he stopped to rest for a moment under the shade of an enormous maple tree growing in the ruins of an old farm when he noticed two men on horseback riding up the lane. Scampering on all fours, he barely managed to slither behind a pile of rotten lumber before they rode into the farmyard and dismounted. The men were Sentinels and had stopped to get water for themselves and their horses from the rusty pump on the ancient farm. From what he could gather from their muted conversation distorted in the hot wind, they were looking for him and they weren't the only ones. Evidently, all of the Sentinels and men from the Brotherhood were out searching. Once they were gone, Eben spent the rest of the day hidden and constantly moving through the corn fields and stands of timber despite the awful heat and humidity.

Eben rubbed his eyes and sighed deeply with exhaustion. All he wanted to do was lie down in the weeds and sleep but time was wasting.

"Keep going," he said forcing his weary body up. "Keep going."

Casting another long look up and down the road, Eben pulled himself over the fence and ran in the ditch towards the bridge. It came closer and closer until he finally thumped across the heavy creosote soaked planks and slid down into the deep ditch on the other side. He'd done it, he'd crossed the invisible barrier between the Community and the English side. Despite knowing he should be overjoyed for making it he only felt the same heavy unease pushing down upon him. After a moment, he stuck his head up and looked around again. The road leading to the paved highway which ran into Kamron meandered into a timber which was quickly becoming dark as the sun set. For a brief moment, he considered simply continuing on and forgetting about everything having to do with the Community but he knew he couldn't. If there was still some shred of hope that he could find Josiah, he'd do it. He had to.

After fighting his way through thick underbrush, thorn bushes and brambles along the river bank, Eben was thankful to reach the bend where the river turned sharply back into the Community. The creek running back towards his home and the Robinsons emptied into it here so he pushed on and slid into the creek bed just as the moon began to rise. Other than the occasional fallen tree to climb over, the going went much more quickly; only a trickle of water filled the once rapidly flowing creek. It also offered perfect cover in some places where it cut deeply into the ground hiding him completely. In others however, it was nothing more than two or three feet deep. In these places Eben made sure to look carefully before ducking low and dashing into a field or stand of trees to hide himself all the while staying on the English side. He knew it wouldn't make any difference which side he was on because if the Sentinels saw him they'd run him down no matter where he was especially this far out in the country where prying eyes were few and far between. Still, he kept to the south side of the tiny trickle of water as there was a small sense of security in not actually being in the Community.

The one thing troubling Eben were the Sentinels his mother had warned him about. Surely, he reasoned, they wouldn't still be there in the timber would they? He'd been gone for hours and wouldn't they have given up by now and joined with the others out searching the roads? Another problem he faced was the fact that he'd never seen the Robinson's house before even though it was only a mile and a half or so from his own. It sat on the edge of a huge tract of timber which separated them from the Community and Eben hadn't ever ventured so far out before. So, his dilemma was twofold: He knew he had to find Wendy and he had to find her uncle's house. The only way to accomplish both of these things was to go back towards the place he had just run away from and pray the Sentinels weren't there anymore.

By ten P.M. Eben finally rounded a bend into familiar territory scratched, dirty, parched with thirst and completely exhausted from his long circuitous journey. There, just down the creek somewhere in the inky shadows was the hollow tree. From there, it was a straight shot to the Robinson's according to Wendy. On the opposite side across the fields was his house in which several lamps flickered in the downstairs windows. He wondered what had happened earlier in the day once his father woke up and realized he was gone. Thinking of his mother up there so alone and so afraid made him want to cry but he boiled with anger too. He was fairly certain she had, and would continue to pay the price for Eben's leaving.

Bastard, he thought to himself. *One day you'll get what's coming to you, I can promise you.*

Eben waited and waited, watching and listening to every noise no matter how small or faint. Nearly an hour passed and nothing moved nor was there any sound. Deciding it was safe, he crept up out of the creek bed and began making his way towards the hollow tree one cautious step after another. Reaching it, he climbed inside and felt around in the darkness but found nothing. The blanket Wendy had brought down earlier in the summer was gone. There was no trace of them ever being there.

Darn it. I hope she's at her uncle's house. Please God, let her be there. Eben stooped down and began crawling out of the narrow opening.

Before he knew what was happening, a shape loomed out of the darkness and hit him savagely in the side of the head. Seeing stars, he fell to the ground. Two shadows pounced upon him and quickly bound his hands and feet tightly with rope. The more he tried to fight the tighter they became until any movement became impossible, painful. He opened his mouth to cry out but before he could do so one of the men stuffed a dirty handkerchief in his mouth.

"Oh, Eben. Damn you," Gideon muttered sadly. For a moment the ropes seemed to loosen but instead, he shook his head and cinched up Eben's hands and feet even tighter. "After what happened with Josiah, I've prayed and prayed that I wouldn't have to do this. You've left me no choice at all."

Eben's chest seized up with panic as he thrashed and kicked with all of his might. He couldn't move and he couldn't cry out.

Gazing down at Eben for several moments, Gideon shook his head once more and covered Eben's with a black cloth bag.

CHAINS

Gideon and the other man dragged Eben through the timber and into what Eben thought was a grassy pasture. Every now and then he could hear them talking in a low voices to one another. The voice of the second man sounded strangely just like his friend John's voice. More dragging through tall, sweet smelling grass until they dropped him on the ground and quickly double-checked the ropes to make sure they were still tight. Next, they picked him up and tossed him into the back of the wagon as though he were a sack of grain, tied him securely to the sides and covered his body with a heavy canvas tarp. Eben writhed about trying to free himself from the ropes but couldn't make them budge until his wrists and ankles were rubbed raw making every little move a torture of pain. A shiver shot through his body as he realized he was stuck; there was no way he could possibly free himself.

The wagon continued on and on for what seemed like an eternity. Eben tried to guess where they were taking him. Could it be to the Sanctuary? Were the penalties in the Obligation real as Gideon claimed? Would they murder him on the same altar where he'd placed his hands on an ancient Bible? If so, Eben knew it wouldn't be a pleasant death.

Other than the sound of gravel crunching under the wheels and the clumping of the horse's hooves on the hard packed road there was no other noise except the pounding of Eben's heartbeat roaring in his ears. Every little movement brought stabbing needles of pain from the heavy hemp ropes which smelled old and musty. The same ropes, he guessed, he and Isaac had carried out of the granary a few days before. Despite the pain, Eben still pulled trying to free himself but they were tied well. Gideon had tied them and he knew how to make good, tight knots which wouldn't slip free.

Hours seemed to pass and still Gideon and the other man rode in silence. Eben finally stopped fighting the ropes and tried to think of something, anything to do to save himself. The thought of simply giving up and letting his father and whomever else do whatever they were going to do repulsed him. If they were indeed going to kill him he knew for certain he wouldn't go down without fighting back.

The overpowering stench of hog manure soon wafted through the black hood covering Eben's head and grew in intensity. The wagon lurched to a stop and Eben could hear the springs on the seat squeak as his father and the other man climbed down. Almost immediately the tarp was ripped off of his body and two pairs of hands untied him from the side of the wagon. He was pulled to the back and lifted into the air, then carried with a grunt of exertion, then another he recognized as being Gideon and the crunch of footsteps on a gravel driveway. Eben thrashed and kicked at the person holding on to his feet but whoever it was said nothing. A rattling of keys, the sound changed; he was being carried inside a building where sounds were dull and muted. His back was thrown against a hard object, he then felt the cold steel of chains being wrapped around his bloody wrists and ankles, finally a click as they were locked together. Finally, the hands undid the knots in the rope and pulled them free.

The cloth bag over Eben's head was snatched off momentarily blinding him in the glare of a lantern. Squinting, was barely able to make out the blurry shapes of his father and Reverend Stohlfutz standing before him. They were in a deep pit of some sort. The floor was hard packed dirt while the filthy walls were constructed of what looked like heavy limestone blocks. The smell in the tiny space was overpowering, a mixture of hog manure and something else he couldn't quite place but it was definitely a smell of rot and decay. On one side, a set of rickety wooden steps led up to a small door. Other than the post Eben found himself chained to, there was nothing else.

"So," Stohlfutz began, "You decided you had to leave eh?"

"I tried," Eben replied angrily.

"Too bad," Stohlfutz said frowning. "You could have saved yourself by simply doing as your father instructed but no, you had to go down the path of your own choosing."

Eben ignored him and stared hard at Gideon. "So tell me Father, what's this old fool going to do? Read Bible passages and insult me while I'm chained to a post in a dung heap? Is this where your friends brought Josiah?"

Stohlfutz shuffled a few paces towards Eben and stopped to lean forward on his cane. "I'm much more than just a simple country preacher, boy. You took the Obligation. Don't you remember? The very words you swore upon the Bible to uphold just two nights ago. Now, you intend to turn your back on it all? The devil is indeed in you."

"The devil isn't in me. He's standing right in front of me."

Stohlfutz threw back his head and cackled with laughter. Gideon only watched completely expressionless, his hands hanging down loosely at his sides.

"Yes, yes, but you said the words nonetheless. Do you remember the penalties? Do you?" Stohlfutz demanded.

Eben tried to remember but he couldn't. He suddenly wished this were all some sort of bad dream but he knew it wasn't. He swallowed hard trying his best to control the fear quaking through his body. "It's all a bunch of bull," he responded trying to sound assertive. "And you're the head crazy of them all if you ask me."

"No, I'm the Gatekeeper. There's more to me than you could ever know."

Eben eyed him suspiciously. "I know you're a nasty old man who steals from everyone and rapes little girls."

Stohlfutz smiled and tapped him with his cane. "I'm your judge and jury boy."

The chains holding Eben to the post were heavy, made up of two-inch round links and were fastened to the post with heavy bolts. He pulled against them ignoring the pain shooting from his wrists and ankles but they wouldn't budge. They obviously didn't want him going anywhere.

"Yes, you've lost your way my young Levite just as your mother and brother did," Stohlfutz said turning towards the door. "Now it's time you accept your punishment."

THE CROW MAN

E ben lay on the filthy dirt floor with his knees pulled up to his chest staring vacantly at a strange depiction of a creature some-one had painted on one of the walls. It was sloppily done and re-minded him of the finger paintings his sisters took so much pride in but it was too frightening to be the work of a child. It looked like a crow with the long, sharp beak and the equally long and sharp talons of its feet reaching out as though it were swooping in for the attack. While he could still stand, he'd stretched as far as the chains would allow to get a closer look at the painting which was visible only when a narrow beam of sunlight shone through a tiny hole higher up in the wall. To his horror, he discovered it wasn't actually paint: It was dried blood.

Searing pain from his bruises kept him from sleeping on the dirt floor of the filthy pit no matter how he tried to lie, while the chains wrapped around his ankles dug deeply into his skin caus-ing open sores which were beginning to fester. His stomach too, howled with pain from the small amounts of the table scraps and dirty water he was given. There were a number of dogs just outside the door, presumably to guard the pit and their barking and howling went on day and night keeping him restless and on edge. For three or four days, he couldn't remember now, Eben squinted his eyes trying to examine every inch of the pit trying to find a way out but finding none, he found himself slowly spiraling into despair. From the scratches on the walls he knew he wasn't the first person to have been locked up here either. There were many, many names carved into the rough limestone: Gabriel Yoder. Ben Wittke, his cousins, Elisa Pohlmann. Jacob Hansaker. Rachel Smyth. He and Josiah's friend, Thomas Sachs, who had disappeared earlier in the year without a trace. Deborah Oster, John Yoder, Noah Hershberger. Too many to count. Eben knew some them. Some, he believed, had fled the Community never to come back while others he had seen in church only a few days before going about their lives as though nothing had happened.

Each morning, one of the Sentinels would come out and force him into a sitting position and tie his hands and feet securely to the post so he couldn't move at all. Once this was done, the Sentinel would leave and Stohlfutz would come out with a basket full of food and a pitcher full of cold, fresh water. Setting both in front of the boy, he began each session with long sermons on the evils of the world, the torment non-believers and sinners faced without God and how total obedience to his Community would set him free. Eben was expected to memorize Bible verses and recite them back. If he failed to do so or made a mistake in his recitations the old man beat him viciously with the cane. Then, he would remove one item of food and throw it out to the dogs. Then, the entire episode would repeat. And again, and again. The beatings went on without end. The old man took special care to beat the soles of his feet with his cane.

If the heat weren't bad enough in the airless pit, the smell of his own bodily wastes on his clothes and where he lay was equally as horrifying. Since he was tied to the post for the entire day he couldn't hold it forever. It shamed him to have to do his business in his pants but there just wasn't any other option. It sat there becoming putrid in the heat. Eben knew he would die in the next few days from the heat, lack of food and water and the beatings. It frightened him to realize he didn't care.

Eben would pray for hours hoping for death until he passed out. "Please God, take me unto Heaven. Please..." he cried. "What have I done Lord? Why is this happening? Please, let me die."

Later in the evening Eben was awoken by the dogs outside barking excitedly as they did when Stohlfutz came out. Sitting up and wiping his face, he did the best he could to look as though he were doing well. The door creaked open and the old man crouched and entered. He placed the basket and pitcher of water on the floor where Eben could see it and approached with a smile.

"And how are you this evening?" Stohlfutz asked cheerfully.

"I'm fine."

"Are you?"

"Yes, as good as expected I guess despite the fact that I'm starving and living in my own crap."

The old man frowned and brought the cane down hard across the side of Eben's face.

"Have you been praying?"

"Yes, all day."

"Good, good. And has the Lord come to you and given you the answers you seek?"

Eben smirked at the old man. "Not yet. I'm still alive. And I know who the Crow Man really is."

The old man howled with rage and began beating Eben with the cane. "How dare you pray for an end to the life God has given you!"

Then just as suddenly as he'd started he stopped and began laughing. "The old myth of the Crow Man. How often I've heard that out here!"

Eben glared at him with hatred.

"Yes, yes, it's real my young boy. The fear he instills in those of weak mind and free-spirit such as you. There has always been a Crow Man in the Community to deal with sinners and malcontents such as yourself. They are chosen from men on the Council, or, the Ten I should say. They're one in the same anyway."

"My father is on the Council."

"Yes. He tried to have me removed as the Head Elder just yesterday but he failed. We'll deal with him soon enough if he doesn't prove himself to the rest of us."

"What are you going to do? Tie him up in here with me? Beat him senseless with your cane?"

The old man shrieked with laughter and beat Eben harder than he'd done so all week.

Eben put his head down and hugged the post until the old man finally stopped. In a wavering voice, he lifted his battered face to Stohlfutz. "I'm sorry Reverend. I think…the evil is coming out. I told you, I've had visions," he lied trying to use a different track.

"Yes? Tell me," Stohlfutz said leaning in close.

"I've seen Jesus standing in front of me with outstretched arms but he doesn't say anything."

"Hmm, interesting, very interesting. You're getting closer," Stohlfutz leaned over and threw an apple towards Eben as one would throw a treat to a dog. "He's trying to welcome you back into the fold. Back into our Community where you belong."

"Yes," Eben said eyeing the apple which had rolled against his leg. "I've realized over the past few days it was foolish for me to believe I could ever doubt God, my father…our Community. I was tempted."

"Yes you were. Your dreams, your insistence that you do what your heart desires despite being initiated into the Brotherhood. Your father was correct, you have sin in you. Your mother had it too. She became distant and brooding, her head filled with thoughts of leaving us. She had many demons inside her vying for control."

Eben gaped at Stohlfutz. "My mother? She's fine. There's nothing wrong with her!"

The old man laughed loudly throwing his head back. "You don't know do you?"

"Know what?"

"Your father's wife, Mary, isn't your mother and your father, well, never mind."

"What? You're lying! She's my mother!" Eben felt his despair quickly turning to anger something he'd been desperately trying to avoid if only to save his energy.

"No, no. Mary isn't your mother. You and Josiah's mother's name was Ruth."

Eben stared at him wondering if this were all part of the torture. "You're a liar you crazy old man!"

Instead of beating Eben with the cane, Stohlfutz leaned down and stared into his eyes. "No, your mother was a fine looking woman. Just fine she was. Such full hips, firm breasts and a beautiful face. Mmm, yes. But she wasn't happy here among us. She and her husband wanted to live in the English world where she desired to do as she pleased."

"I don't believe you! I don't!"

"You should. Think about it, you and Josiah were always different from the younger children. Different looks and much different temperaments."

"What are you talking about? She's our mother!"

Stohlfutz shook his head. "You must have been about one, Josiah, two when she married Gideon so of course you wouldn't know any different. She was much more docile than her sister I must say. A more suitable match for your father, yes, but not without a bit of temper in her as well."

"Her sister? What? She told me she was given to him."

"Oh, she was. Her sister was your mother. It was a true blessing for poor Gideon, but since he knew the family, arranging to have Mary wed to him was easy."

Eben lunged at Stohlfutz clawing at the air with his shackled, bloody hands. "No!"

"I'm afraid so. She failed miserably with Josiah and didn't do much better tempering you and the strangeness you inherited from your real mother."

"There's nothing wrong with me!" Eben shouted. "It's all made up! You're just trying to get inside my head aren't you?"

Stohlfutz cackled and pointed his walking stick at Eben. "You've always been in trouble haven't you? You and that brother of yours."

Eben squeezed his eyes shut while his mind raced about the things Stohlfutz was saying not wanting to believe any of it. He hated his father's strict rules. He hated the Community's rules. He hated the fact that his life had already been decided for him.

"How would you know anything?"

"I know more than you think. You have delusions too my young sinner. You see yourself as picked on and harassed. It's just too hard for you to keep your mouth shut and do what's expected isn't it? You think your life actually matters."

"What are you talking about? You're crazy!

"No, you don't understand. You, your brother, believing you could exist as individuals in spite of everything this Community has given you. No, your future was planned out the moment your parents were put in the ground."

"What?"

Stohlfutz pulled himself to his feet with a grunt and paced back and forth in front of Eben obviously quite pleased with himself. "Yes, your mother was just like you and Josiah. The strangeness and the difficulty just existing as one of us. She didn't want to be your father's wife either and it drove poor Gideon nearly to the devil with rage. He'd pined after her for so long, yes, a long time. But when they began speaking of leaving with you boys… well, we knew then the devil had possessed both of them just as he has you."

Eben lay on the floor feeling anger rising inside his body. "Them? Who are you talking about? You're lying."

"No, my young boy. She had to be taken care of."

"What do you mean? What happened to her?" he cried.

"Oh, your father brought her to me one night kicking and screaming. They hadn't been married long either, a week or two at the most. She was completely possessed and I must say, dangerous. She was a different person entirely."

"What did you do?" Eben shouted.

"Oh, she was right here in this place where you are now. I tried for weeks to cure her but alas, I couldn't. The devil had too much of a grip on her. She was a fighter too. Hmm, yes. Poor girl."

Eben thrashed at the chains trying desperately to break free and reach the old man. "What did you do? Kill her?"

Stohlfutz smiled and waved the cane in Eben's face. "No, I didn't kill her. It wasn't my place and it certainly goes against everything our blessed Community stands for. She was your father's wife and therefore his responsibility to all of us. He killed her."

SAVIOR

Eben wavered between sleep and consciousness never quite asleep but never fully awake either. The drawing of the Crow Man loomed over him taunting him day and night. He knew he would die soon and the knowledge gave him peace. It had been two-days since the old man had last come to the pit and he knew if he were beaten again it would be the last time. The only thing left for him to do was pray.

Hearing a faint noise, Eben opened his eyes to see a young girl in simple Community dress crouching just above him. She reached out to touch his face but he recoiled in fear.

"Who are you?" he rasped.

"That doesn't matter. Here, drink," the girl said quietly holding his head up to a small pitcher. Eben gulped the cool water not caring as it splashed across his face and ran down his chest. After a moment she helped him drink again.

"Can you eat?" she asked. Eben bobbed his head with the little strength he had left. The girl placed his head in her lap and carefully spooned cold corn mush into his mouth. He chewed lightly trying not to irritate his sore gums but the first food he'd had in three days quickly made him forget about the pain. After finishing the entire bowl the girl helped him drink again.

"Do you want more?" she asked. Eben nodded eagerly and the girl produced some bread which he quickly devoured.

"Who are you?" he asked again.

The girl turned to look at the door and moved her head to peek through the cracks in the wall of the pit before slowly removing the hood.

"Katurah."

"Yes. How are you feeling Eben?"

"Horrible, but I'm doing better than I was. Thank you for the food and water, it really helps."

Katurah looked at Eben with the large blue eyes of a child. "You're welcome. I'm just glad you're still alive."

"What are you doing here?"

"I live here."

"Here? On this farm? This is Stohlfutz's? I wasn't sure where I was."

"Yes. You're in the old hog building way back from the house," Katurah replied. "It's hidden behind the barn."

"I guess I didn't know for sure. I had a black hood over my head when my father brought me here," Eben said. He suddenly became fearful for Katurah since she was obviously taking a huge risk by bringing food and water to him. "What if Stohlfutz or his wife catches you out here? I mean, won't he just lock you up in here with me and beat you too?"

"No," she said. Her face immediately turned to one of sadness. "I'm his wife. He doesn't beat me too much anymore. I have to come out and take care of the dogs anyway."

"What?" Eben asked incredulously. "I thought they adopted you. How? Why...?"

"Missus allows him to take us younger girls. She can't, you know, or won't, so she lets him have girls."

A feeling of sorrow overwhelmed Eben as he gazed into Katurah's sad eyes. What she had to live through was a terrible thing to contemplate which made his life seem rosy in comparison. "I never did like how they treated you. So, what people said about what he does to you? It's…true then?"

"About him raping me? Yes. He and some of the other men in the Brotherhood raped another girl who was here before me all the time. Do you remember Caroline Dwyer?"

"Yes, she was three years older than me. We all thought she ran off one night."

"No, she and I lived together in the cellar beneath the house. She was nice to me when I first came her and tried to protect me from him."

"But why was she out here?" Eben asked. "Was she one of his wives?"

"Yes. She told me her father brought her out to Stohlfutz to be reformed but he decided to keep her. Then, after a couple of years he told Arlen to get rid of her one night."

"Get rid of her? What did he do?"

"He dragged her out here and strangled her. Then, he made me bury her."

Eben stared at her with disbelief. "Oh my God! Why?"

Katurah shrugged her shoulders. "I don't know. I think she was too old for him. There were always men bringing girls my age and younger out to him to…test their faith as he likes to say. There were always other men in the Brotherhood who came too, for the same reason. Reverend Stohlfutz in particular, was always delighted when a new girl arrived."

. "So, he killed Caroline? Does he kill the other people out here?"

"No, not all of them. The people in the pit are who they consider to be the troublemakers in the Community. If he thinks he's saved them, he sends them home after he tortures them. Most are frightened into it or have it beaten into them. If not, their fathers have to come and kill them. It's all a secret to keep people in the Community in line."

Eben felt a shiver go through his body. Everything he'd ever been taught and had ever known was a lie.

"The fathers…kill them?"

"Yes, the Reverend won't do it," Katurah said. "He claims he's too holy to be a common murderer."

"He told me my father killed my real mother when I was little. I thought it was a trick of some sort."

Again, Katurah shrugged her shoulders. "I don't know, Eben. There are layers and layers of lies and deceit in the Community."

"But what about Stohlfutz's wife? Does she know what he does out here?"

"I do, but I don't think she chooses to involve herself in anything he does."

"But why? He's crazy!"

"I know, but I think missus would rather tell herself that he's just an ordinary preacher. It's easier for her to live with I think. That and the girls he touches."

Eben stared at her in shock until the reality of his own situation rushing back. Suddenly he was afraid. "Where is Stohlfutz by the way? Is he coming back?"

"No, they're all sound asleep. I made sure of it before I came out," Katurah said. "I want to help you. He's a bad man. Besides, you and Josiah have always been nice to me. Especially you."

A jolt immediately shot through Eben's body at the mention of his brother's name. "Josiah? Do you know where he is? Is he here?"

"Yes, he's in the other pit."

DISCOVERY

E ben could only stare at Katurah. "There's another pit?"
"Oh yes, he's in the one right next to you. Over there."

Yes, Eben thought. It made sense: Stohlfutz was old and couldn't get around too well so he would need to have his victims close by in order to conduct his torture sessions. So Josiah had been here all along, he thought to himself. It never would have occurred to him that he'd be here. No, he knew, he'd have never found him. This new discovery gave Eben a small bit of consolation but it paled in comparison to what he was facing now.

"How is he? Is he still alive?"

"Yes, but he's not doing well. I've been sneaking food and water out to him. He's been beaten pretty badly but the Reverend is keeping him alive for now."

"What do you mean, 'for now'?"

Katurah stole a glance back at the door and turned her attention back to Eben. "They're waiting on your father."

A chill shook Eben to the core. He hadn't believed it when Stohlfutz told him Gideon had killed his mother, that is, if Ruth were indeed his mother. But it seemed as though it were true now. If he had killed her why wouldn't he have any problem doing the same to his boys?

Eben looked at her with pleading eyes knowing what he had to ask. She was his only hope. "Listen to me Katurah, you have to get us out of here. I'm not going to die in this place and neither is Josiah. Will you help us?"

Katurah's suddenly face went pale. She rose to her feet and pulled the hood over her head. "I'm sorry but I have to go now."

"Katurah!" Eben shouted grabbing her arm. "Help us! You're the only person who can!"

"Don't!" she hissed jerking her arm away. "Don't ever touch me! I don't like it when people touch me!"

"I'm sorry. Please believe me. I'm sorry, Katurah, I am. Will you help us? Please?"

Eben watched helplessly as she stormed to the door and slipped out into the night. For a moment he thought she might come back but the click of the lock told him otherwise.

"Please, please don't let us die in here! Katurah! Katurah!"

And she was gone. Eben slumped to the ground and began beating his fists into the hard packed floor while he wept in frustration. All that was left to do now it seemed was wait for the inevitable end.

Eben's outburst continued until using up what little strength he had left, he passed out. Warm, strange dreams came to him and he drifted back to years before when he and Josiah were little and how innocent and beautiful the world was to them then before the horrible secrets about the Community became reality. How could their lives have ended up here in a pit below an unused hog confinement? Where had it all gone so terribly wrong? Why? God had a purpose for everyone in the world but was this it? Deep down, Eben knew Stohlfutz was wrong: His life did matter and so did Josiah's. Eben smiled and fell further into his dream.

He remembering running barefoot through the tall, cool grass bordering the fields one step behind his brother, he remembered them laughing as they jumped into the sweet smelling hay in the barn. Nothing could hurt them, no one could take away the bond they had always shared. He smiled again remembering Mary's loving embrace when he fell down and hurt himself and how her kisses always seemed to make his cuts and bruises magically heal. For just a fraction of a moment he could feel her love for him radiating through his body fortifying him and urging him to never give up. His dream swirled and changed until he found himself in front of a woman he didn't know whose smile and kind eyes reminded him of Mary's. She reached out for him as a bright light came closer and closer until it was just about to envelope him completely. A tear slipped down his grubby face and splashed silently on the dirt floor.

"Eat," came a soft voice. "You need to eat more."

"Mother...?" Eben whispered.

"Shhh, come, you need to eat to get your strength back.

Eben opened his eyes slowly to see Katurah. She was holding his head in her lap. "You came back."

"Yes," she said. "I can't let you and Josiah die out here. I just can't."

"Thank God," Eben wept. "Thank you."

"Can you walk?" Katurah asked pointing to Eben's feet.

"I don't know. I haven't stood up for...I don't know, four days. And he beat the bottoms of my feet with his cane."

Laying Eben's head carefully on the floor, she slid over and gently examined his feet with a frown. Wordlessly, she took a towel she'd brought along and wet it with water from the pitcher and began gently cleaning his bruised, dirty feet. Eben gritted his teeth from the pain it caused but allowed her finish. After drying them off, she opened a jar and pulled out a glob of a strange looking reddish-brown ointment and began gently rubbing it on.

"What is that?" Eben asked doing his best not to cry out.

"It's some salve my mother taught me to make. It helps cure bruises and cuts."

With his feet done, she quickly gathered up the bowl, spoon and other items and hid them inside the folds of her dress.

"Here," she said handing him the pitcher and a small package wrapped in a linen napkin. "Finish the water and here's some sausage and some more bread. Make sure you hide it if he comes out. If you hear the dogs barking and carrying on, it's him."

Eben did as he was told and stuffed the food into his pockets after tearing off a mouthful of sausage.

"Oh, I almost forgot," Katurah said digging into the bun of hair on her head. She pulled out a small key and unlocked the chains around Eben's ankles. Reaching down, she carefully rubbed the sores where the chains had been and applied some more salve. "Keep the salve and put in on your sores and bruises until I come back tomorrow. I'm leaving the key with you as well. Bury it in the dirt right there underneath you."

"Thank you Katurah," Eben said softly.

She smiled faintly. "Remember, if the dogs bark it's him. Put the chains back on if you hear them."

"Do you think he'll come back?" Eben asked dreading the thought of the old man returning to beat him again.

"No, I don't think so. If they can't find your father he'll leave you and Josiah down here until you die. I heard him tell Leroy that."

"Do you have any idea where my father might be?"

"He's gone somewhere, I don't know."

Katurah smiled at Eben and turned to peek through the cracks once again. Kissing her fingers she reached over and gently touched his forehead, then turned and left. Eben heard her lock the door and scrambled over to look through a crack. The dogs obviously trusted her since they sat and sniffed and licked her hands as she walked out of the pen and locked the gate. She disappeared into the darkness.

Throughout the rest of the night and the next day Eben managed to sit up and began wiggling his toes trying to help them heal. The food Katurah brought had saved him, he was certain of it. The salve too, seemed to be some kind of natural miracle. He dutifully rubbed it on his feet, ankles and the other bruises and cuts he had. Eben prayed and thanked God for sending her. Now he had a newfound purpose: Save himself and save Josiah.

As the day turned to evening neither Stohlfutz, his Sentinels or Gideon showed up. Eben sighed with relief happy with the short reprieve he'd been given but how long would it last? He prayed Katurah was sincere about helping him escape. What if Gideon came back to kill him and Josiah? Maybe Stohlfutz knew she was sneaking food out to the boys and was simply waiting to make his move whatever that could be.

WICKEDNESS

Throughout the next day and well into the evening, Eben sat and continued to rub and stretch his feet and wrists waiting for Katurah to come back. Despite what she'd said to him the day before, worry began to cloud his mind wondering if it really had been a trick all along but still, he wasn't so sure. She'd seemed too sincere, too confident in her hatred of Stohlfutz to just leave him to die.

Outside, the barking and whining of the dogs suddenly rose in intensity and a key rattled in the lock. Scrambling to put the chains back on, Eben managed to just lie down as the door opened. What he saw made him want to retch. Instead of Katurah, a lantern lit up Stohlfutz slowly making his way down the steps. He approached cautiously to stand just beyond Eben's reach and poked at the boy in several places with his cane grunting as he did so.

"So, still with us eh?"

"Looks that way," Eben muttered without raising his head.

"You've hung on much longer than most have. Yes, you're strong, like your mother was."

Eben didn't move but kept his eyes on the old man.

"Tell me, have you seen the error of your ways? Do you feel God's love for you? Are you ready to take your place as a man in the Community?" Stohlfutz asked.

"Sure," Eben replied realizing he might still have some glimmer of hope however faint it might be. Whatever Stohlfutz was up to, he knew was a long shot at best so he decided to play along. "I thought you were going to let me die out here. What do I have to do?"

Stohlfutz smiled maliciously. "Nothing really. Just a simple show of your faith."

"Really? I don't like the sound of that at all."

"Well, you shouldn't, but if you ever want to leave this pit you'll do it. If not, well then, you can rot to death down here. It doesn't matter to me in the least."

A loud shuffling noise caught Eben's attention. He looked up and was shocked to see Leroy and Arlen dragging Gideon between them. Once down the rickety steps, they led him to the center of the room and dropped him heavily on the ground. Eben gasped once he was able to see his father's face in the light of the lantern. His appearance was appalling: Blood ran down from a large gash in the side of his head and his face looked as though it had been battered with a rock.

Stohlfutz poked at Gideon with his cane and nodded to Leroy and Arlen who stood smirking like naughty children. "It would seem that your entire family has a problem following the rules around here wouldn't you say, Gideon?"

Gideon only stared at the floor breathing heavily without answering. Eben thought he could see tears streaking down his cheeks.

"Go get the other one. I want to get this over as quickly as possible," Stohlfutz ordered. Leroy continued hanging on to the ropes binding Gideon's hands behind his back while Arlen disappeared out the door.

Eben forced himself up to his knees careful to keep his hands holding the unlocked chains in place. He wondered if he could somehow run out the door without being caught but what then? His feet still screamed in pain and surely Stohlfutz or the other two would catch him before he got far. His mind raced trying to think of something, anything to save himself and Josiah but he was fast running out of options.

"Your *father* here made a grave mistake in thinking he could get the best of me," Stohlfutz said poking Gideon in the chest. "Tried to convince the other men on the Council to oust me didn't you? Well, Gideon, no, you underestimated how much power the Lord has given me."

Arlen returned with Josiah. Chains were still fastened securely around his wrists which Arlen used to pull him along. Eben caught his breath at the sight of him when he was dumped next to Gideon on the floor. Like their father, Josiah's face was battered and bruised. Dried blood was caked on his face, on his hands, arms and ankles where the chains had dug deeply into his skin. And worse, he looked dangerously thin. So thin in fact, Eben could see the outline of his ribs showing from beneath the torn shirt he was wearing the night he left.

"Josiah!"

Josiah looked up at Eben with vacant, lifeless eyes. "Hey, little brother."

"Are you okay?"

"Not worth a darn," he replied. "You? You look like I feel."

"Enough of the family reunion!" Stohlfutz barked. He tottered over to stand between Eben and Josiah. "We were just about to enlighten your brother here on a little family history. Gideon, why don't you tell these fine young men all about it."

Gideon continued to stare at the floor. "I'd rather not."

"Do it!" Stohlfutz shouted. "At least let them know what really happened so long ago. I think it's the least you could do for them. Wouldn't you agree?"

Leroy slapped Gideon hard enough to knock him face down on the floor but Gideon forced himself back up in defiance. "Tell 'em damn you! I ain't got all night!"

Eben and Josiah looked on as Gideon swallowed hard and squeezed his eyes shut trying to find the courage. "I'm…I'm not your real father boys."

The only sound was a light summer breeze whistling through the cracks and holes in the pit.

"What are you talking about?" Eben finally asked not quite believing anything anymore. Josiah gaped at him through his swollen eyes.

"Your real father…well, he, your real father was my brother Dan. Your mother was Ruth, Mary's sister."

Eben rocked back on his knees as though someone had hit him in the stomach. Josiah pulled himself up to his knees and looked at Eben with a mixture of anger and confusion evident on his face. "What's he talking about, Eben?"

"It's true," Gideon continued. "Your mother, Mary, and I took you in after they died."

Leroy and Arlen laughed obviously enjoying the pathetic show going on in front of them.

"Go on," Stohlfutz commanded. "Tell them the rest of the story."

"Do you both remember the Ten Commandments?"

"Um, yes, I think so," Eben said flatly. "What do they have to do with anything?"

"No," Josiah replied crossly. "I don't."

"I broke the sixth, the ninth and the tenth."

Eben's mind raced trying to remember the Ten Commandments. "Let's see, the ninth is, *Thou shall not bear false witness against your neighbor* and the tenth is *Thou shall not covet your neighbor's house; thou shall not covet your neighbor's wife.* And um, the sixth is," Eben felt himself go limp once it came to him. So, it was true after all, he thought to himself. "The sixth is, *Thou shall not commit murder.*"

"Yes," Gideon said softly.

"What? It's a lie!" Josiah shouted breaking the silence. "All of it! Lies! Mary is our mother!"

Eben looked at his brother with mournful eyes and shook his head slowly from side to side. "No, Josiah, it's true. I thought it was a lie too, but it's not."

"Eben's right," Gideon said. "You boys were never supposed to know. Yes, I did those horrible, awful things but in my case, it wasn't my neighbor. I bore false witness against my own brother. I coveted his wife, Ruth. I lured him down to the creek and I murdered him when she wouldn't leave him for me. And...I murdered her when she refused to stay here with you boys and live as my wife."

Eben and Josiah could only stare at Gideon with mournful, hateful disbelief.

Stohlfutz strutted around as though he were out for a fine Sunday stroll with a smile creeping across his face. "Yes boys, Gideon's brother Dan decided he didn't like living here. He was like the two of you in many regards. He was temperamental and fought with his father, your grandfather, God rest his soul. And, he was the oldest son. He took the Obligation as was his right, his duty. He could have been next in line to be the Head Elder by now but he wanted to live with that whore of his out in the English world. Didn't he Gideon?"

Gideon nodded and choked back a sob. "Yes. When you boys were little Dan and Ruth decided they were going to leave with you both and I knew I had to do something but I didn't know what. I went to my father and Stohlfutz and they presented me with a solution. If I stopped Dan they'd give Ruth to me and I'd get the farm, the animals, and a chance to be on the Council, all of it. I could have the life intended for Dan and not be a common laborer or worse, a Sentinel, as was my destiny."

"So you killed them?" Eben shouted stretching against his chains. He wanted to throw them off and tear Gideon to shreds. "How could you kill your own brother? And the woman you loved? My God!"

"I don't know..."

"Yes," Stohlfutz added continuing to enjoy himself. "It's just like I began to tell you the other day boy. There is a secret law here which states that family must deal with problems on its own which has been in place since our forefathers first came here. We must do what's necessary to protect the Community from strife and internal conflict. Once your father had taken care of Dan he was presented with Ruth but she knew what had happened and wanted no part of it. Gideon brought her here in the hopes that I could talk some sense in to her but alas, she wanted nothing to do with the new arrangement."

"Killing your own family? That's insane!" Eben yelled. A chill swept through his body causing goosebumps to rise on his arms and on the back of his neck.

"No, it's quite effective in keeping order. Until now, that is," Stohlfutz said with a shrug.

"Please!" Gideon blurted out suddenly. "Take me Reverend! Let them go! They were only fighting back against me! They're just boys! They don't know any better!"

Stohlfutz shook his head and clucked his tongue. "No, no Gideon. You know I can't be involved in such a thing. I'm a man of God after all! No, it's already been decided by the Council and we must do as the Council dictates. Our laws and traditions are indisputably clear. You of all people should know that."

"No! Leave me here and let me starve to death then. Please, just let them go!"

"I'm afraid it's come much too far for that dear Gideon. Now, bring the tall one here and place him in front of Eben."

Arlen grabbed Josiah's chains and began to pull until Josiah reared back and kicked him in the groin. With a roar, Arlen began beating him with his fists until Stohlfutz intervened.

"Stop! Stop it now! Get him up and put him on his knees over here."

Arlen swore under his breath and did as he was ordered. Eben and Josiah were now face to face.

"If you want to live through the night," Stohlfutz said to Eben, "you only have to do this one thing just as I told you earlier. You have to prove your faith to us."

"What?" Eben spat. "Hit him? Beat him some more?"

"No. Kill him. And when you're done, you must kill Gideon too."

JUDGEMENT

Eben stared at Stohlfutz with horror knowing there was no way he would kill Josiah or Gideon for that matter. "No."

Stohlfutz swung the cane with lightning speed hitting Eben across the face. "This is your only chance! Do it!"

"No, I'd rather die."

"So be it! All three of you will be fed to the pigs and shit out! That's what you deserve you disgusting, damned sinners. You'll rot in the depths of Hell where you belong!"

"We'll see you there then Stohlfutz!" Eben shouted.

Again, the cane smacked into the side of Eben's face splitting his cheek open. Blood ran freely down his face but he didn't flinch. Stohlfutz scowled and stepped in front of the lantern leaving Eben hidden in the shadows for just a moment.

"It's too bad you chose this Gideon, too bad in deed. Oh, and before I go, I thought you might like to know that your wife and other children will be well taken care of once you're gone."

Eben raised his left foot slightly allowing the chain to slide off, then did the same with his right foot. Thankfully, no one saw him do it and the chains came off silently.

Gideon tried to stand but Leroy pushed him back down. "You leave her alone you bastard!"

"I don't believe you're in any position to do anything about it. You surely know of my son Jonah's little problem don't you? We've already discussed it with his wife who unfortunately, can't bear him any children and she's willing to accept Mary as an equal. A fine looking young widow such as her will need a good strong husband to take care of her and the children. Your daughter, Miriam, she's what, almost thirteen now?" Stohlfutz asked with a smile.

"No!" Gideon roared thrashing at Leroy and the ropes. "No! I'll kill you Stohlfutz! Kill you!"

As Stohlfutz said this he stood with his back to Eben who had already begun to slip the chains off his wrists.

"I've enjoyed our time together, I truly have, but I must go. We have much to attend to in the coming days. Take Gideon and the other boy and tie them to the post with Eben," he commanded. "Let them die together."

Stohlfutz cackled to himself and turned towards the door. Eben knew it was time.

Ignoring the searing pain in his feet, he leapt onto Stohlfutz's back catching him completely by surprise. The old man hit the dirt floor with a grunt as Eben's fist smashed into the side of his face. A second punch landed with a crack fracturing Stohlfutz's nose and cheekbone. Leroy and Arlen looked on in surprise for moment, long enough for Gideon to stand and smash the back of his head into Leroy's nose. Josiah, though weak and frail managed to get away from Arlen and charge into him headfirst with all the strength he had left. It wasn't enough; Arlen recovered quickly and hit Josiah sending him sprawling into a corner where he lay dazed and breathless. Eben ignored Stohlfutz for the time being and jumped onto Arlen's back and dug his fingers into his eyes until he felt them give with a fleshy pop. Arlen screamed in pain and fell hard to his knees, his hands covering his bloody eyes. Josiah had managed to pull his bound hands under his feet so they were in front of him and wielded them like a club battering Arlen even further. Gideon took several blows from Leroy's club and fell onto his back but as Leroy charged in Gideon's heavy boots kicked up breaking his jaw. He cried out in pain but he wasn't done. With a shriek, he swept Gideon's legs aside and continued pummeling him.

Eben cast a quick glance at them and wavered. Should he help Josiah or should continue with Stohlfutz? The old man was up on all fours scrambling to the door and Eben knew if he made it out of the pit he'd call for help. Not knowing if there were other Sentinels around, he ran and caught Stohlfutz from behind just as he reached the bottom step. Suddenly out of nowhere, a brown blur brushed past his face and raced down the steps. Eben reared back in surprise realizing it was one of the dogs from the pen outside charging headlong into the pit. In an instant, the dog went for Leroy's neck giving Gideon the chance to scramble out of the way.

Sensing Eben's hesitation, Stohlfutz let out a howl and snatched up his cane wielding it like a club landing a few blows on Eben's hands and shoulders. Eben deflected the blows sending the cane clattering away into the darkness. Rage overcame him: He intended to kill Stohlfutz and this gave him a strength he'd never felt before. Strangely, as if some miracle had just occurred, his battered body could no longer feel any pain.

"You're going to die Stohlfutz!" he screamed.

Stohlfutz squirmed to scramble away but Eben held him down. With another roar he savagely slammed the old man's head into the step.

"Please!" Stohlfutz cried. "Please, no!"

Eben wrapped his hands around Stohlfutz's neck and squeezed tightly hearing bones crack. The old man choked and flayed about catching Eben's face with his fingernails. They tore deeply into his skin but he didn't care. He squeezed harder.

"You better pray old man because God isn't going to save you."

Stohlfutz gasped loudly and continued clawing at Eben's hands but he didn't loosen his grip despite the pain burning in his arms. The old man's breathing became slower and slower.

A hand touched Eben's shoulder but in his frenzy to finish the old man he ignored it. There was only Stohlfutz and he was going to die.

"Stop," Gideon said pulling Eben back.

"Get off me!"

"No, Eben, stop," Gideon persisted. He reached down and pulled Eben's hands away. "You can't do this, you're not a murderer."

Eben jerked his hands away from Gideon and glared at him with seething hatred. "Go to hell damn you!"

"Is he...dead?"

Eben and Gideon jumped from the sound and looked up to see Katurah watching intently from just inside the doorway. She stood uncertainly, her eyes never leaving Stohlfutz.

"No, he's still alive," Eben said stepping away from Gideon. He still trembled with anger.

"Come here, Molly, here girl," she said snapping her fingers. The dog looked up from the bloody mess that was Leroy's neck and growled. "Molly! Get over here now!"

The dog hesitated and with a whimper, trotted over to sit sullenly at Katurah's side.

"Good girl."

After a moment, she slowly walked down the steps, picked up Stohlfutz's cane and caressed the smooth, worn wood. With one tentative step, then another, she slowly approached the Reverend. A cry escaped from her mouth, she began beating the old man slowly at first, until all of the pent up rage and shame she had been forced to live through spilled out.

"No, no, no!" she screamed.

Eben limped across the pit to Josiah who sat with his legs splayed unnaturally beneath his body. Each time he tried to pull himself he kept falling back with a curse. Even after being starved and beaten for over a week, he was still stubborn as ever.

"Can you walk?" Eben asked kneeling by his side to unlock the chains binding his wrists.

"Not too well I'm afraid. My feet hurt like the devil and I think some of my ribs are broken but other than that, I should be fine."

"Good, we're getting out of here, the two of us. Come on, I'll help you up."

Josiah relented and took Eben's hand crying out in pain when Eben tried to pull him up. "Oh my God, that hurts. Easy…"

Pulling Josiah's arm around his neck and wrapping his arm around his brother's waist, Eben struggled to his feet nearly losing consciousness as pain flooded back into his body. After the events of the past two weeks and the knowledge he'd just barely escaped death, exhaustion overcame him as the adrenaline in his body faded away.

"I hate you! I hate you! I hate you!" Katurah screamed each time the cane thudded into Stohlfutz's prostrate body. The cane snapped in two but Katurah continued beating with the broken end until Stohlfutz suddenly moaned loudly, then went silent. Drained, she fell to the floor in a heap, her sobs filling the small space.

Both boys winced from the pain in their feet and hung on tightly to one another as they began slowly hobbling to the door. Other than freeing himself from the ropes, Gideon still hadn't moved. He watched the boys with infinite sadness etched on his face. Josiah refused to make eye contact but Eben looked back at him with contempt. Upon reaching the steps, he paused and knelt down next to Katurah.

"Katurah," he said softly. "We need to go. Are there any more Sentinels outside?"

She nodded and wiped her face with her shawl. "Only one and the last I saw of him he was in the bunkhouse eating but there are two more coming out to help cut up Josiah and your father and… you before they feed you all to the pigs."

Josiah stiffened. "He's not our father. He's a beast!"

Eben nodded his head knowingly. "I figured as much. He was going to have Arlen kill me too wasn't he. After I killed Josiah and him," he said gesturing to Gideon.

"Yes, I think so."

Gideon remained quiet and unmoving. Instead of standing tall and proud as he'd always done, he looked small and helpless in the yellowish light dancing off the walls of the pit. The erect posture, the hard eyes, the confidence he'd always exuded were all gone, replaced by a bent broken man neither boy had seen before.

"One thing's for sure, we're not going to be able to go on foot. Do you think you could get to any of the horses in the barn without being caught?" Eben asked turning his attention back to Katurah.

"I took Leroy and Arlen's horses out to the back pasture just before I came out here," Katurah replied. "They're already saddled and besides, when the other two show up they'll think they've left if their horses aren't up by the house."

"Good thinking. Are you ready?"

Katurah rose to her feet slowly never taking her eyes off Stohlfutz. She wiped her face again, went to Josiah's side, took ahold of his other arm, the three shuffled to the narrow door of the pit.

"Boys," Gideon finally said. Eben stopped and turned his head to look at him but Josiah's eyes flickered with hatred.

"Come on Eben, don't mind him. Leave him here to rot like he deserves."

Eben knew he should continue out to the horses and leave Gideon behind without another word. He was the worst kind of person there could be in Eben's mind, nothing more than a murderer who committed his sins out of lust and greed. But something held him back, the finality of the moment perhaps, a desire to hear what he had to say.

"When you get to the horses stay off the roads until you make it down to the river bottom but don't stop until you get to town."

"I thought you were on his side," Eben said gesturing to Stohlfutz. "Why should you care about us now?"

Gideon could only shake his head slowly, methodically back and forth. "What I did...it was wrong and how I've always treated you both was wrong. I can't begin to tell you how...sorry I am Eben. Josiah, I'm sorry."

Eben eyed him incredulously. "You brought us out here knowing Stohlfutz would have us killed! You killed your own brother and our mother! Do you really think saying you're sorry is going to fix that? Do you?"

"No, I don't."

"The only reason you're standing there now is because you refused to kill us! You're pathetic!"

"I've prayed and prayed, Eben. After I brought you here I realized I couldn't do it to either one of you. I've had to live with what I did to Dan and Ruth and it's torn me apart for fifteen years and...I raised you both. You're my sons. I refused to accept that for a long time but... I know I'm going to hell. I couldn't kill either of you!" Gideon cried. "There's nothing for me here anymore. I've been kicked out of the Brotherhood and removed from the Council, now this," he said waving a hand around the pit. "If the Sentinels don't kill me I'll be a pariah for the rest of my life. You boys need to go. I won't stop you."

Josiah pulled on Eben drawing him towards the door. "Let's go. The devil can have him."

Giving Gideon one last look, Eben grasped Josiah tightly and ducked through the doorway into the cool night air blowing through the deserted farmyard. It washed over their bodies soothing hot, bruised skin and cleansing the foulness from their lungs. They inhaled deeply gulping it in. Eben shivered from the sudden change in temperature but managed a smile until a low growl came out of the darkness in front of him.

"Get down, bad dogs!" Katurah hissed. "Down!"

Sniffing at Katurah and hoping for food, the dogs backed down and watched in a chorus of whines and whimpers. Once out of the dog run, the three made their way to the edge of the building covering the pits and peeked around the corner to see an expansive barnyard spread out before them.

"Oh, no," Katurah muttered before quickly ducking back.

"What?" Eben asked.

"The other Sentinels are here. They're up by the house with the lantern. Do you see them?"

"Yes, darn it!"

Five or six men stood by the house visiting with the other Sentinel who'd been in the house earlier. Eben couldn't hear what they were saying but judging from the way they kept pointing and nodding in the direction of the pit, they were waiting for Stohlfutz, Leroy and Arlen to come back to fetch them.

"How far to the horses?" Josiah wheezed. "I can't walk at all."

"They're just back on the other side of the windbreak," Katurah replied. "Not far, but we can't cross here, they'll see us."

"Can we go around behind the barn and hog lot?" Eben asked trying desperately to look around the darkened farmstead. There were enough buildings to give them plenty of cover but it would be a long way around.

"Yes, but it's going to take a while especially since you two can barely walk and by then they'll start wondering where the Reverend is."

"Let's go then, we don't have time to waste."

Despite the searing pain in his feet, Eben gritted his teeth and continued slogging away with Katurah's help. After only twenty feet, both boys collapsed in a heap.

"Darn it all!" Eben muttered breathlessly. "It's going to take us all night!"

Just then, Gideon appeared in the darkness and stooped down to lift Josiah up from the ground. "Lead the way Katurah. Eben, I'll come back for you in a minute."

"Put me down!" Josiah said angrily. "I don't need any help from you!"

Without saying anything, Gideon threw Josiah over his shoulder in a fireman's carry and followed Katurah around the corner of a grain silo. A few minutes later, he reappeared and helped Eben up.

"Here, get on my back, it will be easier."

Knowing he didn't have any other choice, Eben reluctantly obeyed and put his arms around Gideon's neck when he squatted down. The two headed off into the darkness making sure to stay behind the farm buildings and out of direct sight of the house. Following a small trail between the canopy of overgrown tree branches they came out into an isolated pasture where they could just make out the silhouette of two horses. Gideon trotted through the tall grass to Leroy's horse Daisy and helped him up into the saddle behind Josiah. To Eben's surprise, Katurah sat atop Arlen's horse holding the reins.

"Are you going too?" he asked.

"Yes, why wouldn't I? Once they find the Reverend out there they'll kill me. I'll be buried in the windbreak like all the rest of them."

"That's what they do with the bodies?" Eben asked incredulously.

"Some of them, others are cut up and fed to the pigs. Others, well, they're taken away by their fathers and buried somewhere else."

"My God."

Gideon ran his hand over Daisy's soft muzzle and looked back towards the house. In the light of the rising moon he looked like a man who'd lost all hope but had accepted with what lay before him.

"You three get going. Remember, stay off the roads and don't stop until you get to town."

"What are you going to do?" Eben asked.

"Once those Sentinels find out what's happened out there all hell is going to break loose. With any luck, I can get to one of their horses and hopefully, lead them on a wild goose chase."

"Why are you doing this?"

Gideon shrugged his shoulders and looked up at the moon. "I can't live with the things I've done any longer. I have to do this to save you boys and you as well, Katurah. Maybe God can find some way to forgive me but, I doubt it."

Eben stared at him for several moments before speaking. "You know they'll kill you."

"Yes, I know. I've known that for a long time," Gideon said releasing the bridle and stepping back. "Take care of yourself boys."

With a click and a gentle nudge, Eben and Katurah rode down the hill away from the house and crossed a small creek into another pasture. Once they were a good two miles into their journey they brought the animals to a trot and headed towards the river.

"He's crazy," Josiah said turning his head back to look at Eben. "I bet as soon as we were out of sight he ran right back up to the house and told the Sentinels where we're at. I bet it's another one of their damned games."

Eben peered back over his shoulder and saw nothing but darkness. There was no sound other than the chirps of crickets, frogs and the wind gently blowing through the grass. "No, I don't think so. I don't see or hear anyone."

"Why do you think he just let us go?"

"I don't know, Josiah. Maybe he really does feel guilty but more than likely, he knows it's the end for him and he's afraid."

Josiah grunted in agreement. "So, where are we going?"

"I've been thinking about that. We're going by home first."

"What? Are you insane?"

"No, think about it. They caught both of us at the creek didn't they?"

"You got caught at the creek too? Just like I did? How stupid are you?"

"Would we be stupid enough to go the same way again?"

EXODUS

The three rode silently each reflecting on what had transpired for the next two hours passing darkened farms and lonely fields along the way until they reached the river bottom. Here, they traveled nearly three miles in the thick underbrush before changing direction again and setting out across the Beiler's land. The dull roar of hoof beats and muted voices carrying in the night air told them the Sentinels were searching and this knowledge made Eben tense with worry. There was absolutely no going back now.

Eben began to recognize the landscape the nearer they came to home and rode up a narrow waterway to the next road. Suddenly, Katurah stopped her horse, slid off her back and pulled both animals into the first two rows of a cornfield. "Sit absolutely still and don't make a sound."

Both Eben and Josiah held their breath. Just a few feet away they watched a single man on horseback riding low in the saddle who they recognized as Gideon go tearing by. He was soon followed by a group of several men also on horseback chasing close behind. They thundered along the gravel road raising an enormous cloud of dust and soon disappeared over the next hill. Eben breathed a sigh of relief listening to the sound fade away. They were going away from the creek and home. Katurah swung herself back onto the horse and sent her off at a trot across the road into another field with Eben following close behind. They were getting close.

"We're going to swing out away from the house right here," Eben said pulling the reins to guide his horse into one of Gideon's pastures. "We can cut across down by the pond and come back up to the creek without being seen from the house or the road. I think it will be faster too."

"You sure about this?" Josiah asked anxiously. "Because I'm not. If we get caught again I'll never forgive you."

Eben smiled. "We should be across the creek and halfway to town in another hour or two. Besides, we're going to cut across the edge of father's land over to Yoder's."

"Will the horses be able to get across? The bank is fairly steep."

"Yes, and that's about the only place I know of where it's not too wide. They should be able to walk right across it."

Josiah shook his head. "I hope you know what you're doing, Eben."

"I do too," Eben replied. As they rode through the pasture he could barely make out the timber and creek down from the house in the inky darkness. A sudden pang of longing shot through his body staring at the timber because it reminded him of Wendy. He wondered how she was and if she had been thinking about him for the past week since he'd seen her last.

"So tell me, Josiah, did you ever see Wendy the night you took off?" Eben asked softly. "Because I haven't seen or heard a thing from her since before that night. I...miss her."

"No, I got across the creek and had taken maybe five steps before Leroy and his brother caught me. It was bad, Eben, they beat me senseless. I hoped she was there and saw the entire thing so you'd find out about it. But later on, I woke up in the pit and fig-ured I was done for."

"I hope she's still here," Eben said examining the shadows of the timber carefully. "When I met her she said she was staying with her aunt and uncle for a couple of weeks and well, it's been over a month."

"What if she's not?"

"We keep going until we get to Kamron."

"What then?" Katurah asked. Other than telling the boys to sit still an hour earlier, these were the only other words she'd spoken since leaving Stohlfutz's farm. Her silence conveyed apprehension and fear to Eben. He could feel it radiating from her.

"We go straight to the police."

"Tell me, Eben," Josiah asked, "What if they're just like the Sentinels are here? What if they just laugh and haul us all back out here? Have you thought of that?"

Eben scowled. He had thought the same thing and it was a cause for concern. Without Wendy and her knowledge of life in the outside world to ask about how the police outside the Community operated, he simply didn't know. "I have, and we're just going to have to have faith that they aren't bad people. Heck, all they have to do is look at the two of us, which should be enough I'd think," Eben said.

Eben looked up to see the moon sinking lower in the western sky and turned back to gaze at the pastel morning light spreading across the eastern horizon. As he turned he thought he saw some-thing moving behind their group in the direction they'd just come from. He waited, pulled the reins to his left and towards the creek, and turned to gaze into the in blue-black shadows again hoping and praying it was just the long early morning gloom playing tricks on his eyes. Then, again, something moved again ever so slightly.

"We're being followed," he said softly. "Katurah, kick your horse up into a trot, we're going straight for the creek right now."

Katurah immediately kicked her horse hard. Her small body bounced crazily in the saddle as her horse strode out quickly outpacing Daisy in their race towards the creek. Eben turned to look back again and was horrified to see several dark shapes spreading out into the pasture behind them and they were riding hard.

"Go! Right now!" Eben cried digging his heels into Daisy's sides. The horse, clearly surprised not to be kicked with the sharp spurs Leroy had worn, responded sluggishly at first and slowly picked up speed. Josiah leaned forward and hung on to her neck and mane tightly. Eben snapped at the reins trying to make her run faster but she seemed to have reached her limit.

"Come on Daisy!"

Suddenly, the creek was directly in front of them. Katurah's horse saw it and glided over almost effortlessly and continued running through the trees. Hearing the heavy breathing of a Sentinel's horse closing in upon them, Eben clung to Josiah tightly and prayed Daisy could make it.

"Come on girl!" Eben shouted. "Go!"

The boys ducked to avoid low hanging tree branches as Daisy charged blindly through the timber. Just as she reached the creek, Eben's eyes grew large knowing she wouldn't make it.

"Hang on!"

The horse leapt just in time but years of abuse and the weight of the two boys pulled her down. With a shriek, she hit the opposite side of the ravine heavily and rolled over Eben and Josiah and down into the trickle of water at the bottom. The force of the impact knocked Eben senseless. A sudden snap in his leg sent waves of pain shooting through his body. Panic began to set in as he tried to move but couldn't. His hands pushed feeling hair and warmth – Daisy lay on top of him shrieking and thrashing in the narrow creek bed trying to get up but each time she tried to stand she fell back on Eben's legs. Finally, somehow, he managed to somehow pull himself away and Daisy managed to regain her footing and crashed away into the timber. Eben moaned in agony and reached out to a face looking down upon him.

"Josiah…" he mumbled but winced from the crashing sound his voice caused inside his head. It hammered his brain and crushed his eyes, a jumble of voices and a roaring in his ear melded into one continuous cacophony.

"Eben!" a female voice cried. "Grab my hands!"

Eben reached up to see more outstretched hands but they were too far above him.

"Wendy?"

"You have to stand up Eben, darn it!" Josiah shouted. "We can't reach you!"

A pair of rough hands pulled him away from Wendy and then there was a gruff voice yelling in his ear. Before he knew what was happening, Eben found himself on his back face to face with Lev Fisher who held him down with a knee dug into his chest.

"I got him!" Lev yelled punching Eben savagely. "I got him!"

Four shadows appeared in the early dawn light and stared down at Eben. They were Sentinels. *It's all been for nothing*, Eben thought to himself. *I'm going to die after all of this.* He shut his eyes tightly and waited for what he knew wouldn't be a pleasant end.

"What are you doing Eben?"

Eben opened his eyes and stared with disbelief at the man squatting next to him. It was John, his friend since childhood. He reached over and gently placed a hand on his friend's leg causing Eben to jump and cry out. "Hmm, looks like it's broken."

John licked his lips and smiled as though they were telling stories after church. "Come Eben, we'll get you picked up take you over to Doc's. You'll be fine, you'll see."

"No," Eben rasped. "I'm going with them."

John turned his head to look at Wendy, Josiah, Katurah and a clean-shaven man Eben didn't know standing across the creek in the hazy light filtering through the trees. With a barely perceptible shake of his head, he turned his attention back to Eben still smiling. "No, my friend. You need to come with us."

"No! Let me go John!"

John gripped Eben's face tightly and leaned in close. "You can't go with them because you're staying here. Someone has to be held accountable for the mess you've made and I've been put in charge of doing it!"

Eben tried to raise his arm to strike John but Lev restrained him. "What's wrong with you? They're going to kill me!"

"Let him go, John!" Josiah shouted. "Let him go or it's the end for you!"

"What in the hell are you going to do about it Josiah?" John shouted. "What? Looks to me like you're crippled up and those two harlots aren't going to be much use either. Why don't you come over here and stop me?"

The other man, who Eben guessed was Wendy's Uncle David, stepped in front of Josiah and the girls and held a thin rectangular box up in one hand, his other arm cradled a shotgun. "Let the boy go. I've called the police and they're on their way out here as we speak."

John and the Sentinels looked at one another and broke into a chorus of laugher.

"This ain't none of your concern. This is a Community matter!" Lev retorted angrily. "Him, and him, they killed my brother and blinded another man so we have the right to take'em."

David raised the shotgun and pointed directly at Lev. "Like hell you do. These two," he said gesturing to Josiah and Katurah, "are on my property and none of you son of a bitches are going to set foot over that creek. But, you are going to let the boy go."

John and the Sentinels laughed again and mumbled amongst themselves. Eben raised his head far enough to see that he was right on the edge of the embankment. He tried moving his leg but the pain was overwhelming. If only it would cooperate...

"Are you going to come over here and get him?" John asked standing to face David. "Because if you try, I'll have these men rip you to shreds because this is Community property. You can't do a thing and you know it."

David stomped to the edge of the embankment and pointed the shotgun at John's face. "Let him go right now you little prick."

John threw his head back and laughed while he kicked Eben's leg with the crazy smile still plastered across his face. He looked back down at Eben, pulled his long Brotherhood knife out of the sheath on his belt and examined the blade with his finger for a moment. "As Sentinel Lev said, this is a Community matter. Eben and Josiah there murdered his brother and left another man blinded. And worse, they almost killed our dear Reverend Stohlfutz. He's hurt badly but he'll recover, God willing. No, someone has to pay and it's going to be one of these two."

John knelt down and grabbed a fistful of Eben's hair forcing his head back.

"No!" Wendy screamed. "Leave him alone!"

"Josiah! Come over here or I'll slit Eben's throat! It's your choice! You, or him!"

"Don't Josiah! Stay there!" Eben croaked. The blade he knew, was sharpened to a fine hone - tiny rivulets of hot blood ran down his neck when John pressed it tight against his neck. He suddenly didn't care if he died as long as Josiah stayed where he was and would be able to get away "Go ahead John, do it. What did they promise you? Land? A second wife? Lots of livestock? Maybe you'll take my father's place on the Council, eh? But what if you don't? You know as well as I do, Lev or one of them will kill you eventually."

"Shut up, Eben."

"No, John. We've been friends since we were little and now you're going to murder me? For what? It ruined my father. Don't you think you'll regret it someday? Come on!"

For a moment the pressure on the knife lessened. Eben watched John carefully. His eyes kept darting back and forth between the Sentinels and David, then back to Eben. He was having doubts.

"Kill him!" Lev yelled. "Do it!"

In the distance the wailing of sirens could be heard piercing the morning air. Eben hoped they wouldn't be too late. He gulped and looked at John with tired eyes.

"John, what's your decision?"

John roared in frustration, slapped Eben across the face and gestured towards the Sentinels. "Put him on a horse and take him to the Sanctuary!"

Seeing his chance, Eben pushed off on his good leg and fell down into the ravine. Luckily, he was able to grab ahold of a tree root growing out of the opposite side which he used to begin pulling himself up. With a shriek, Wendy rushed forward and took ahold of his arm trying desperately to pull him up and was quickly joined by Josiah and Katurah. John screamed again and jumped down beside him knife raised intending to strike. Just as he was about to plunge it into Eben's body a shotgun blast blew him back against the opposite wall of the ravine. David immediately cycled another round and pointed it back at Lev.

"If you try, I'll blow you away fat boy. I've been hunting deer out here for thirty years and I don't miss, ever."

Lev and the Sentinels raised their hands and quickly disappeared on their horses as several police officers came charging through the underbrush with guns drawn.

With the help of David, Josiah and Wendy, Eben was carefully pulled up out of the ravine and gently laid on his back.

"Eben," Wendy cried gripping his face gently. "I was so worried about you, I thought something awful had happened to you!"

Eben wrapped his arms around her and held her tightly. For a moment he considered telling her just how correct she was but he quickly thought better of it. "I'm sorry I made you worry."

"You should be mister. I'm…I'm just so happy you're okay."

"How did you know we were going to be coming through here? I mean, we were planning on going further on down the creek to cross but the Sentinels caught up to us."

"When Josiah didn't show up I freaked out and told Uncle David and Aunt Shelley what was going on. Thankfully, they were willing to help. We've been out here every night since I saw you last."

"But I thought you were only going to be here for a couple of weeks. It's been almost a month since we first talked and I was afraid you were long gone."

"Well, I talked to my parents and told them the story. Oh, Eben, I had to stay! I've been coming down here every day since the last time I talked to you hoping you'd show up but you never did. I found your handkerchief and hung it up so you'd know I was here. See?" Wendy said pointing.

Eben's eyes wandered to the hollowed out tree to see his red handkerchief, now faded and torn from the weather, hanging on the branch just above the opening. "I'm sorry, Wendy, after that night I couldn't get away. I tried and tried but couldn't."

"Those awful men were down here all the time too. I figured they were looking for you. David wanted to run them off especially since they were on his property but I talked him into waiting to see if you'd come back. We thought that if they were still here then that meant you were still over there somewhere."

Eben and Wendy hugged each other again not wanting to let go.

"Look," Wendy said softly.

Eben looked up and was surprised to see Josiah sitting on the same log he and Wendy had sat on the month before when they'd first met. To his surprise, he was rocking back and forth crying like a baby.

"Hey little brother, looks like we made it," Josiah wept. "I can't believe it, I just can't."

"We're free, Josiah, we're free."

"Thanks to you, Eben, you got us out."

"Where's Katurah?" Eben asked raising his head.

"Over there," Josiah said pointing.

Katurah sat with her back against a tree staring off into the distance ignoring the police officer trying to question her. She was perfectly still, her face showing absolutely no emotion but her arms were wrapped tightly around her tattered teddy bear.

"Who's she?" Wendy asked.

"Her name's Katurah. She's the reason we were able to escape from where we were being held. If it wasn't for her, Josiah and I would both be dead."

Wendy suppressed a sob and hugged Eben again. "I never believed a lot of religious stuff until I met you. I prayed for you Eben. For an angel to come and find you and Josiah and keep you safe because I didn't know what else to do. God really does listen to people's prayers, she's proof."

Eben managed a smile despite his exhaustion and the pain coursing through his leg. "Yes, I think he does. Thank you for not giving up on us, Wendy."

David, who had gone to talk to the police, approached the couple and squatted down by their side. "Hey young man, we have an ambulance coming out to take care of you, your brother and the girl. You going to be okay?"

Eben looked over at Katurah, then at Josiah and finally brought his gaze back to Wendy. Honey-colored morning sunlight filtered through the trees illuminating the creek bottom while a cool morning breeze whispered through the leaves above. Turning his head, he looked back in the direction of the house he'd grown up in but it was hidden from view. He knew then that he'd never see it again but instead of feeling fear, he felt a strange sense of peace, something he hadn't felt since he and Josiah were little. The timber looked different Eben realized, as though all the horrible events of the past month were suddenly washed away and replaced by a hopeful calm. "Yes, finally, I think I am."

The Des Moines Register
August 27, 2011
Two Men, Charged in Community of God Murders, DCI and Local Authorities Investigating Generations of Murder and Abuse

Kamron, IA – Amongst the gently rolling hills and farm fields of southeast Iowa dotted with quaint farms and churches a reclusive religious order has charmed outsiders with their way of life free of all modern conveniences such as electricity, cars, appliances and cell phones for generations. Members claim to live a simple life they say God has commanded them to live. To many outsiders it was a tranquil, peaceful place where God and family were the two most vital aspects of life, a place which harkens back to our rural roots so admired by Thomas Jefferson and the Founding Fathers.

All of this changed this week when two men, Judson Z. Stohlfutz, 72, and Gideon J. Wittke, 48, both of rural Kamron were charged with multiple counts of First Degree murder. Stohlfutz has also been charged with False Imprisonment, Kidnapping, Child Abuse, Sexual Abuse of a Minor and Rape. His wife, Anna C. Stohlfutz, 72, is charged with Second Degree Murder, Aiding and Abetting Murder, Exploitation of a Child, False Imprisonment, Kidnapping, Sexual Abuse of a Minor and Rape.

According to Washington County Sheriff Don Repp, a tip from three teenage members of the Community who managed to escape led them to the home of Judson and Anna Stohlfutz.

"We were not prepared for what we found on the Stohlfutz farm," Repp said. "It's a charnel house."

Authorities have uncovered the remains of nearly one-hundred bodies buried around the farm while thousands of human bones litter the one-hundred and fifty acre site. Seven more bodies were uncovered on a wooded creek bottom near the home of Gideon Wittke and have been tentatively identified as the remains of his brother Daniel Wittke, 20 and his wife, Ruth Wittke, also 20, who were said to have disappeared in 1996. Five other sets of skeletal remains were also found on the creek bottom have yet to be identified. According to Repp, Gideon Wittke turned himself in to the Washington County Sheriff's Office early Sunday morning.

"We were looking for Mister Wittke but he showed up in town, walked in and confessed to killing his brother and wife. Evidently, he murdered the brother so he could be 'given' his wife Ruth but she fought him and in turn, he murdered her."

He went on to say that the creek bottom wouldn't have been searched if not for the heavy rainfall Saturday evening.

"The creek hadn't had much water in it for nearly two-months but the rainstorms Saturday night and early Sunday washed out the south bank for nearly fifty-yards unearthing several sets of human remains. We're guessing the Wittke family had been burying family members and others down there for years."

Gideon Wittke reaffirmed his guilt while undergoing questioning.

"He honestly doesn't believe he did anything wrong," Repp stated. "He claims he was doing the Lord's work for the good of the Community. He intended to save it by becoming what they called, The Gatekeeper, a position held by Judson Stohlfutz."

Gideon Wittke's wife and younger children have been removed from the Community and taken to an undisclosed location.

"Hopefully we can identify some of the victims from the farm and creek and give them a proper burial but with no dental or medical records it's not going to be easy." Iowa DCI Special Agent Rick Larson said. "And worse, these people out here absolutely will not talk to us."

When asked why member of the Community are so close-mouthed Larson only had one explanation.

"Along with the three minors who came to us Saturday night we've had several ex-Community members contact us in the last week telling us what's gone on out here for many years. Evidently leaving and telling isn't an option for these people. If they refuse to join the Church, marry and follow the Community's strict laws they're murdered by the head of the family, in most cases, the father. It's done to maintain order and to ensure the survival and the secrets of the Community. Stohlfutz was an enforcer, what they called the 'Crow Man', and backed up by a secret group of men known as the Ten along with their police force known as Sentinels. In many ways, they're much like the Gestapo in Nazi Germany. He and these men tortured and raped young people in an attempt to force them to conform to the Community's rules and murdered others."

Led by Zebadiah H. Yoder, the Community of God is an ultra-conservative religious sect believed to have broken away from the Eastern Mennonite Church in Pennsylvania in the late 1840's and settled in the rich farmland surrounding Kamron in 1849-50. The Community chose to stay virtually unchanged in the years since denying themselves any modern conveniences. Tourists were charmed by their simple way of life using horse and buggy for travel. Their only industries were farming, logging, the crafts and produce they sold in the Kamron Farmer's market and the world-famous cheese factory south of town. Members wear simple home-made clothing, married men sported long beards and straw hats while the women wore simple blue or black dresses and covered their heads with lace bonnets. But behind the peaceful lifestyle lay a deadly secret. Whispered rumors of murder, torture, child abuse, forced marriages among families and rape have gone on for generations but could never be proven until recently.

At its height in 1900, the Community is believed to have had two- to three-thousand members living in their sprawling homeland north and west of Kamron. Over time, the older generations of large families died off while young people began leaving in droves during the 1960's and 70's to live in the modern world free of the strict laws and rules of the sect. Along with the decline in population the pool of available marriage partners has dwindled significantly leading many to either never marry or to marry first- or second-cousins. Recent estimates have guessed the population has declined sharply to less than five-hundred today.

Wittke is currently being held in the Washington County jail and has been refused bail. Stohlfutz has also been refused bail is being held at the Oakdale Prison Hospital recovering from wounds received in an altercation with Wittke late Friday and will be transferred to Washington County once doctors determine he is well enough. Anna Stohlfutz is being held in the Johnson County jail and has also been refused bail. According to Washington County Attorney Robert Hoffman more charges may be pending as the investigation continues.

FREEDOM

Greencastle, Indiana – Eighteen months later

E ben scowled at his reflection in the mirror and tugged at the tight collar hoping to let a little of the heat out of the uncomfortable dress shirt he was wearing. If the shirt wasn't bad enough, the tie was worse forcing him to hold his head up so it wouldn't choke him. Deciding there was no way around not wearing the shirt, tie and awful pants, he threw his hands up in frustration before padding down the carpeted hallway to the kitchen of the small townhouse his family shared. Wonderful smells of cooking food and pastries filled the air. Hoping to snatch a cookie or two, Eben quickly rounded the corner nearly knocking Miriam down in the process.

"Sorry, Miriam."

"What the rush?" she asked brushing long blonde hair out of her eyes. "Somewhere to go?"

Eben smiled. "Maybe."

In the living room just off the kitchen Isaac sat tearing through a bowl of Captain Crunch while watching an Animal Planet show on T.V., his favorite channel.

"What are you watching, Isaac?" Eben asked.

"It's a show about lions in Africa. I wish I could have a lion. They're awesome."

Eben laughed at his little brother. "Yeah, it would be a fun pet until it ate you."

"Nah, I'd train him to be good. He wouldn't eat me."

"I'm sure you could," Eben laughed. The smells from the kitchen were beginning to be too much for him to stand any longer. "I'm going to grab something to eat. Want anything?"

"No thanks, I'm good," Isaac replied raising the bowl to slurp noisily.

Eben peeked around the corner to see Rebecca and Lydia busy spooning cookie dough out onto a baking sheet while Mary opened the oven to take out a fresh batch. Seeing Eben she set the sheet down and approached him.

"My, my, don't you look nice," Mary said slicking his hair to one side.

"I don't know why I have to wear these stupid clothes, they're uncomfortable," Eben complained pulling at the collar again. It already felt as though he were suffocating.

"It's only a couple of hours. After it's done you never have to wear it again."

"Promise?"

"Well, yes. They won't fit you in another six months anyway the way you've been growing this year."

Eben eyed his mother's famous oatmeal chocolate chip cookies cooling on a rack next to the stove with desire. They were his favorites.

"Go ahead," she said. "Take two and go outside so the girls and I can finish."

"Thank you, Mother," he said shoving one in his mouth, then picked up two more and had them eaten before he walked the fifteen feet to the front door. Chewing noisily, he flopped down to put on the stiff leather dress shoes sitting by the front door of the townhouse but paused weighing them in his hands. "Stupid shoes."

Instead of putting them on, he pulled his socks off, bolted outside and ran through the freshly clipped grass to stand where he could see down the long driveway coming into the Deer River Center from the highway.

"Is she here yet?" Josiah asked from the lawn chair he lounged in underneath the shade of an expansive old maple tree. He had rolled the sleeves up on the dress shirt he was stuffed into and was busy whittling on a stick he'd found in the yard. Two huge, scarred bare feet shot out of the bottoms of the black dress pants he wore and he rubbed them contentedly back and forth in the grass. Like Eben, he hadn't had worn shoes much while growing up and being expected to wear them, especially when the weather was nice, was a torture for both boys.

"No, they must be running a little late. She said they'd be here by noon but it's almost twenty after."

Josiah smiled. "You're sweating like a whore in church. Nervous?"

"No! It's just hot."

"I think you're nervous. Gonna see your girlfriend?"

"Shut up, Josiah, she's just my friend."

Josiah hooted with laughter and went back to his stick. Eben blushed and turned away so his brother wouldn't see that he'd gotten to him. His eyes went back to the long thin line of highway and continued watching.

The tiny shape of a car turning off the highway began the long snaking drive towards the Center. Eben stood up straight and absently fiddled with the tie hoping he looked as good as his mother said he did. His anticipation soon turned to disappointment when the car swished by and continued driving towards the main buildings further down the road. Eben exhaled sharply and sauntered back to Josiah where he flopped down in the grass next to his brother.

"I guess I am a little nervous," he said.

Josiah looked up from his stick and grinned. "I know you are. Heck, I am too."

"You are?"

"Well, yes. Everything's happened so quickly in the past year and a half. It seems just like we came here yesterday. Now, we're going to graduate from high school, you're going to college and I'm going to keep working at the A & P. Heck, if I keep saving I'll have enough to buy a car in a few more months. We're doing things we never, ever thought we'd do and sometimes it's a bit overwhelming."

"Yeah, I know. It's exciting but when I think about all I just want to wet my pants," Eben replied.

The boys continued sitting in the shade thinking about the events which had brought them, their mother, Isaac and the girls to Indiana. After leaving the Community, the Iowa Department of Human Services placed the entire family with the Deer Creek Center thanks to the insistence of Wendy and her parents while the lawyers and prosecutors tried to sort out the mess Stohlfutz and Gideon had brought upon them. It was a torturous time for everyone; Josiah, Eben and the rest of the children were placed in the Center's school with other children who had escaped from abusive religious orders and cults. It was a struggle being so far behind academically and socially but all of them eventually caught up though Josiah and Eben struggled more than the younger children. Mary spent her days doing her best to make a home out of the small three bedroom townhouse on the parklike campus of the Center while trying to reassess her life and undergo job training. But for all seven, the outside world was a big, confusing, often frightening place compared to the rural backwardness and isolation of the Community. Even simple things such as using modern appliances, indoor plumbing and grocery shopping were completely foreign and bewildering to them. Mary, Isaac and the girls, Eben knew, cried themselves to sleep every night for the first few months of their strange new lives. Things were hard but they improved bit by agonizing bit thanks to Mary's determination to make her children's lives better and the compassion shown by Todd, the director of Deer Creek, and his staff.

Then, it was back to Iowa for several weeks to endure the trials and all of the nastiness Stohlfutz's state appointed defense lawyers dragged Josiah and Eben through before finally, his guilt and subsequent sentence of life in prison freed the family from some of their ghosts for a time. The mental scars took longer for Deer Creek's counselor's to work through.

"Do you still have the dreams?" Eben asked.

Josiah stopped whittling and thought for a moment. "Yes, sometimes, but they're not as bad as they used to be. Every now and then I dream I'm back in the pit chained to that damn post while Stohlfutz beats me but I can't die, I just lie there in pain forever and ever. You?"

"No, not so much anymore. I sleep pretty well these days except the nights when you're snoring like an old hog."

Josiah cackled with laughter and began grunting like a pig.

Eben watched two robins hopping through the branches in the tree above going about life without a care in the world. He knew what he wanted to ask his brother but he wasn't sure if he should or not.

"What are you thinking?" Josiah asked shooing a fly away from his face.

"Oh, it's nothing."

"No it's not, I can tell from the look on your face. Say it."

Eben took a deep breath and picked at the grass. "It's strange, Josiah, I miss some things about it. It was, I don't know, so perfect in my mind when we were younger. I guess not knowing anything was easier."

"Yeah, but it wasn't. It's okay to remember the good things but you have to think about what was really going on. It was all a lie, Eben. They were going to kill us."

Eben took a deep breath and nodded his head slightly. "I think about how easy it would have been for you or I to go down the path father, I mean, Gideon did, and that scares me."

Josiah brushed white and green wood shavings from his clothes. "Yeah, it is scary. I wouldn't have been able to live with myself and you wouldn't have been able to either. But we didn't. Besides," he continued, "He's where he belongs. From what I've read on the internet, Anamosa is a bad place to be locked up."

"I don't know, I still feel like I should have done more you know, sooner," Eben said. According to his therapist, a man named Rick who Eben liked enormously, he suffered from post-traumatic stress disorder and anxiety. "You're right though, I knew I couldn't have ever done what he did. I would have let them kill me before I'd have killed you or even…him."

"That's the difference between us and him," Josiah said. He never referred to Gideon as anything other than 'him' which suited Eben just fine. "And, old buzzard nose is in hell where he belongs. Too bad they didn't lock him up in one of those pits like he did to us. It's taken me a long time to get over how badly I wanted to stick him with this," he said holding his knife aloft. "But, it's all worked out because of you Eben, don't ever forget that. You saved all of us."

Eben exhaled slowly trying to make sense of it all which after a year and a half, was still hard to do. Stohlfutz's lawyers had managed to convince the judge to place him in protective custody due to his age and the severity of his offenses against children but he didn't last. Only two months into his life sentence another inmate caught up with him somehow and brutally stabbed him to death with a homemade shank. From what Josiah and Eben had managed to learn about the incident, Stohlfutz had been stabbed nearly forty times and bled to death on the floor of a bathroom. His body was buried in the prison cemetery with nothing but a number marking the grave.

The sound of a car pulling up in front of the townhouse caught both boy's attention. Eben looked up to see a blue Toyota Camry slow and stop. His heart immediately leapt into his chest. Sunlight reflected off the windows making it impossible to see who it was but just as he stood the back door flew open.

"Hey you!" Wendy cried.

Eben grinned and quickly walked towards her trying his best to adjust the tie so it wouldn't choke him. Just as she had before, Wendy wore one of her colorful dresses, this one pink and red with multi-colored flowers splashed all over and there were the strange shoes, sandals he knew now, on her feet. Other than her hair being a little longer and done up a little differently since the last time he'd seen her, Eben thought she still radiated beauty, especially when she smiled.

"Hi Wendy," Eben said hugging her warmly. "I'm so glad you and your parents could come."

Wendy gave him a quick kiss on the cheek. "I wouldn't miss seeing you get your high school diploma for anything. I'm so proud of you. And Josiah too!"

"I told you, Eben, she came to see me, not you," Josiah said sauntering up to the car.

"Shut up, Josiah!"

Wendy laughed and hugged Josiah.

"Mr. Harrison, Mrs. Harrison, it's nice to see you again," Eben said extending his hand.

"It's good to see you too young man. I've told you, call me Jeff," Wendy's father said shaking Eben's hand.

"Oh, Eben!" Wendy's mother Annie exclaimed as she crushed him with a hug. The family resemblance between Wendy and her mother was striking; the red hair, the freckles splashed across her face and the bright blue eyes. "It's so nice to see you again! Congratulations!"

"Thank you Mrs. Harrison, it's nice to see you too."

"Oh, you! Call me Annie!"

Eben blushed. "Yes ma'am, sorry."

A new chorus of voices joined in as Mary, Isaac and the girls poured out of the townhouse to greet Wendy and her parents. As they mingled together Wendy returned to Eben and gently took his hand.

"Are you excited about going to college?"

"Yes, I think so. I never thought I would so it's a little strange to think about."

"You're going to the community college in Greencastle aren't you?"

Eben smiled. "Um, no. I've decided to go somewhere else."

Wendy looked at him with surprise. "You have? Where?"

"Well, I've given it a lot of thought and I'm going to go to State Fair Community College in Missouri. The one in Sedalia."

Wendy's eyes grew large in surprise and for a moment her mouth hung open as what Eben was telling her began to make sense. "What? But that's only about half an hour from the University of Missouri...where I go!"

Eben kicked at the grass with his bare feet hoping, praying he hadn't made Wendy angry. "I hope you're not mad at me...I um, I guess I like it out there."

"I'm not mad at you! I think it's wonderful!" she cried hugging him tightly.

"Are you sure? I mean, if you don't want me so close I'll go ahead and stay around here."

"No! It would make it a lot easier to talk to you since you're not too handy with a cell phone yet. I'm excited about you being out there, I really am!" Wendy said.

Eben blushed and exhaled with relief. "You're sure?"

"Yes!"

"It's just that, I um, I want to be closer to you, Wendy, I..."

Wendy looked up at Eben with suddenly wet eyes. "I do too. I've hoped you'd say that to me for a long time.

Eben smiled and avoided looking her in the eye. "There's one more thing I want to ask, um…"

"You can ask me anything, you know that."

"When you all go back to Missouri in a couple of days could I, um, get a ride with you? I haven't been able to get a driver's license yet and well, I don't have a car."

Wendy smiled and took his hands in hers. "Of course."

Eben hugged her again and breathed deeply while the sun warmed his face. *Freedom,* he thought to himself, *is a wonderful thing indeed.*

AUTHOR BIOGRAPHY

Robert Denton Brownell (born March 2, 1968) is an American author who lives with his wife Braedi, their two children and Yorkie in Iowa. He received his BA in history from the University of Iowa where he immersed himself in fiction writing classes taught by students in the world famous Iowa Writer's Workshop. By day, he works for his family's business, Brownells Inc. as a copy/content writer and writes fiction whenever he can. His first novel, *Harold's Dreams,* was published in 2012.

www.ingramcontent.com/pod-product-compliance
Lightning Source LLC
Chambersburg PA
CBHW070554130626
46556CB00001B/160